HIDDEN SEEDS

Jessica Brodie

Book Three in the Dahlia Series

HIDDEN SEEDS

a novel

Jessica Brodie

Valor Publishing Group, South Carolina

First published in the United States of America in 2026

Library of Congress Cataloging-in-Publication Data
Hidden Seeds
p. cm.

Cover Design by Hannah Linder Designs

ISBN 979-8-9929008-4-2

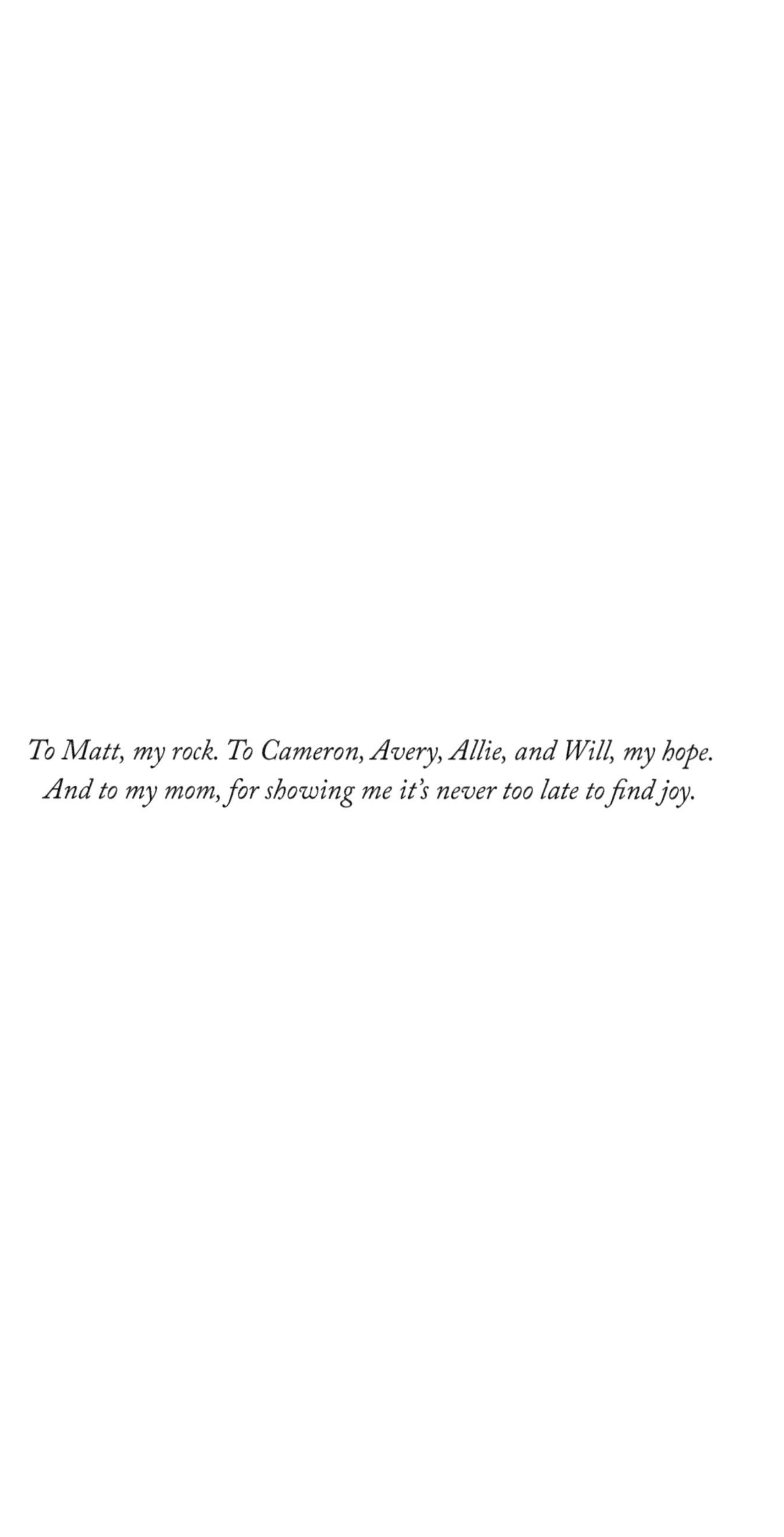

To Matt, my rock. To Cameron, Avery, Allie, and Will, my hope.
And to my mom, for showing me it's never too late to find joy.

CHAPTER 1

Natalie

In Natalie's dreams, Stace was always still alive, still beautiful, her long dark hair thick and waved just right—not matted with blood and harsh against the white slab in the county morgue.

Dream Stacey hugged Natalie there in the street, crying thick ugly tears that soaked Natalie's shoulder as she whispered apologies over and over. Broken glass and shards of metal surrounded them as they clutched each other in the dark night. The coppery smell of smoke and the faint hint of gasoline crept over from the burning car, but Stacey's hair was soft on Nat's cheek, familiar.

Like home.

"I didn't mean it, Nat. You can have him back, or we can both ditch him, start fresh. Go to California, like we talked about. I don't even know what I was thinking . . ."

Only it was all make-believe. Even in the middle of the dream, Natalie knew the truth. And so she stroked Stacey's hair, let her cry in her arms until the weeping became sobbing and finally Natalie was the only one left, sobbing and shaking all on her own.

Stace . . . don't go . . .

But she was gone. And Natalie was alone. Cold. Broken.

Everything in her life suddenly over with the clink of a glass and the turn of a key.

Funny how all the warnings, all the worries, everything just faded away until nothing was left but you and the truth in the darkness.

Now, slumped in her car parked outside the small shopping plaza, Natalie closed her eyes against the memory of the dream, the same dream that plagued her night after night. The heat of the sun felt like bliss as she counted back, just like her therapist taught.

Ten Mississippi, nine Mississippi, eight . . .

The longer it was since the accident, the longer it was since she moved back home to Dahlia, the easier it got. Natalie rested her head against the car window, hand still poised on the key in the ignition, forcing her shallow breathing to settle and her heart to wind down.

A knock against the car window startled her.

"Miss Motts?"

It was an older man, and he peered in at her, his face a mask of concern. She reeled in her thoughts—*Mr. Sweeney, the rental property.*

Natalie sighed, gathered her purse, and opened the car door.

"I'm all right, Mr. Sweeney. Just a headache."

She clicked the lock on the door and plastered on that Motts Megawatt, the smile that earned her Homecoming Queen and a date with pretty much any boy she wanted back in high school.

Way back before Stace and Tucker and Nashville and everything else that had turned her whole world upside down.

Mr. Sweeney looked relieved as she slid out of the car, and he held out an arm to guide her across the street.

She swallowed past a smile and accepted the arm. Sometimes Natalie forgot how old-fashioned Dahlia still was, at least compared to Nashville. Here, it was ma'am this and if-you-please that, as if manners and Southern grace really could keep the boogeymen away.

Of course, Natalie knew better.

They crossed the street and stood on the sidewalk, staring up at the vacant storefront.

Mr. Sweeney unlocked the creaky old door and stepped through the space, which used to be a karate studio, and before that a hair salon, and a boutique even farther back. But the sensei moved to Charlotte, the hair salon went under after Rennie Pierce got so sick from chemo, and the boutique fizzled when the mini-mall opened in Aberville, the next town over.

Natalie's sandaled heels clicked across the laminate flooring, tuning out Mr. Sweeney's warnings about wiring glitches, peeling vinyl, and old buildings. Wide-beam shelves, which once held hats and ladies' heels, lined one whole wall, and a tiny alcove at the back still held a couple of dilapidated sinks from Rennie's old shampoo station. The front boasted wall-to-ceiling glass, letting in tons of natural light, and the place began to take form in her mind.

I see it. She hugged herself. There, she'd stack the rows and rows of paint, along with brushes and canvases and palettes. There, the cleanup station, and over there, she'd arrange clusters of tiny tables for private groups. In the front, she could picture the easels for the more experienced painters, and then some long rows of tables and chairs, classroom-style, where people would follow along and create their masterpiece. She knew it could work—knew it *would* work.

Mr. Sweeney cast a glance at her.

"I hate to ask, being as I know your daddy and all, but we do require first, last, and security. After that, the rent's due the first of every month. And we need at least six months' notice to vacate."

She nodded, mentally calculating. She'd spent the entire morning crunching the numbers, weighing the risks. Yet now, all her rationale had suddenly and inexplicably fled.

"If you need some more time, I can certainly—"

"I'll take it." Her words surprised even her.

"You . . . will?"

"Absolutely. You'll get those two sinks fixed, and install that counter like we discussed?"

His eyebrows knitted, but she knew what he'd say even as he said it.

"You have yourself a deal, Miss Motts."

"Thank you, Mr. Sweeney."

They went over the final details and she signed the lease, adding an extra swoop at the end of her signature.

At the door, he handed her the key and gave her a kind smile.

"I think an art studio will be a real nice addition to Dahlia." He put a grandfatherly hand on her shoulder. "You holler if you need anything, darlin'. We'll get the signage changed first of the week."

She gazed at the storefront, where you could still see "Karate Kicks" emblazoned across the top. Near the road a smaller sign listed the shops—hardware, boutique, insurance, coffee. Soon, hers would be there, too. The plaza was already used to a steady flow of people in and out. Even though this place, her place, wasn't karate, it wasn't too far off.

She waved as Mr. Sweeney shuffled off, back toward his sad little pickup truck, then hugged herself tight. *My own business—me. I'm doing this.*

A flash of Stace high-fiving her seared though her mind, but she pushed it away.

Forget the past. Focus on right now, this new thing, this plan. She, Natalie Motts, former Dahlia hotshot, might have gotten her tail nipped and then some this last year. She might have come home crying in a fit of grief and tears and a whole lot more.

But her fight wasn't over.

CHAPTER 2

Natalie

It was as if she'd never left.

Late that afternoon, Natalie stood in her parents' kitchen, the counter jutting hard into her midsection, chopping scallions and trying not to nick her index finger. So far, so good.

Early-summer sun cast vivid beams through the French windows, the ones Mom redid the year before Natalie headed off to college, the familiar yellow-flecked countertops and painted sunny cupboards still crisp. They reminded her of Easter and baby chicks and bouquets of daffodils, all the things Mom loves. The backdrop of her youth, surrounding her once again.

Everything the same. Yet everything had changed. And now, the shop! Her shop.

A lump knotted in her throat, and she swallowed, forcing a deep breath. *I need to tell them.*

Beside her, Ashley cracked a handful of fettuccini in two and stirred them into the pot in batches, her sister's white-tipped fingernails glossy and perfect against the tarnished silver.

"Late night?" Ashley gave her the side-eye.

Not by choice, though Natalie certainly didn't want to share any of that with her sister. No matter how many sleeping pills her doctor prescribed after the accident, the nightmares persisted.

"Didn't sleep super well, but it's nothing. Guess I'm still . . . getting used to everything."

Ashley stuck a bowl and a block of cheddar into Natalie's hands. "Just 'cause you're binge-watching late-night TV doesn't mean the rest of us have to pick up the slack."

But Ashley's tone was teasing. Sweet.

"You're just jealous because I get our old room to myself." Nat stuck out her tongue but took the cheese and bowl, fumbling in the drawer for the grater. "Remind me again why you didn't get the already-shredded kind?"

"Because it tastes better . . ."

". . . and Mom likes it that way," Natalie finished their standard line, and the sisters giggled.

And suddenly it was like eleven years had come and gone as fast as Ashley could snap her manicured fingers.

Natalie grated the cheese in a slow, steady rhythm just like the old days, the ting of the grater on the ceramic bowl a percussion beat, keeping time. Outside the window, she caught a glimpse of Ashley's husband, Matt, playing catch with the twins. She could hear the ball game on in the other room, pictured her daddy snoring in the big cream recliner while Mom scurried around, setting the table, probably glancing nervously at the street in hopes Hayley would be home on time.

Their youngest sister Hayley, now a junior in high school, had some track thing after youth group, and Mom had fretted this way and that. How Hayley needed to get her "fanny home pronto" because Saturday dinners "are a priority in this house, part of our family identity." Natalie was the one who'd convinced Mom to let the girl go.

After all, childhood only lasted so long. That's something Natalie knew all too well.

"What?" Ashley gave her that soft-eyed look again, the one she'd started when Natalie moved back home last year—a worried mama hen who wanted to pry but didn't dare.

"Other than the kitchen, I think this house hasn't changed one bit since we were born."

"Why fix what isn't broken?"

"Of course you'd say that." But Natalie said it in the soft tone she'd adopted, another something-new that started between them since she moved back.

Thinking of Ashley as an ally instead of the competition wasn't easy, but her older sister hadn't been anything but good to her since she came home. Really, since Ash got married, had kids, and became a real, live grownup. At least one of the Motts sisters was doing her job right.

Natalie crossed the room for a spoon, ruffling Ashley's ponytail as she passed.

"You know, I'm here for you," Ashley said quietly. "What you went through . . . after what Tucker did to you. And with Stacey, your best friend. I can't even imagine your pain."

"I know you are."

The moment lasted a beat or two longer between them than normal. Faint tears welled in Ashley's eyes, and she opened her mouth like she wanted to say more.

But then the door slammed open and Hayley burst in, all pink-flushed cheeks, swinging high ponytail, and mud-caked sneakers, and the moment was gone.

"I'm starving! Puh-leeeeease tell me you're making that cheesy pasta thing. And that Nat's not the cook." Hayley, the only brown-haired girl of the bunch, batted her bright-blue eyes exaggeratedly.

"Yeah, yeah." Ashley shook her head, the tears like a distant memory. "And those shoes stay outside. You know Mom's been cleaning the house since you left."

Hayley huffed out a breath. "It's just *us*."

"You know Mom."

Thirty minutes later, they were all gathered around the big oak table in the dining room, Daddy saying the blessing and Ashley's kids Paisley and Peter doing their six-year-old level-best not to break out into a fit of giggles like last time. Natalie was stuck between Paisley, who kept giving her looks someplace between adoration and wary study, and Hayley, who was eying the platters like a ravenous horse. Natalie suspected her little sister could out-eat all of them and still stay skinny.

"Any luck on the job front?" Daddy looked at Natalie across the table.

Her heart fluttered so fast she was sure the whole table could see it. *Just tell him about the shop.* Why, at twenty-nine, she still cared so much about what her father thought remained a mystery to her.

But her mouth felt like it was coated with flour, and she knew she couldn't. Not tonight.

"Nothing yet." Natalie waved a hand like she was shooing away some annoying kids. "But there may be a PR position at the retirement home this fall."

Daddy shook his head. "You'd think with your grades, a bachelor's in marketing, and that swanky big job on your resume you'd have landed something by now."

"Daddy. Dahlia, South Carolina, isn't exactly Nashville."

"Or Charlotte," Ashley offered.

Natalie nodded gratefully. "Good marketing jobs in a small community aren't exactly spilling over. Plus, I'm picky."

"Well, maybe over in Aberville, or even the next town." Daddy stabbed a forkful of pasta.

"Maybe I don't even want to go back into marketing." Her fingernails dug into her palm. *You've practiced this a hundred times: I want to open an art shop, a place where people can come and be creative, take classes, have some fun. I have a business model, I've saved up the cash, and I found the right place . . .*

But the words just wouldn't come.

"Not go back into marketing?" Daddy looked almost scandalized, and Natalie had to bite back a giggle.

Mom cleared her throat. "You know, the local school's always looking for good teachers."

"We'll see." *No thanks.* Natalie glanced at Hayley. "So, Hay, still set on USC?"

Hayley, her hair damp from the shower, nibbled on her bare nails and shrugged. "Hard to turn down a full ride if I can keep my grades up next year. Besides, Kiki and I want to room together."

"Kiki? That's the girl from that . . . other school?" Mom's tone was mild and her eyebrows were raised like it was an innocent question. "And don't bite your fingernails."

But Natalie could see the concern. If she remembered right, Kiki lived on the other side of town, and her family didn't have a lot of money.

"Oh, Mom, she goes to our church." Hayley rolled her eyes.

"This meal is so good, Ash." Natalie lifted her fork and caught her brother-in-law's eye, hoping he'd read her mind. *Time to change the subject.*

"Hope there's enough for seconds," Ashley's husband, Matt, said. "So, Jim, how's business going this month? I might have a client to send your way."

Natalie shot him a thank-you look across the table, jabbing at a chunk of broccoli.

After dessert, Daddy took his favorite position in the recliner in front of the television.

The twins started making poor Matt give them bear rides around the living room, though he didn't seem to mind. Natalie hadn't given much thought to Ash's husband when they'd first gotten married, but he'd proved to be a nice guy, and funny. Not nearly the boring accountant her dad seemed desperate for him to become, even if she'd been certain at the time Ashley was marrying a carbon-copy of their father, right down to the profession.

Hayley excused herself.

"If it's okay, some friends are going to pick me up so we can study for finals."

Mom gave Hayley the look. "*Which* friends?"

"Just Chelsey, Zoe, Mike, and Ben."

"Ben Smathers? Bobby's little brother?"

"Yeah, Mom." Hayley rose to clear her plate, then caught herself. "I mean, yes, ma'am. I'll be home by nine-thirty. We're just going up to the diner."

Mom nodded approvingly. "Ben Smathers is a nice boy. I like him."

"So does Hayley." Ashley poked her sister.

Mom sighed at Natalie when Hayley left. "I almost wish you were still dating his brother."

"Mom!" Ashley looked horrified.

Natalie snorted. "That was ancient history. Besides, he's *married*." She would be, too, if not for . . . well, everything. She jutted her chin and gave her best effort at a sassy smile.

"Well, I didn't mean *that*. I just mean they're a good family. Did I ever tell you Arlene Smathers and I always talked about how we hoped one of my girls would marry one of her boys?" Mom got that faraway romantic look she always got when they watched girly movies. "Who knows—maybe Hayley will end up with Ben? They'd be a good match . . . "

"Hayley's sixteen, Ma. And this isn't 1827. I think she's perfectly capable of finding her own husband without a matchmaker—when and *if* the time comes."

Ash giggled and Mom swatted at her, the tension diffused.

But that night in bed, long after Ashley and her family went home and she could hear Hayley banging around in their shared bathroom, getting ready for church tomorrow, Natalie stared at the ceiling.

Years ago, she and Ash had put up stars, the glow-in-the-dark kind that only showed when all the lights were out. She'd scraped them all off her senior year, convinced they were babyish, but she must have missed one. Now in the darkness, Natalie focused on that single, solitary star, just a yellowy fuzz against the black ceiling.

Don't you think about him. Don't you dare . . .

A tear welled up. She squeezed her eyes shut and, clenched her teeth hard. *God, help me.* But either God wasn't listening, or he didn't want to let her off so easy tonight.

Tucker's eyes appeared in her mind first, those golden brown, laughing eyes that grabbed her tight even before her fresh-from-college heart even registered all the other stuff—handsome, charming, single. That warm, always slightly tanned skin a popping contrast beneath the collar of his crisp white shirt and blue tie. Slightly disheveled hair, just a little too long for corporate, but perfect for the Nashville music scene, both edgy and little-boy-wild all at once. Hair she once ran her fingers through long, long, long ago . . . a lifetime ago.

Oh, Tucker. *Why?*

Of course, she knew why. Stacey knew, too.

And it didn't matter how many months passed or how many miles she put between then and now, there and here. He was weak. He was selfish. Stacey, too.

They betrayed her. Broke her heart. He would have done the same to Stacey had they lived long enough, Natalie knew that now.

But they hadn't. One drink too many tipped their fate when he got behind the wheel of the car, and now they were both dead and gone, together. Forever.

Together forever.

The irony hit her like a punching bag, and she rubbed the spot on her finger where her engagement ring once lived. All her dreams, demolished.

The tears came now, ugly tears that spilled up and out, wetting her cheeks and neck and the thin summer coverlet Mom bought for this room where she now slept. The guest room. A guest in her own childhood home.

This isn't how my life is supposed to turn out.

She wanted to scream the words until she choked, but instead just let them wash over her along with the tears until her breathing settled, her raw throat relaxed, and her heart tumbled slowly back into place. *Oh, God. Help me.*

A single sunflower began to form in her mind. She focused on it, on the petals all thick and lush, like an overgrown dandelion or a lily, only thicker, bigger, bolder. Stronger.

Sunstrokes—that's what her shop will be called. She could picture the logo in her mind, bold black script with a vibrant full-grown sunflower, petals golden-yellow and wide open, the stem curving to become a paintbrush at the bottom. She'd designed it years ago, even shared it with Stace, who loved the idea of a brushstroke at the end, like a flourish. Later, the name settled on her heart—instead of brushstrokes, sun-strokes, like painting with light instead of color, only the light had all the colors.

Natalie saw the stem now in her mind. Sturdy but graceful, rising up and up as the yellow blossom lifted its face toward the sun, petals like arms, calling out for all the world to see.

See me. See. Me.

Black soil far beneath churned, fragrant with life, and Natalie pictured all of this—soft lush dirt, green healthy stem, butter-yellow blossom gently fading into orange and then brown and then finally black at the very center, like an eye that couldn't look away. No matter how hard it tried.

After the accident, that sunflower wouldn't leave her alone. It haunted her mind as if it were the only thing she had to hold onto, the only thing that could get her through. She'd dream about it night after night—first the accident, then the sunflower.

It was like God were speaking to her through that sunflower: *Your dreams are wrecked, baby girl, but I have something more in store for you. Just hold on tight.*

The click of the ceiling fan wrapped her now in its steady, easy rhythm. In the room next door, she could hear Hayley puttering around, getting ready for bed. Outside her window, the wind picked up, and a dog barked its warning, or maybe its hello, from a few houses down. The sounds of summer. The sounds of home.

That night she didn't dream for the first time in a long while, at least not that she could remember. Maybe God was answering her prayers after all, taking the memories away. The pain.

Free. At last.

Though when she awoke, all she could think about was Stacey, and Tucker's convertible, Stacey's long dark hair flowing wild in the wind.

CHAPTER 3

Natalie

THE MAY SUN FELT GOOD on her arms Monday morning as Natalie stood outside the shop, looking the building up and down. Something about the painted wood against the rich red brick called to her creative spirit, whispering promises of what could be in what once was.

"You really think it can be ready by then?" She didn't know if she was asking old Mr. Sweeney or herself.

The landlord gave a one-shouldered shrug. "Could be, give or take a week. See that door, though? That'll have to be fixed, plus those floors in back are starting to warp. And it does get drafty in winter. L.J. will be here any sec. He'll work up an estimate, tell us what we're in for."

"You're not trying to talk me out of this, now, are you, Mr. Sweeney?" She said it in her sweet-as-sugar voice, the one Mom instilled in all her girls, but she put a gentle hand on his arm to show she meant business. "I've got big plans for this place."

"Your daddy'd run me up one side of the street and down the other if I ever wronged one of you Motts girls." Mr. Sweeney shook his head. "Bad for business. I just want you to know what you're getting yourself into."

I hope I'm getting myself into a killer moneymaker. But Natalie just smiled.

His eyes softened. "You sure you want to do something as big as starting a business? A pretty lady, young like you, might be married with a baby in another year. Priorities change."

She hoped her grin masked her frustration. "I don't have a ring on my finger yet, Mr. Sweeney. Besides, if I do get married—not that I plan to anytime soon—I'm certain my husband will be supportive of whatever business I choose to start."

He made tsking noises. "Don't wait too long, hon. These are the best years of your life."

After he'd gone, and the contractor had come and gone, she walked through the space once more, going over her supplies list and calculating dates. Her yellow cotton sundress made swishing sounds as she walked, and she shook her head, loosening the headband.

Time for a giant cup of coffee—and some decision making.

She stepped outside, turned toward the smell of java, and almost ran smack into a stroller.

"Natalie Annabelle Motts, why if it isn't the Homecoming Queen herself!" The voice, a female's, was friendly, warm enough to be genuine, and probably was.

Still, Natalie's back stiffened. She knew moving back home again meant a nonstop reminder of who she was. But it felt like being reminded every single day that she used to be Somebody. *I'm not even sure who I am anymore.*

Much less who she wanted to become.

But when Natalie met the woman's eyes, her own eyes were warm to match. "Well, hey there, Shelly! I'm not such a queen these days. But look at you!"

Shelly giggled, her belly large with child and her cheeks flushed with color, probably the prettiest image of a pregnant woman Natalie had laid eyes on. A toddler perched in the stroller, all decked out in one of those fussy blue-plaid smock things people dressed their kids in these days, and a mini Shelly lookalike peeked out behind her mom, passing her brother a tiny gray rabbit.

"Brianne, say hello." Shelly caressed her daughter's honey-brown locks, nudging her forward. "This is Miss Natalie, Mommy's old friend. Wow, it's been a long time."

Brianne murmured a greeting and ducked back.

"You are the perfect picture of motherhood." Natalie said, and meant it. She smiled. "I'm so happy for you."

"I'm really blessed. How about you?" She gestured toward Natalie's left hand. "Let's see that ring."

Natalie's stomach dropped, and on reflex she grabbed at her ring finger, rubbing at what once was. Funny how that finger still felt naked, exposed.

"Ah, we . . . it didn't work out." Natalie shrugged like it was no big deal.

Shelly's eyes widened like she'd just seen the mayor's underwear. A delicate hand flew to her mouth. "Oh, Nat! I . . . I'm so sorry! I didn't kn—"

"No, it's totally fine. Really." Natalie gave her megawatt grin. *Perfectly okay, no heartbreak here. See?* "I'm just glad to be back home, with my family again."

"I hear Nashville's pretty hectic." Shelly's brown eyes reminded her of a doe's, liquid and filled with sympathy.

Natalie wrinkled her nose. "Oh, yeah. Nothing like Dahlia."

Shelly put a hand on her back and winced. "Going to go rest awhile. Little Robbie's in a kicking mood today." She looked Natalie up and down appreciatively. "I don't know how you do it. You look the same as you did in high school! I mean, I don't think you've gained a pound!"

Natalie just waved a hand. "All an illusion. See you soon, Shelly. Nice meeting you, Brianne!"

At the door to the coffee shop, Natalie took a breath and realized her hands were shaking. *Is it going to be like this every single time someone asks about the wedding? About Nashville, my old life, why I'm back home after all these years?*

Maybe this was a big mistake. Maybe coming home to get her bearings—let alone start this business—wasn't so smart, after all. Why did she tell all those people her big news last winter, let her parents send out save-the-date announcements like she was some debutante?

Natalie's insides wiggled like a goldfish had gotten loose and was swimming around beneath her skin.

"Allow me." A wrinkled hand, thick blue veins beneath gnarled knuckles, clasped the door handle to the café before her, and a gentle hand on her shoulder nudged her ahead.

Natalie looked up to thank the man, but he'd already slipped past her, heading toward the newspaper stand.

She stepped into the cozy café and took a deep slow breath, inhaling the nutty spiced aroma, the soothing swirl of cinnamon and java and pure sugar, as her stomach settled and the lump in her throat began to subside. *It's a good place.* She didn't know Finn McCafferty, the owner, too well when they were in high school together, but clearly, the guy was smart. Or maybe he had a lot of help behind the scenes. That's something she could use—a helper. But not yet. Phase Two, she reminded herself. Besides, she had Hayley.

Ten minutes later, a large caramel cappuccino before her, Natalie perched at a small bistro table, her back to the wall, sizing up the town where she grew up. Joe Mama's arrived in Dahlia after she left for college, and she could tell it did a good business. The tables were mostly full, a few moms catching up over coffee, a little

Bible study in the corner, a cute old couple holding hands by the window. The old man who'd held the door for her was chatting with two younger men by the door, a newspaper tucked under his arm, and the purple-haired barista rushed to get a large order ready for someone at the counter. In the back, she could see Finn cleaning one of the machines, so intent on his task he didn't seem to realize his back was getting soaked from runoff. Either that, or he didn't care.

Natalie gazed at the shelves lining the walls, the artsy knick-knacks and perfumed soaps and lotions on display for purchase.

Local artwork would do well here. She'd seen it in other coffee shops, funky landscapes and flowers, farmhouse scenes, colorful and priced competitively, good both for the artist and the shop itself. Natalie pulled her blue-striped notebook from her purse, clicked the pen, and added it to her list.

Someone cleared her throat, and Natalie looked up. Two women her mom's age, women she'd seen at church, stood before her.

"Honey, I'm so sorry for your loss." The lady's icy blonde hair was streaked, and her big chunky earrings swayed with her concerned expression.

Natalie had to force her shoulders to stay relaxed. Her thumb instinctively reached toward her ring finger. *Not again.*

The other woman leaned down, her face level with Natalie's, and put a hand on hers. She smelled like gardenias, the scent cloying.

"Don't you forget your church is here for you. Always."

"Thanks, Mrs. Leman, Mrs. Carpenter." Natalie gave what she hoped was a grateful smile.

The second they left, she gathered her purse and stood. In a way she was a widow, of sorts. But it felt wrong, false, now that she knew the truth. Now that she knew her whole life back in Nashville was built on a lie. She thought she'd be Mrs. Tucker Armstrong, heir to Armstrong Communications.

Instead she was a joke. At the funeral, Mrs. Armstrong barely met her eyes. Gone was the charming little banter they'd shared, the jokes about how they looked so much alike they could be mother and daughter. With their son gone, it was as though Natalie hadn't really existed. No one had even put up a fight when she gave her resignation. Forget the fact that she'd worked there since graduating college, been lead on a dozen of their bigger marketing deals in the last year alone.

She became Girl Who Was.

Best forgotten.

But back home in Dahlia, it was like no one could forget who she was a decade ago.

"Here." Someone stood in front of her, his hands on her coffee cup. Finn. "I've got that for you."

"Thanks. Ah, how's it going?" He was taller than she remembered, and not nearly as gangly.

At her smile, he gave her a wary look, like they were still in high school.

"Not bad. How long are you back in town?"

A breathless laugh escaped her lips. If only she knew. "Assuming business goes well, hopefully a long time." At his questioning look, she nodded toward the length of the plaza. "I just rented out Karate Kicks, or at least what used to be. I'm opening an art place."

"You? Art?" He gave her a doubtful look.

She maintained the smile. "Yeah, me."

I'm more than just Homecoming Queen, Motts girl, and Bobby Smathers's ex-girlfriend, she wanted to say but held her tongue.

"Hopefully we can partner up sometime, do some events that generate business." She could feel the weight of the blue-striped notebook in her purse, all the ideas swirling, and she gestured to the shop around them. "It could be a good fit."

He moved away now, heading toward the back with her coffee

cup. "Maybe. Good luck getting started."

"Thanks."

She stared after him, watched as he disappeared into the back. Why she cared she didn't know, but suddenly she wanted to convince him she knew what she was doing. She wasn't some silly girl, opening some art shop on a lark with Daddy's money.

This is my place, my dream, my money. Daddy had nothing to do with it.

Natalie squared her shoulders and headed for the door.

If she was going to be successful, she needed to take a cue from what was working—this place, for starters. For she did indeed aim to be a success, and there was one thing no one knew about her yet, but they'd sure know soon:

Natalie Motts was the hardest worker around, and the most driven.

And there's nothing that would stop her once her mind was made up.

CHAPTER 4

Natalie

An hour later, Natalie paced the living room, working hard to keep the exasperation out of her voice.

"I wasn't trying to keep it from you."

Daddy crossed his arms. "Well, you did. Your mom had to find out at the grocery of all places."

"I was planning to tell you both tonight. I . . . was just waiting for the right time."

It was the truth. If she'd hesitated at all, nervous about their reaction, it wasn't from anything besides timing. If there was one thing Mom taught her, it's that timing was everything.

That, and Daddy's moods ruled the house.

And, oh, was he in a mood today.

She squeezed her eyes shut. *It's not like you need their permission. You're a grown woman, a college graduate.* But Daddy was still Daddy, no matter how old she got. And even if she didn't need his permission, she craved his blessing.

She looked at Mom pleadingly. "I'm sorry. I shouldn't have waited. I just wanted to show you my plans, make you both proud."

Mom sighed. "You don't have to work to make us proud, Nat

honey. We're just worried about you, and we want to help you. And it's, well, embarrassing to find out about this from somebody else. I had to pretend to Mr. Sweeney I knew what he was talking about just to save face."

Natalie's palms grew sweaty. Save face—that was always the issue here.

Daddy's recliner creaked as he shifted. "And why in the world you're opening some silly art studio instead of using your college degree is beyond me."

"It's not silly."

Mom put a hand on her arm. "That's not what he meant."

Sure. Natalie sighed. "May I at least get the plans, show you both what I have in mind?"

"By all means." Daddy didn't even look at her.

In her room, Natalie gathered it all in a neat stack—the marketing plan, the business proposal, the quote from the landlord, even her bank statements. On the very top rested the updated logo she'd sketched out last night, shaded in with buttery yellows and greens and a pop of vivid pink, homage to Dahlia's own town logo, designed after its lush flower namesake.

She laid it all out downstairs on the coffee table.

Mom took a seat on her right, peering over. She fingered the logo, mmm-ing appreciatively.

Natalie looked Daddy in the eye and spoke slowly but succinctly, just like she'd done hundreds of times with clients. *Forget that Daddy's no client—you've got this.*

"Sunstrokes is something I came up with a few years ago, before Tucker even asked me out, right after I got that promotion," she began. "And it's a good business model. With just rent and basic supplies, I don't have to worry about major overhead, so the profits can go right back in as long as you're letting me live here. And you've both been so gracious about that."

"This is your home, Nat." Mom squeezed her knee. "We love having you here."

Natalie gave her a grateful look. "Not only that, but Dahlia's, well, ripe for this kind of place. Moms and kids, afterschool art lessons, ladies nights, church groups, homeschoolers and teen nights."

She could picture it all. And with the hardware store next door, another idea hit her—a woodworking offshoot. The back room was a good size for lessons, and surely Mr. Ray or one of his sons wouldn't mind teaching a class or two. Especially if she paid well. Besides, she'd tutored Mickey Ray, his youngest, through most of high school science. He kinda owed her, not that she was keeping score.

Daddy snorted. "Sunstrokes. Sounds like people will be falling over inside."

"Daddy . . ." But it was a start. He'd said "will be."

"I just don't think it's a good idea." Daddy had that look, the one where he thinned out his lips and squinted his eyes all analytical, like he was cracking some ancient code deep in his mind.

Natalie kept her voice calm. He liked all the facts first, needed to see all the possibilities before he could wrap his mind around something new. Eighteen years under his roof taught her well.

Natalie smoothed the business plan, handing it over. "It's the least risky business venture possible, other than a consignment store, and Dahlia doesn't need another one of those."

The second one just opened this spring out on west Main Street, and it was doing well, but two in one small town was a bit much. Plus—*art*. But she needed to keep emotions out of this, especially when it came to Daddy.

"I took all your advice in Nashville. I saved and invested, just like you taught me. I won't even need a bank loan, and Mr. Sweeney's willing to do half-price rent for the first six months."

Daddy blinked at that.

"That's awfully good of him." Mom tucked a stray lock of hair behind her ear.

"I think so, too." She pointed to the paper in her father's hands. "As you can see, I have all the numbers right here, and projections through not only year-end but next summer, all the way down to office supplies and trash bags."

He scanned the sheet, the line between his eyes creasing.

She reached out a hand and laid it gently on his arm. "And I'm not asking for a thing. Just your support—and your blessing. You and Mom are already doing me a kindness by letting me stay here."

Mom wriggled a little in her chair, and Natalie could tell she was pleased.

Daddy needed facts. Mom craved manners. As for Natalie? She was still figuring that out.

But she suspected it started with standing on her own two feet, and Step One was her own business.

"What about medical insurance?" Daddy frowned. "Investing?"

"I already talked to Jason over at Payton Insurance. There's a group medical co-op I can do. And investing will be on hold till I start turning a profit. But speaking of profit, look at the margin." She pointed. "That's the most conservative projection."

Tucker would be proud. The thought, unbidden, was like a punch to the belly. She swallowed, keeping her eyes on the paper.

She'd done these sit-downs a gazillion times, at first just watching, but by the end, leading. She knew the suits were always impressed someone like her—all blonde and young and innocent-looking—could not only crunch numbers like a pro but explain it so seamlessly. Her boss, Tucker's dad, called it their "poker face" move. A little surprise usually sealed the deal. People always needed a shove to spend marketing dollars, though in truth she knew that was the very thing that drove sales—and made the difference between a skyrocketing promotion and "just okay."

But this was Daddy. He'd changed her diapers, or at least passed Mom the wipes.

The tick of Nana's wall clock kept time with her heart.

Finally, Daddy looked her in the eye. "You've certainly done your homework."

From him, that was high praise.

She let out a hint of a breath. "Yes, sir."

"You know I'm not one for start-ups, but you have saved the money, I'll give you that. And the location is strong." He eyed her. "Just be smart, Natalie. And it wouldn't hurt to have a backup, just in case."

Of course he'd say that. But her heart felt like it was softening, loosening in her chest.

"Yes, Daddy. I will."

Mom scooted her chair back. "How about I put on some decaf?"

Daddy nodded. "That'll be nice, Mary Lynn."

Natalie joined her in the kitchen, leaving him with all her papers. He'd want to read everything.

"Who knew all that fingerpainting would pay off," Mom teased at the counter.

Natalie bristled but forced a smile, passing her mom the coffee container. She'd come a long way since fingerpainting.

Mom leveled out four scoops, put them in the carafe, and pressed start. Finally, she handed the container to Natalie, but not before she looked her deep in the eye.

"Honey . . . are you sure you want to do this?" Mom's brows looked nonexistent in the kitchen light, and for the first time Natalie noticed small lines creasing her mother's mouth. "I mean, insurance and pension, weekends off, vacations. You know, that's how I met your Daddy. I was just a typist at the firm, helping in the summers when school was out and I wasn't yet teaching summer school. Swept me off my feet, he did." Mom got that faraway look.

"I just worry . . ."

"You don't have to worry, Mom."

"Pfft." Mom huffed out a breath. "Do you know how hard it's going to be for you to meet a man, a *good* man, when you're spending your life getting a small business off the ground?"

Natalie's jaw tightened. "I don't need a man, Mom."

"You say that now . . ."

"No, really. I don't!" She took her mother's hands in hers. Tucker, his sandy hair and his never-met-a-stranger grin, loomed like a ghost in her brain. "I had all that. It didn't work out. And I realized—I don't need a man to be happy!"

"Now, Nat, that's not what I'm saying—"

"You, and Ash? You both lucked out. God sent you your perfect mate when you were young enough to enjoy it. But maybe that's not what God wants for me, Mom."

Maybe that's not what Natalie wanted anymore, either. She thought she did, once. But now . . .

She took a deep breath and swallowed, like she was trying to swallow back all the words she wanted to say. *Happily-ever-afters aren't all that matter.*

But looking at her mom's hunched shoulders, the sheen to her light eyes, and the disappointed droop to her mouth made Natalie's heart flutter.

She pulled her mom in for a hug, surprised to find her own eyes moist. "I love you, Mom. If God wants to send me a husband, my little business venture certainly isn't going to stand in the way."

She felt her mother give a shaky sigh. "You got that right, sweetheart."

After the coffee finished and Mom and Daddy were sipping their pre-dinner mugs, Nat retreated to her room.

She slipped on shorts and an old T-shirt, twisted her long blonde hair into a topknot, and pulled a fresh canvas and her dropcloth from the closet.

I don't need a man. The words echoed as she squeezed a glob of green neatly on the palette. She didn't even need a best friend.

Natalie had herself, she had Jesus, and she had a fierce, sharp, creative mind. Not just that, but she was willing to put in the hard work to make it all happen.

And yet. *More. Something more.* She didn't know what. But she knew it was out there. Calling to her. Waiting for her.

Sunstrokes. It was an easy business to open, really, and perfect for the town. Six years at Armstrong Communications taught her the ins and outs of not only what makes good press but a solid business, and she'd graduated near the top of her class, anyway. She had the smarts, not to mention the chops from one of the best publicity firms in town. She worked her tail off those six years—seven, if you count the internship—and rubbed shoulders with some of the biggest names in town thanks to her job. Well, that and Tucker.

A shiver ran down her spine, and she pushed thoughts of him aside, dipping her brush into the deep green, swirling in a dab of white so the shade was just right, vivid as the trees outside her bedroom window.

Tucker had helped her, taught her, mentored her, but she did the heavy lifting. Running, fetching, always learning. Always listening.

And more importantly, she had the passion. She'd minored in art mostly because it gave her access to the university's art studio, where she could lose herself in the canvases and the colors when homesickness hit so hard it made her want to run back home where she'd always known everyone and everything. She wasn't good enough to be a full-on artist—she wasn't deluded enough to dream of that. Natalie was nothing if not practical.

But art . . . creating . . . the whirl of texture and color and pattern and silhouette, the play of light upon dark, how the shadows and intricate lines could create just enough mystery to delve into the beauty underneath. That's what she'd been after, always. She could lose herself in creating, forget all about Natalie Annabelle Motts—Homecoming Queen, head cheerleader, church choir leader, and all-around-town-princess—and just be Nat. Girl in the world. Daughter of humanity. No one.

Free.

If she could, she'd give everyone that experience.

But it ran deeper than that. Natalie knew it in her bones—art was something Dahlia *needed.* Something every prospering community needed, like a good library and a strong church base. It wasn't just fun to "mess around with paint," but an outlet for expression, a way to free the soul and the mind, a place where people could come together and laugh. Wholesome.

Like the coffee shop, it was yet another place where Dahlia could bring people together. With all the craziness in the world today, Lord knew everyone could use some of that.

After all, art had opened her own mind to things she'd never experienced growing up the sheltered, well-loved daughter she was. Race and class issues. Poverty and pain. Mental illness. Betrayal and passion. Anger and fear.

A shiver ran through her again as she realized maybe that was why she'd been leveled but not obliterated after the accident.

Sunstrokes has to work. She squeezed her eyes shut and swallowed hard. *It just has to.*

CHAPTER 5

Laney

Laney peered at herself in the smudged mirror over the bathroom sink. Dark circles framed dark eyes, and a puffy red spot she could tell would become a pimple stared back at her as if challenging.

She splashed cold water on her face and grabbed her toothbrush. Its bristles were bent, reminding her of the trees back home where she'd grown up. Central Florida live oaks, all graceful beneath their burdens.

Laney wasn't graceful, not for a minute. She was clunky and jumpy and scattered, she knew this. *And I will be for a long time, after everything.* Maybe always. But she knew a thing or two about holding her own beneath burdens.

Those oak trees have nothing on Laney Ricks.

"Mommy . . ." A little hand grabbed at her pajama shorts.

Laney ruffled the girl's chestnut hair, hair so much like her own if she hadn't dyed it purple with those black streaks and cut it so short. But change was good. Change was something she could control, the counselor taught her. She might not be able to get rid of the tattoos from her old life, or Ethan's brand, the memories.

But hair color? That was a cinch. That, she could definitely manage.

"Ready for breakfast?" Laney asked her.

In the tiny kitchen, Laney poured a bowl of cereal, tossing the empty box in the trash. *Thank goodness for food stamps.* She made a mental note to go by the grocery after work.

At the table, Alissa focused so hard on coloring Minnie's dress a vivid red that she didn't even notice she was dribbling milk from her spoon onto the cheap coloring book. She was still so little her legs weren't close to reaching the floor, and she swung them back and forth in time with her crayon, like it was a game.

While the girl was occupied, Laney threw on jeans and a clean shirt, grabbing Alissa's small backpack with the change of clothes for camp. The backpack was yellow with that creepy SpongeBob and his toothy grin staring up at her, nothing that should have triggered the memory. Still, it came. The day she'd crammed her own backpack full, jammed a fistful of cash from Ethan's wallet deep inside, and zipped it up tight.

The first time she'd tried to leave The Life, leave Ethan's and the other girls. She could still hear the slam of the cell door, still feel the relief that came from being behind bars. Out.

Free.

She giggled at the irony, that being locked up inside a jail cell could mean freedom for one while it was supposed to mean the opposite. But it didn't matter. She'd gotten out, and while the ghosts might linger still, they were just ghosts. They couldn't hurt her anymore, and they surely couldn't hurt Alissa. *That's the most important thing.*

A honk sounded outside the window.

"Come on, baby girl. Cha Cha's waiting."

Laney locked the apartment door and they clamored downstairs and into the waiting car. Cha Cha drove a clunker, but it ran and got her to work on time. Joe Mama's coffee shop was a good place, and the owner a nice guy, even if she didn't trust him for a hot minute. Men and trust might be one thing she never got back, but that was okay. She had Alissa, and the apartment, and for the first time in maybe her whole life, hope for the future. If only she could keep holding on.

"You got the letter?" Cha Cha gave her the side-eye once the car door slammed.

"What letter?"

"Jacking up rent prices. Again." Cha Cha let out a shoo-weee and pursed her lips like she'd just eaten a sour lemon. "They stuck it in the door crack."

No. "Hang on a sec."

Laney's heart thudded as she raced up the stairs and saw the envelope, upside down near her front door. Another hundred a month? *How in the world . . . ?*

Maybe Finn would let her work a few more hours, or maybe the hardware shop needed some help. Of course, Joe Mama's was a sweet situation. He let her bring Alissa when there was no camp or school, let her plop down at a table and color for hours.

Her hands shook as she climbed back into Cha Cha's brown clunker and fastened the seatbelt. Cha Cha had the music all cranked up, and Alissa was singing off-key, grinning and oblivious.

God will make a way. Laney squeezed her eyes shut as they rumbled toward town. *He's got to.*

CHAPTER 6

Natalie

Two weeks later, Natalie pulled open the door to the newspaper office, the bell tinkling as she breezed inside.

The one-room office smelled like coffee and perfume, and she waved at the receptionist and the ad lady, both on the phone.

Tiff Smathers looked up, her smile considerably warmer than when they'd met a few months ago.

Natalie didn't blame her—back then, the reporter thought Natalie had her sights set on Tiff's husband. *Nope*. Nat might have dated Bobby Smathers all through high school, but truth be told, he was like a brother. And besides, she didn't think she'd ever seen a guy look at his wife the way Bobby did at Tiff.

"Hey, Nat." Tiff gestured to the chair beside her desk.

Natalie sat, clutching her blue-striped notebook. "I'm mostly here to see Dinah about an ad for the shop." She nodded toward the spray-tanned ad rep still on the phone. "But I was wondering . . . do you do articles about new businesses?"

Tiff looked thoughtful. Her dark lashes were thick and gorgeous, and Natalie suddenly felt extra blonde beside her.

"We do that rundown list you've probably seen once a month,

and of course your standard ribbon-cutting grand openings, but that's about it."

Natalie bit her lip. She'd figured as much.

"Well, if you think of anything, any way I can get some extra news coverage beyond all that, would you holler? I'm not asking for special favors or anything," she added quickly. "Just trying to get creative."

Tiff grinned. "Well, you're in the right business for that with an art shop. I'll say if you end up doing any events tied to newsy stuff, that would be fair game. Like, a benefit fundraiser, or some partnership with a nonprofit?"

An event. That's something Natalie hadn't considered. "Now you've got my wheels turning."

Tiff leaned in. "How close are you to opening?"

"L.J.'s just about finished with the counter repair, and the sign goes up tomorrow." Natalie wanted to wriggle with excitement, but instead she folded her hands around the notebook. "Maybe Monday?"

Tiff looked impressed. "That's great! Let me know if Bobby and I can come help with the open house. I'm sure Smathers Grocery will cut you a deal on platters."

Dinah gave her the ad rates, and Nat signed the contract. The *Dahlia Weekly* was the only paper in town, so a small ad was a no-brainer. Plus, it helped legitimize her. Still, it was another chunk in the expense line.

That's okay, Natalie told herself as she bid her goodbyes and stepped out into the sunny morning. It would take two good years to turn a profit, if she got lucky. But it was all part of the plan.

By the time she pulled up in front of the shop—her shop—she could see L.J. already inside, his apprentice helping him lift what looked like a heavy countertop in place. She watched them, taking a step back and peering through the glass to survey the work she'd completed last night. She'd stayed past dinnertime putting a final coat on the walls, and when she left it was too dark to see the full effect. They looked good, she decided. Sunflower yellow, of course, with one accent wall a royal blue and another fern green. And the wide glass windows let in a ton of natural light, perfect for an art shop.

She could picture the rows of canvasses there on the left, filled with people playing with color. Already she'd bought and set up the long tables over on the right. Soon they'd be lined with chairs, and on top, palettes and brushes and cups of water all taking up residence as colorful, practical centerpieces.

It's all coming together. She wanted to hug herself, or jump up and down or do something girly and totally not like the professional small business owner she now was, so instead she just grinned. Monday. So soon and so far away all at once.

But first: coffee, and a chat with Finn.

Joe Mama's was filled with customers as usual, even though it was already ten-thirty.

The same girl at the counter, the one with the purple and black hair and the tiny stud in her nose, rang up customers, sending the fancier orders down the line but pausing to prep the light stuff, pastries and the daily brews.

"Caramel latte, right?" the girl asked when it was Natalie's turn.

Natalie was impressed she'd remembered. But she shook her head. "Can I try the lavender? Extra whipped?"

"You got it."

Natalie paid, lingering a moment to watch the other barista make her latte.

Hair-color girl glanced over at her. "You're opening the painting place."

It was a statement, not a question, and Natalie caught her eye, recognizing the interest. "Yeah. You paint?"

"No, but I'd like to."

"Come on over sometime. I'm hoping to open Monday."

The girl shrugged noncommittally, then turned her attention to the glass door, which dinged as a couple entered.

Natalie took her latte to a corner table, swiveling her seat like before so she could watch the room. Tucker always did that, too. His dad had served in the Marines ages before he'd launched the firm, and he'd always said he couldn't sit someplace unless his back was against the wall and he had eyes on the whole room, just in case. Just in case of what, Natalie didn't know. Bomb threat, or some military coup? Tucker and his brother had picked up the habit, and apparently so had she, but she did it for the people-watching. That, and it somehow made her feel in control. After everything that had happened, finding out all those secrets, all concealed so carefully from her by those who were supposed to love her most, well . . . control felt perfectly appealing.

It's not my fault, she reminded herself for what felt like the five-hundredth time as she stared into the tiny foam heart the barista swirled atop her coffee. *I'm not a fool just because I didn't see it coming.*

Still, being able to see things coming—that felt good right now, whether that was business projections or just being able to see who walked in Joe Mama's front door.

Finn emerged from the back, a long tray of pastries in his hands. She watched as he paused to chat with his employees and share a few words with the couple at the counter.

When she caught his eye, she motioned him over.

Like last time, his expression was guarded but polite. "How's it going? All set up over there?"

"Almost. I was thinking this Wednesday evening I'd host a small drop-in. Just for this plaza. You, your employees, Ray from the hardware store, Mimi at the boutique and her girls, that sort of thing. We can all paint, have snacks, get to know each other. You know, so we can talk each other's businesses up."

Finn scrunched up his face. "It's a nice gesture, though I'm not much for art stuff. But I'll tell Laney and Bev."

She could tell he didn't plan to come. "Think of it like team building. A chance for you to spend a little time with your employees."

Finn's eyes grew thoughtful. "I'll spread the word. I'm not super social. But I might pop by."

"Thanks. I know you're busy." She could tell he wanted to get back to whatever he was doing, twisting the dish towel in his hands like it would squeeze out liquid gold.

He looked relieved and took a step toward the back. "Catch you later. Good luck with all your final prep if I don't see you before Monday."

Natalie gazed after him when he'd gone. While a nice guy, he didn't seem to like her much. Or maybe avoid was the better word—like he wanted to avoid her. She hadn't known him well when they were in school together, just knew he'd hung around with the Miller brothers a little but mostly stuck to himself. She'd never seen him at youth group stuff or sporting events. Come to think of it, besides a handful of classes together, she'd never seen him much, period.

Almost like he had one foot dipped into adulthood already, ready to jump out of this town the first chance he got.

And yet he'd stayed in Dahlia, unlike most of the kids from school. Unlike her.

She wondered at that, wondered what it would've been like had she stayed, done college close to home, married some local boy. Like Shelly, with her two gorgeous kiddos and a third on the way. Would she have been happy, had a mess of kids right now like Shelly? Like Ash?

Ash. Natalie checked her watch, remembered her sister was meeting her to do some decor stuff around lunchtime. She wanted to fix that one splotch on the wall before Ashley arrived.

Natalie slugged the rest of her latte and brought the cup to the counter.

"Thanks," she told hair-dye girl on her way out, passing her a few flyers. "I hope to see you Wednesday. I'm hosting a drop-in for all the shops in the plaza. Finn's got all the details, but just in case he forgets."

The girl bit her lip. "Any chance kids can come?"

She's a mom, too. Seemed like every female her age was these days.

"Sure. How many you got?"

"Oh, just me and Lissa. She's four. I'm Laney, by the way."

"I'm Nat. Yeah, this is definitely a kid-friendly place."

"Awesome." Laney looked relieved, and Natalie didn't blame her. Finding a cheap babysitter wasn't exactly easy.

Back in her shop, L.J. and his guy were just about finished.

Natalie had fixed the goof and was on a ladder, tacking in some crisp white shelving, when the bell over the door tinkled.

"Can you believe I'm on time?" Ash laughed and set some bags on the counter. "And I got you a present!"

"Because I'm clearly your favorite sister," Natalie teased, climbing down the ladder.

"Actually, I got you two presents."

Natalie watched as Ashley hoisted two fluffy green ferns and hooked them on either side of the front door.

"Ooh, I love those!"

"Me too. I got three more for my front porch."

Natalie giggled and hugged her sister. "Thank you."

"Any time. Daddy been in to see the place yet?"

Nat stuck out her tongue. "Nah. Says he's waiting for Monday, when it's official."

"Well, Mom said she thinks it's 'just darling,'" Ash tossed her head dramatically, making air quotes with her fingers. "Even if she thinks the two odd-colored walls are a little weird. But I love them."

Natalie shook her head ruefully. *That's Mom.*

"So, I'm ready." Ash gestured to her old jeans and T-shirt. "Put me to work."

A half hour later, they had the chandelier installed, and Ash was holding the level while Natalie positioned some of the art. Right now it was mostly her stuff, but she planned to incorporate as much student work as possible. She closed her eyes a moment, picturing the room in a year—swirls of color on canvas taking up every square inch, if she had it her way. This one was a giant Japanese Cherry Tree, its chocolate-brown trunk rising from a soft haze of green into tendrils of vibrant pink, blossoms dancing like fairy lights into the sky above.

"I just had no idea you were this good." Ash shook her head.

Natalie wrinkled her nose. "I'm really not."

"Well, *I* think you're good. Just because that one professor said, well, whatever he said."

The professors at school had been encouraging but honest—Nat didn't have what it took to go pro, didn't have that commitment to composition and light and study, that extra-special . . . whatever it was . . . that made someone an artist. She didn't mind that, truthfully. Still didn't. It had never been about "being good enough" or "being an artist" for her. Natalie just liked to play with paint.

Still, she liked this piece. It meant something to her—strength. Beauty. Rising from far, far below.

They tapped the nails in place, carefully set the canvas, then moved to the next one. This one was a fish with a sassy wink.

Natalie held it in place while Ash worked the level. They made a good team, she realized.

"Hey, you remember Finn McCafferty?"

Ash peeked down. "The Joe Mama's owner? Sure do. Super nice guy."

"Do you remember him at all from school?"

Ash tapped a nail into place, blowing a stray lock of hair from her eyes as she did. "Not really. Didn't he work at that gas station on the edge of town, like, forever?"

A flash of a young Finn, all skinny and serious at the cash register, came to mind, and Natalie smiled.

"Now I remember."

Ash's phone rang from her purse on the counter, and she made a face.

"They can leave a voicemail if it's important." She pounded the other nail home with a flourish and hammed a bodybuilder pose. "I'm on a ladder with a hammer. Nobody gets to mess with me."

But a moment later, Natalie's phone rang. She pulled it from her back pocket and locked eyes with Ash. *Mom*, she mouthed, hitting the speaker button.

"Are you girls together?" Mom sounded out of breath.

"Yeah. What's wrong?"

"Hayley's in the ER."

CHAPTER 7

Natalie

Hayley's bright blue eyes were rimmed red, her expression miserable. Natalie gazed at her kid sister in the hospital bed, a rush of pity washing over her.

"It's a nasty break." The doctor pointed to the X-rays, speaking mostly to their mom. "A couple of them, really. Here," he pointed, "and here. Looks like she'll avoid surgery, but she'll have to stay completely off the right leg. Right now the concussion is my main concern."

There went summer track. And probably any hopes of Hayley helping at Sunstrokes when school got out.

"But what about practice?" Hayley gripped the thin hospital blanket. "I'll lose my scholarship if I can't compete in the fall."

Dr. Diaz leaned down. "Sorry, kiddo. You stay off it completely till the cast comes off, and I'm reasonably certain you'll be okay come September. Maybe August. You're not the first athlete to break a leg at Dahlia High. Comes with the territory."

Mom shook her head. "You're lucky it wasn't worse. Why they decided to do your class trip at a trampoline park is beyond me. Those places—"

Ash put a light hand on Mom's arm. "—are perfectly safe and a total blast. It just happened." She turned to the doctor. "Thanks, Dr. Diaz. We'll make sure Hayley doesn't push it."

When the doctor had gone and it was just them, Natalie gave Hayley the side eye. "Trampoline park? That's way better than our class trip. I think we did the zoo in Columbia."

"We did a nature hike." Ash sniffed.

Mom smoothed Hayley's bangs in place. "Well, those two sound like far safer options. I'm sorry this happened to you, baby."

Hayley groaned, but it managed to sound like a growl and a whimper all in one. "I just . . . that's my whole summer. Gone, just like that! All my friends'll be at the track, or the town pool, every day. Chelsey and Zoe are gonna kill me."

"You can help me with the quilting for church."

"*Mom.*"

Hours later, they were back at the house, Hayley settled in bed upstairs on pain medicine. Ashley'd gone to get the twins from school, and Mom was in the kitchen marinating the chicken for dinner.

Natalie joined her, pulling two tall glasses from the cabinet and filling them each with plenty of ice and lemonade.

"You didn't have a fun day." She handed one of the glasses to her mom, who took a long swallow.

"Thanks, sweetie. Your father's liable to throw a fit when he gets home and hears all this."

"Daddy doesn't know?"

Mom waved a hand. "I don't like to trouble him with all this when he's at work."

Natalie blinked. "But *you* were at work."

"Oh, Mrs. Jenkins got Gloria to cover my classes. It was fine. Speaking of work." Mom gave her a pointed look. "What are you going to do now that Hayley's on bed rest awhile? I know you were counting on her to help at your shop. Oh, and please tell me you changed your mind about those . . . odd walls."

Natalie made a face. "I like my walls. But yeah, Hay getting hurt does change some things. I mean, if she were just behind a cash register it'd be one thing."

Hayley was supposed to be her helper, stocking paint and teaching the kid camps, but Natalie didn't see how she'd be able to do all that back-and-forth stuff hobbling around on crutches all summer. Poor Hay. Summer job, summer plans, everything out the window.

Natalie shrugged. "I'll handle it alone mostly, but I'll just see if I can find a part-timer. Maybe someone on Saturdays and afternoons, when it's the busiest."

Mom gave her that concerned look. "But isn't that going to be expensive? And you know Ash committed to helping that church camp the twins are doing all summer."

Natalie wiggled her fingers. "All in the budget. I'll just wait till I absolutely have to, that's all."

Weeks later, Natalie wanted to eat those words. It was Saturday, she'd just finished leading her second two-hour class of the day, and here stood yet another customer who couldn't understand why her brushes cost triple what they cost at the big-box store the next town over.

"For the kids?" she asked the lady, who had two children in tow and a skeptical look on her face. "Look, those are our high-end brushes. Artist quality. But we also have these inexpensive ones, down over here."

She showed the woman the budget brand.

But the woman pursed her lips. "Those last once or twice and they're done."

"I'm getting some more in Monday, way better quality than these, but not nearly as expensive as the top brand here. Can I call you Monday?"

The woman hesitated.

"And I'll give you ten percent off."

"Mommy, I want to paint todaaaaayyyy," the little boy tugged his mom's hand.

Natalie snagged the cheap brushes from the shelf, put them in the woman's hand.

"Here. You can have these for today, no cost. And I'll have the brushes you want here Monday. Sounds like a plan?"

"With the discount?"

"Deal."

When they'd gone, Natalie propped open the door for some fresh air. Then she let out a breath and sank into the stool behind the counter. *Note to self: Order better-quality cheapy brushes, and lots more mid-grade.* Now if she could only remember this at closing when it was time to put in the order.

Still, she couldn't help but smile. "Lack of customers" was one worry she could officially cross off her list, at least for now.

Since she'd opened two weeks ago, the place had been a swarm of people—the curious, come to say hi and check out what she's doing. The moms and kids come to take art classes, the random hobbyist there for more paint or brushes or canvasses, and yesterday she'd booked her first party. Not bad for brand-new.

Swiveling in the seat to survey the mess behind her—paint-spattered tables, brushes rinsed and drying by the sinks, chairs askew where just an hour before a sea of elementary-aged kids had painted starfish and seahorses, a cacophony of color and cluttery disarray—she hugged herself. *It's happening. It's really happening.*

"You look happy." The voice, a female's, drifted from the open door.

Natalie looked up to see the purple hair-dye girl from Joe Mama's. Laney.

An involuntary giggle escaped, and Nat smiled. Her real smile, not the Motts Megawatt. "I guess I am."

Laney hesitated at the door, as if she wanted to come in but didn't at the same time. She carried a black tote, and in the other hand was a Joe Mama's bag that looked like it had a few pastries inside.

Natalie's stomach growled, and she remembered she'd never stopped for lunch. "If those are the blueberry scones from the other day, I envy you."

Laney looked down and shrugged. "Think so. Finn lets us all take home what doesn't sell that day, so maybe I lucked out. My daughter loves the chocolate chip ones."

"Ha, my sister Hayley would fight her for those."

Laney grinned. "So business is good so far?"

"So far. I've got one more class at five, and it's been steady."

Laney eyed the big sign: Grand Opening: Half-Off Paint-Party Classes.

"At those prices, I bet," she said. "That's pretty cheap for this kind of thing."

Natalie arched a brow. "Well, hopefully they'll try it out, get sucked in, and can't resist coming back." She nodded to the Joe Mama's bag. "So you work Saturdays, too?"

"Not normally 'cause of my daughter, but she's at a birthday party today, so I picked up a shift. Landlord jacked my rent—again."

Natalie considered. "Any chance you might be looking for extra work? I could use some help. Saturdays mostly, and a few afternoons."

The girl scrunched up her nose. "Ah, man, I wish, but I don't have anyone to watch Lissa."

"You can bring her." The words shot out before Natalie could think, but it was true. There was plenty of space, and it wasn't like another little kid would hurt anything.

An old brown car pulled into the lot, music cranked up so loud the windows vibrated.

"That's my ride." Laney's brows knitted, and she looked at Natalie hard. "You sure?"

"Positive. Just think about it, what hours might work for you, that sort of thing. We can talk in a couple days."

Laney's eyes grew thoughtful. "Thanks."

Natalie watched her climb into the car. She could see a child's car seat in the back. As the girl slammed the car door, Natalie could see the driver's giant hoop earrings sway.

CHAPTER 8

Laney

THE JOB SOUNDED good, Laney couldn't deny it. But instead of hope, which she knew she should be feeling, all that welled up inside was panic.

You've gotta tell her about your record, and the situation with Lissa. And what if she says no or asks questions? And it's just too much too fast too hard too . . .

In her lumpy bed that night, Lissa snoring softly across the room, Laney pressed the heels of her hands to her brows. She knew she had to take the job, knew there was no way she'd say no, but the worries brewed like a pot of spaghetti noodles on the burner, cresting over the rim and sizzling.

She could see the letter from the landlord in the dim moonlight, still on her dresser where she had to look at it every single morning. Couldn't ignore it, run from it, pretend it wasn't there, none of the stuff she'd spent all those years doing back with Ethan, her and all those other girls all blissed out on whatever substances he'd been feeding them.

Laney squeezed her eyes shut and swallowed past the lump in her throat, which seemed to come more often these days. Crying was something she hadn't done much of since she was just a kid, just a little older than Lissa. But after Mama passed and it was just her and Zeb, she'd learned to stuff the tears down deep. Locked away tight like that stupid pink box she used to keep her treasures in underneath the bed.

Zeb was a piece of work. Not that he'd ever laid a hand on her. Her stepdad wasn't Man of the Year, but he wasn't *that* kind of bad. Still, there was no way she'd ever let Lissa get exposed to the things she'd seen at her age. The bars, the booze, the guys and all their groping hands and disgusting leering drunk howls and stinky hot breath.

Laney shuddered. Dumb. Dumb to get all PTSD over a lost and messed-up childhood when all the really, really bad stuff hadn't even happened to her yet. That stuff came after.

Still, she'd taken enough get-your-life-back-together coping classes between the prison and the halfway house after to know: probably every cockeyed decision she'd ever made in her whole darn life came from those early days, the things she saw, all she heard and knew way too young. Way, way too young.

Ethan jumped into her head then, and she wanted to punch him. Swift and hard. Make him pay. Good—anger's not a bad emotion. Miss J taught her that at the house. *God gets angry, righteous angry. The good kind of angry.*

And her anger was one hundred percent righteous. Laney knew that without a doubt.

Only, she didn't know whether it was anger at him or her or Mama or Zeb or the johns or everything, all rolled into one ginormous catastrophe.

Nah, it was anger at Ethan. *He gets it all.*

It was easy to pin it all on him, and he deserved it, too. "Grooming," that's what they called it. He'd started it when she was, what—fourteen? No, thirteen. Making her feel like she needed him, like she was special. Like he could get her out of there and out in the world where she could start living her dreams and making it happen. He'd given Laney her first pill that night, the Fourth of July, two days before her fourteenth birthday. It felt like a lifetime ago.

It'd made her feel good, too. Grown up. A little dangerous. Made her walk taller and toss her hair like the girls behind Zeb's bar, the same bar she'd been working—on the sly, naturally—since she was eight and Mama first hooked up with Zeb. Before the baby that wasn't, and the hospital, and Mama's far too quick descent into la-la land. Overdose, that's what they said was Mama's official cause of death.

But Laney knew Mama really died of a broken heart, broken dreams. Dreams of a real family, her and Zeb and Laney and Baby Henry.

But Baby Henry didn't make it. Mama'd had to push out a stillborn knowing he was already gone.

Laney rested her hands on her own tummy, still flat like a girl's even though she'd popped out Alissa almost five years ago. Only those two tiny red squiggles across her stomach, and the kid across the room, evidence it'd happened at all.

A ping of longing clutched in her chest, and Laney rolled over to gaze at her. Lissa. Her baby girl, even if she wasn't a baby baby any longer. All that wild hair, those long limbs and cute freckles and skinny little girly feet that Laney hoped to God with every ounce of want and need and bone-crunching longing in her soul would never ever ever feel the ache of stilettos on cold pavement.

Please, God. You know I don't got a clue what I'm doing here, but I know what not to do. And I know you're looking out for us. Help me do this mom thing right. Help me do what I can't possibly do on my own. And this job thing . . . the art place . . .

Alissa sighed in her sleep and hugged her stuffed dog tight as if she could hear her mama's prayer.

Laney rested her head back on her pillow, pulled the blanket up to her chin snug and secure. Safe.

We're okay now, she reminded herself. Ethan was long gone, him and all his crew. Locked up, hopefully for good. She had a new name, a new look, even her own apartment.

And Nat didn't have to know about the record. It's not like it was in her file. Somehow Miss J got that all to go away under the release conditions.

If she could just hang on and keep paying her rent.

It's not fair what her landlord did, and she knew it, but it wasn't like she had another option, not unless she wanted to pick up and go to . . . well, where would she go, anyway? She had a good job. Lissa was in a good school. Worse came to worst, she could always find a roommate, or—something.

God, she pleaded in her mind as she drifted off to sleep, *if that art shop's where you want me to be, I'm in.*

Laney's palms were sweating so bad Monday morning she was afraid to wipe them against her jeans, just in case they left a wet mark. Standing outside Finn's office door at the coffee shop, she had her hand raised, ready to tap.

Beverly brushed by on her way to the back, arms laden with a big tray of scones for the oven.

"Works better if you actually knock." The older woman's tone was wry, but she gave Laney a wink.

She was right. Laney rapped on the closed door before she could talk herself out of it.

"Come in," her boss called.

But when Finn took a look at her face, he raised an eyebrow. "Please don't tell me you're quitting."

"No!" Laney blinked. "I, ah. Just wanted to see if . . ." *Out with it.* If he said no, he said no. "Would you be okay if I took a second job, at the art place? After I get off work here."

"Of course." Finn's tone was far gentler than she'd expected, as if he knew how hard it was for her to summon the nerve even to ask in the first place. "Just don't ditch me on the morning shift. Bev'll kill me if she heard, but you're the best barista we've had since we opened."

"I heard that," Bev hollered as she sailed by.

Finn made a face. "But you're the best scone-maker!" he called after her.

"Yeah, yeah," they heard from down the hall.

Laney couldn't help but giggle at the exchange, the relief running off her shoulders like rain on a slanted roof.

"Thanks, boss."

"Anytime."

Between orders, Laney peeked out the window, watching for Natalie's silver SUV, which pulled in like clockwork at nine forty.

She darted over to Sunstrokes on her break, her mini backpack clutched in her hands like it was gold.

"So, ah, yes," Laney blurted before Natalie could even say good morning. "Yes, I'd love to work here. That is, if you still need someone."

"Oh, thank goodness!" Natalie's smile widened.

"I just had to run it by Finn this morning, make sure he doesn't mind. But he's fine with it."

They worked out the schedule—she'd help Monday, Wednesday, and Friday when she got off at two, and then from ten till whenever on Saturday.

"And you're sure it's okay if Lissa comes? She won't be any trouble."

Natalie waved a hand. "I don't mind in the least, truly."

Walking back to Joe Mama's, Laney let out a breath she didn't realize she'd been holding. With the extra money, she'd be able to afford not only the rent increase but also pad her slender savings account. That was another Miss J idea—all the girls in the house needed to open their own savings account, with the idea that they were supposed to contribute a little each paycheck just in case.

"There's one way into debt quicker than you can clap your hands and that's having no emergency fund when you find yourself in an emergency," the older woman had told them more than once.

She'd personally taken Laney to the local branch herself, deposited a crisp hundred-dollar-bill right there and then.

"To get you started," Miss J'd said. "One day, you can pay it forward, do for someone else the way you've been helped."

But Laney had only been able to tuck aside five bucks a paycheck lately. Quickly calculating in her head, she realized she could do ten times that, now, plus have enough for extras.

"Things lookin' up, sugar?" Bev tossed her a look when Laney'd washed her hands and joined her coworker once again behind the counter.

For now, Laney thought, swallowing back a grin. *For now.*

CHAPTER 9

Natalie

Daddy had that look on his face, the one that said he thought she was making a mistake. All he said was "pass the French bread," but Natalie knew that look all too well.

It was Saturday night, they'd all gathered around the table for the Motts weekly dinner, and Natalie had just told them about her brand-new hire.

Mom finally sighed and offered a smile. "Well, sweetie, I'm glad you hired some good help. I'm sure you know what you're doing."

"Don't you think it's smarter to wait till you're turning a profit?" Daddy said, smearing a hunk of butter on his bread like he meant business.

"I can't do it all myself, Daddy. Besides, she's good with kids. Maybe better than Hayley." Natalie made a face across the table at her sister.

Hayley stuck out her tongue in return. "At least she's not on crutches all summer. That's one plus."

Mom shook her head. "Hayley Suzanne, you are one lucky young lady it wasn't far worse. You could be stuck in that bed all summer. At least you can walk."

"At least." Natalie could see the annoyance flicker behind Hayley's smile.

"Well, at least promise me you won't rule out Golden Acres. I talked to Mr. Van Buren the other day. He tells me they're saving that marketing job just for you."

"Daddy, I've told you before I don't want to go back into marketing. Sunstrokes is a good business model, a solid effort." Natalie could feel her shoulders tense, and she forced herself to smile politely. "But I appreciate it. I really do."

Mom thinned her lips. "The insurance benefits alone would make that job worthwhile."

Ashley held up a hand. "I think Nat's doing just great on her own. And Peter, Paisley. You guys said that was your favorite camp week yet, didn't you?"

The twins' summer camp had finished a weeklong session at Sunstrokes Friday, where Natalie hosted twenty-five first-graders from the town's rec camp for two hours all week.

"Can you be my teacher at school, too, Aunt Nat?" Paisley reached into the depths of her purple T-shirt and pulled out a ceramic heart, which they'd hand-painted on Day Two.

Nat giggled. "Sorry, kiddo. But you can come take art lessons any day you like. Deal?"

"Deal."

After dinner, Daddy called her in to come sit with him while Ashley cleared dishes with Mom. She perched on the ottoman as he got himself positioned in the recliner, listening as Hayley thump-thumped on her crutches all the way up the stairs to her bedroom.

"I really think you're making a mistake with this art place. I talked with Mr. Sweeney, and he told me how much rent you're paying. That's way too much."

Natalie frowned. Mr. Sweeney had no right to discuss her rent agreement with her father, even if they had gone to high school together.

"Daddy, I promise you I'm doing fine. All the projections are lining up just as they should. And other than Hayley's injury, we've had no surprises. I mean, I was going to pay her, too."

Daddy's jaw tightened. "I just think you're getting in over your head. And with inflation, and all this talk about recession—"

Natalie closed her eyes, measuring her words. "There is risk involved in every business. Any business, Daddy. You know that."

"But why my daughter needs to even be throwing herself out there on some, some common *risk* like anybody else is beyond me. You're a Motts, for gracious sake. I raised you better than that."

Two hot points prickled her cheeks. "Daddy, you and Mom raised me to think for myself, not be some fearful little tail-between-her-legs puppy-dog afraid to make a business move. Come on."

She had enough doubts swirling her around like a circus tiger, leaping with the snap of a whip. The last thing she needed was to get it from her family, too.

Daddy sighed. "Just say you'll think about it. Really consider it."

"Fine."

Daddy nodded like he'd won. "Good."

Ashley gave Natalie an extra hard squeeze when she and Matt left with the twins.

"Don't let Mom and Daddy get you down. You know they hate change. You're doing a great thing with that art shop, sis. Just keep it up."

Natalie was surprised when unexpected tears blurred her eyes, so she just leaned in to hug her sister longer.

When they'd gone, she laced up her worn sneakers and slipped out the back door, her feet slapping against the uneven sidewalk as she eased from a walk into a glide and then a jog.

Dahlia looked even older at twilight, so old it was almost timeless, the kind of classic Americana you'd see in some history book. When she was a kid, she'd thought it boring. Heck, they all did—that's why pretty much everyone she went to school with got out of town as fast as they could after graduation. Well, everyone except Finn and Ash and Shelly and a handful of others who didn't seem to mind the slow pace.

And after Nashville, a slow pace was exactly what Natalie wanted and needed.

Natalie shifted from a jog into a full-on run, heading down Long Street over to Church, past Main and then toward Harding. If she squinted, she could see her plaza in the distance, just barely able to glimpse the blue neon coffee cup logo on the Joe Mama's sign. Other than porch lights and a few streetlights on the corners, it was one of the few unnatural lights she could see.

It used to bother her, but she realized now it was almost a comfort. Everything else in life changed—jobs, friends, the economy. Tucker. But not Dahlia. Never Dahlia.

Tucker's sandy hair and grin materialized unbidden in her mind, and for a second she wanted to smack that stupid, self-assured grin right off his face.

Deceiver. The word loomed, hovering on her lips, and she wanted to shout it. Instead, she just let it echo on repeat in her head as her feet pounded the pavement. Deceiver. Deceiver. Deceiver.

That's what he was. He'd taken her heart, her love, all she'd had to give. All her dreams.

And he'd turned them into dust. Not only that, but he'd taken her best friend, too.

As if one loss weren't bad enough—nope, Natalie had gotten both courtesy of Tucker Langston Armstrong Jr., spoiled-rotten, pretty-boy, pampered son of the largest media mogul in Nashville.

The man she'd thought she'd marry. The man she'd thought was a good guy.

Boy, was she ever wrong and then some.

Deceiver.

Hands balled into fists, she closed the distance to the end of the street, aiming for the only bright lights she could see—Nico's Gas and Go. The very edge of town. After that, it was just a handful of farms and a whole bunch of nothing. In the distance, she could see a plot of land cleared, and a sign advertising some company's construction effort. But that was about it. Farmland, tractors, fields of cows, stretching out for miles.

She paused at Nico's to catch her breath, sucked in the summer evening air in hot gasps until her heartrate settled and she could see clearly again.

"Still a runner, huh."

The voice startled her, and she glanced over. It came from one of the gas pumps.

The man stepped into the light, and she realized it was Finn. He was wearing a deep blue T-shirt and jeans, and his teeth looked surprisingly white against the dark night.

"Barely," she huffed out. "Don't think I'd make the track team if they had a sudden reunion, though."

He laughed, and she looked up at the station.

"This is where you worked, isn't it? All through high school."

"It is."

Silence stretched out, and she wanted to fill it, jabber on, but there was nothing to say, and even if there were, she didn't think he'd want to hear it. Probably had her pegged as silly since way back in the day, just like everyone else in this town. That was okay. They'd figure it out soon enough. Or not—she wasn't sure she cared one way or the other.

She realized he was still looking at her, and she cocked her head.

"You doing all right?" he asked. "At the shop?"

Natalie shrugged. "Pretty good. Hey, thanks for letting me share Laney. She's been a great help."

"Just don't steal her away for good." It took her a second to realize he was kidding, and she grinned.

He finished pumping gas, then gave a slow wave, hopped in his truck, and headed off into the night, toward the middle-of-nowhere side of town.

As he drove off, she stared after him, wondering where he lived, who he had at home. A wife? A roommate? Maybe a housecat, perched on a sofa waiting for him to toss some crunchies in a bowl and scratch its chin.

The thought made her laugh, and she was still smiling when she got back home. Mom and Daddy were already in bed—naturally—and her clothes felt soaked with sweat.

She slipped off her sneakers as she bounded up the stairs two at a time, heading for the shower.

At Hayley's door, she knocked. "You still up?"

Hayley was on the phone, but she covered the receiver and looked at her sister. "What."

It was more a statement than a question, and Natalie blinked. "Everything okay?"

Hayley rolled her eyes and shot her a killer glare. "Could everyone in this family *please* stop asking me this? I'm fine. Everything's fine."

All right, Miss Moody, Natalie wanted to say, but instead just raised her brows and slowly backed out of the room, hands raised as if to say "yes, ma'am" as she shut the bedroom door.

"Just my sister. I wish everyone in this house would just leave me alone," Natalie could hear Hayley say behind the closed door to whoever she was talking to, her tone petulant. Hayley laughed at whatever they said in reply, her voice changing so it became almost a purr. "Riggghhht?"

Natalie couldn't blame her, even if it did sting. She'd been seventeen once, too, though she was far more used to being adored by her kid sister than despised.

After her shower, Natalie wrapped her hair in a towel and pulled the canvas from her closet. She'd been working on a portrait of Ash, figured she'd give it to her for her birthday if she could ever get the eyes right, which so far she'd had no luck on.

She played around with it for twenty minutes before giving up and shoving it all back in the closet. Instead, she burrowed in bed and grabbed her sketchbook and charcoal, jumping back into the one thing she could seem to draw right now, even though she wished she couldn't.

Stacey.

If anyone saw her sketchbook they'd think she was obsessed, and maybe she was. Page after page—Stacey laughing, her feet in the lake. Stacey on the couch, glass raised in a toast. Stacey with her black cat, Edgar, the one she'd had since college when he was just a fluffball of kitten.

Stacey on the cold slab that last night in the morgue, dark hair limp and piled around her in a tumble, eyes closed, face a mask of emptiness.

Natalie closed her eyes and found herself sketching her friend's dark hair, smooth skin, long arms, just looking at her. Looking, her gaze even and flat. Guilty.

Hayley's telephone purr echoed in her mind as Natalie worked on the cheekbones, the hollows beneath Stacey's eyes, the pool of shadow outlining her collarbones.

When she'd finished, Stacey gazed back at her, eyes now hard and cold. Challenging, almost.

All this time, Natalie'd blamed Tucker, almost as if Stacey hadn't made any choice in the matter.

But oh, she had.

Hard tears welled in Natalie's eyes as she stared back at Stace, willing herself to meet her friend's gaze. *I still love you, Stace. But you were wrong.*

Dead wrong.

A tiny bubble of laughter threatened, but instead Nat willed the tears to come. Therapy these last few months taught her the anger was just sadness in disguise, and even if she was furious—which she was—she still grieved her best friend. The sister of her heart.

Yeah, they're both jerks. Nat switched off the lamp and closed the sketchbook, setting it on her nightstand. *Dead jerks. But jerks, nonetheless.*

The single glow-in-the-dark star on her ceiling gazed down at her, steady in the restless night.

"I'm going to do this," Nat whispered aloud to the star, as if it could hear her. "Just you watch me."

But in the night, she was haunted once more by dreams of the wreck, the morgue, the flames.

CHAPTER 10

Natalie

On Sunday, Natalie slipped into the pew behind her parents, Hayley grudgingly bringing up the rear. Ashley and Matt were already there, the kids nowhere to be seen—probably in children's church. Natalie half wished she could join them. She liked their church. After all, their family had gone there since before she was even born. But after the big contemporary megachurch she'd gone to in Nashville, Dahlia First felt . . . stuffy. Old. Almost like nothing ever changed, or ever would.

But today, there was a buzz. Up front, someone had tied festive balloons all across the kneelers, and if she wasn't mistaken, the big cross behind the altar had streamers and sparkles. On the sides of the altar, Natalie could see several easels, each covered with a heavy white sheet.

"Are we having a party and someone forgot to mention it?" Natalie murmured under her breath to Hayley, who giggled like the old days.

"Oh, that's the pastor's big 'announcement.'" Mom sighed. "I guess it'll do some good."

Before Natalie could ask more, the choir began, and they all rose to join in the opening hymn.

When the pastor walked out, everyone gasped. Instead of the trim brown beard and black minister's robe he normally wore, Pastor Dave sported a fresh white robe and a cleanly shaven face.

"So I know I said I wouldn't shave my beard until the Gamecocks won a perfect season, but I'm making an exception," Pastor Dave said, the room thrumming with energy. "Because today is Celebration Sunday, a brand-new start and the kickoff of a brand-new ministry, and I figure today we need an extra-fresh and exciting way to celebrate."

"He looks ten years younger," someone said.

"I heard that," Pastor Dave called back good-naturedly, and laughter erupted. "Helen and Eddie, would you mind?"

Nat looked around as two of the congregation's older members, Helen Chastain and Eduardo Perez, began to take the heavy sheets off the easels. What looked like architectural renderings adorned two of the easels, while another had a timeline and another a set of fundraising numbers.

"For a long time, we've been raising money for a new contemporary space. But over the last year, God has laid something important on my heart—it's time to stop looking within, and start looking outside our doors. Thankfully, our church council has felt that same divine nudge. Together, we all began to pray, and you know I've been asking you all since Christmas to join us in prayer about what the Lord can do through us, his people. And today, I'm excited to unveil what I believe is an extraordinary opportunity for God to use this congregation. But first."

Pastor Dave motioned to Eddie, who dimmed the lights. On the big screen behind the altar, a video started. On the screen, a solitary young woman began to speak.

"My name is Effie, and last year, I finally had the courage to escape my abusive husband. It took me seven different attempts, and each time he found me. The last time, they took me to the emergency room, and I barely made it out alive. But thanks to the Chrysalis Center, today I have a new life—and new hope. And so do my children."

The video cut to Effie and her kids on the playground, walking through a small apartment, shopping in a small clothing store, and cooking a meal with another family.

It closed as Effie and her children gathered on a sofa in a small apartment building, smiling at the camera.

"Thank you," the little girl on Effie's lap said directly into the camera lens. "Thank you for our new life."

The lights rose, and a smattering of applause stirred the room.

Pastor Dave took a moment and gazed at the room. "Last month, I learned about twelve acres of land that have come available on the edge of Dahlia after the passing of one of our oldest members, Mr. Wayne DeLuc. Wayne and his late wife, Cherry, have apparently deeded this land to the church to sell or to do whatever we wish. My first thought was that we could sell it to finance the rest of our contemporary building. But when I brought it to the committee, the Holy Spirit led us elsewhere. Helen, if you would?"

Helen Chastain, a steely gray-haired lady in a light summer dress, approached the pulpit.

"You've all seen this video," Helen began, "and many of us have volunteered a long time at the Friday Night Giveaway, hosted at Dahlia Community Church. We all know Dahlia might be a small community, but it is no stranger to the problems of this broken world, whether that it is homelessness, hunger, poverty, drug abuse, and much, much more. And we, the Church Council and the Futures Committee at Dahlia First, have prayed and come up with what we believe is a beautiful, God-inspired way to be God's hands and feet in this world. We'd like to partner with some other churches in the community and start our very own version of the Chrysalis Center, using the property Mr. DeLuc deeded our church. And we're calling it . . ."

She stepped back and gestured to the men beside her.

"The Tikvah House," they all said in unison.

Helen held up a hand. "Now, most of us are not Hebrew scholars, myself included, so I don't expect you to know this. But the word 'tikvah' means 'hope' in Hebrew. And for us, it is the perfect name for a place we can come together and create as a community of faith—a place of hope for women, women in crisis, where they can start over, start afresh, start anew."

"We're not asking for a churchwide vote today," Pastor Dave added. "We're just excited, and we want to share the plans with you. We're only asking you to go home and begin to pray about this. Does this feel like a good fit for our church? Does this seem to be a good way to honor the memory of a man who cared deeply about our church and its role in our community?"

After the service, Natalie approached the easels with others from the congregation to look at the plans. As she gazed at them, the woman from the video—Effie—wouldn't leave her mind, her dark brown eyes staring deep into hers. From the map, she could tell it was the land just north of Nico's Gas and Go where she'd gone running last night. *It would be a perfect spot, truly. And what a good thing to start here.*

On the other pages, she saw a list of the types of women who might be a good fit at Tikvah House—abuse survivors. The formerly incarcerated. Those fleeing sex trafficking and other harmful cycles. Women struggling to stay sober.

Even though she'd heard all her life how "untarnished" Dahlia was from the evils of the world, especially from Mom, Natalie knew it wasn't exactly true. All she had to do was drive a few miles east and there was a far-poorer section of the community, and just like everyone else, she read the headlines week after week in the

Dahlia Weekly.

As she peered at the plans, a tickle began to swirl in her belly. *I want to help. I want to be involved.*

And she knew exactly how.

Beside her, Mom sniffed. "I was really hoping we'd get that new church center. Our ladies group has been meeting in Louree Kinley's house since the fall. It would be so nice to have a good dedicated spot for Bible study."

"I think it's a good idea," Natalie said, plans zipping through her mind as Effie's eyes still echoed. "It could help a lot of people. What do you think, Hay?"

Hayley was busy on her phone, but she looked up long enough to mutter, "Yeah, why not? Dahlia's got enough of a dark side. It's about time."

The next morning, Natalie walked into the *Dahlia Weekly* right at nine. Not only was Tiff there, but so was her boss, the publisher, Rebecca Chastain Jamison—granddaughter of Helen Chastain.

"Your granny goes to my church, and she and the pastor told us all about the new project she's hoping to launch," Natalie said, shaking Rebecca's hand.

"The Tikvah House!" Rebecca grinned, gesturing to the chair between her desk and Tiff's. "How'd it go over? Granny's over the moon about it."

"I don't know about the rest of the church, but I love it. And I want my shop to help. Tiff, you said a fundraiser for a good cause might be newsworthy, right? Well, I want to do whatever I can, use Sunstrokes, partner with whoever, and do something really big to help."

Tiff's smile matched her boss's. "You don't know how happy this makes me. A girl I went to college with introduced me to Chrysalis, and we used to volunteer. To think there could be something similar, right here in Dahlia? Count me in."

"I volunteered at a similar place, in Nashville. How about I get all the details together, get some partners, and get back with you soon? If you know anyone who wants in, send them my way. Deadline is tomorrow at noon, right?"

Rebecca nodded. "Yep. Count our paper in, too. Looking forward to it."

Before walking into Sunstrokes, Natalie swung into Joe Mama's, a folder of papers and her blue spiral notebook tucked under her arm.

"Finn around?" she asked Laney.

"I'll grab him."

When he walked out from the back, his expression was wary but amused. "Looks like business."

Natalie motioned him over to a table. "I just came from the *Dahlia Weekly*. The publisher's granny is a member of my church, and she's part of a team spearheading this new home for women in crisis they're hoping to open right by that gas station where you used to work."

"On Old Man Wayne's place?"

"Yeah, something like twelve acres." She showed him a booklet they gave out at church with all the plans, what Tikvah House would do, who it would help, everything. "I'm planning some sort of fundraiser, and I figured you might want in. The newspaper's joining in, too."

Finn blinked, considering. He opened his mouth to speak, then closed it. Finally, he looked through the papers a long time.

"Yes," he said finally, a funny expression on his face. "I'm most definitely in. What do you have in mind?"

She wrote down her number on the church booklet and slid it over.

"If you have time tonight, come on over when my shop closes at seven. I'm hoping to gather whoever wants to help for planning."

He was still poring over the booklet when she left, an odd gleam in his eye.

Laney caught her eye as Natalie headed out the door.

"I'll tell you all about it later." Natalie waved at Laney. "I'm so excited!"

CHAPTER 11

Laney

LANEY SLUNK AS FAR DOWN in the seat of Cha Cha's brown clunker as she could get as they headed toward Lissa's day camp.

Cha Cha eyed her. "'Sup with you?"

Laney closed her eyes. "Hard day."

"Hmpf. Well, you know I gotta little sumpin' in my purse if you ever need to unwind."

Laney opened her eyes long enough to shoot her a glare. "You know I don't do that stuff. Besides, you better not have anything in your purse that doesn't belong there if you're toting me and my kid around."

Cha Cha snorted and let out a shoo-wee. "Girl, I'm just messin' wit' you. But seriously. Let it go." She put her thumb and middle finger together and whooshed out a long, drawn-out sigh. "Peeeeace."

"I'm trying."

Laney took a series of deep breaths as Cha Cha turned left and then right, headed toward the church where Lissa went to camp.

It was a good thing, what Natalie told her about Tikvah House. Even Finn thought so. She should be glad a place like that would be coming to Dahlia. A place like that had saved her life after she got out of the slammer, and The Life itself, helped her birth and keep Lissa, get situated here in Dahlia with all she needed to make a brand-new life, far away from everything and everyone. Brand new.

But sometimes, reality hit a little too close to home.

Laney shifted so the seatbelt wasn't cutting off her circulation as Cha Cha slammed on the brakes at a red light and honked her horn at whatever driver had done her wrong.

"Peace, Cha Cha." Laney breathed.

Cha Cha let out a roaring laugh as they zipped through the light and into the church parking lot.

"My baby girl!" Laney wrapped her arms around Alissa, whose ponytail was now half-drooping and had something sticky and red down the front of her Barbie T-shirt.

"Popsicle Day, sorry." Britt, the freckle-faced camp counselor said, giving Lissa her usual goodbye high-five. "But we got the kind that washes out with regular laundry soap, I promise."

Laney giggled in spite of herself. "Hey, she's happy, I'm happy. It's all good. Thanks, Britt."

Britt waved at Alissa. "See you tomorrow, cutie."

Lissa was asleep before they got to the red light, and Cha Cha nodded toward the back.

"Want me to keep driving a few so you get a little quiet time?"

Laney wrinkled her nose. "Nah. She'll never fall asleep tonight if I do that. Just head home."

When they pulled up, Laney pulled a ten out of her pocket and passed it to Cha Cha, then slid Lissa from the car seat.

"Gas for the week. Thanks again, Cha Cha."

"You got it, girl."

Upstairs, Lissa told her in full detail about every aspect of the day, including the five snails they'd rescued from the puddle near the oak tree behind the church.

"Britt let me name them all but the last one."

"Oh? And who got to name him?"

"*Her*, she's not a him, Mama. BB named her."

"And what'd he name her?"

"Michelle."

"So, Toopy, Saylo, NeePee, Shila, and . . . Michelle?"

"That's right!" Lissa stabbed a hot dog with her pink fork and grinned. "You have a good memamy, Mama."

"Memory," Laney said, enunciating every syllable. "And thank you, baby girl."

Oh, did she ever have a good memory. Long after Lissa fell asleep for the night, Laney lay there, remembering. Remembering it all.

Zeb. Her own Mama. The day she'd met Ethan. All the promises he'd made.

Every one broken.

By then, she didn't care much about anything but the pills he was feeding her. Somehow, the line between what was real and what wasn't had blurred into one big hazy fog.

And by then, nothing mattered, really. Not who she'd been, not where she was going, not even who was by her side.

"Everything's survival, sugar," Ethan liked to say, taking a long drag on his smoke and puffing it out in perfect popping rings that sliced through the night air like magic.

Of course, some things she blocked out, chose not to remember. In her own way, that was survival, too.

How could a girl like her, a girl who'd once had a home and a mom who loved her, a life and a school and dreams of her own, have wound up part of Ethan's crew of hustle girls? That was beyond her.

"Part of my magic," Ethan liked to say.

He'd called himself the pied piper. Not everyone could hear his call, but the ones who did? They belonged to him. Got sucked in. Into The Life.

Most would never get out. They'd die there, whether from hooking up with the wrong guy or overdosing on the wrong pills.

But her? At first she'd called herself lucky for getting out, but Miss J, she said it was something else. She was blessed. God picked her out of the mess, plucked her out, put his own Big Papa hand on her, and led her to safety.

Safety might have looked like getting busted half-on-purpose by the cops for a broken taillight and winding up in jail on too many outstanding warrants, but it was safety nonetheless.

Now, in her narrow bed, listening to her sweet baby girl snore softly across the room, Laney knew Miss J was right. *I am blessed.*

That's where her name came from. Her new name, not the one from the old days. Eliana Ricks was the one Miss J helped her select. Laney for short, but in her heart, it was Eliana. It meant "my God has answered," and that was exactly what God had done with her—answered her desperate prayers, given her the miracle she never thought she'd experience. Not only the miracle of getting away from Ethan and The Life, but the miracle of Alissa, of starting over somewhere new and fresh, of experiencing joy.

Miss J'd helped her pick out Alissa's name, too. Alissa meant "joy," and that's what she'd brought to Laney. Not surface joy, either, like plain-old regular happiness. The real kind of joy—hope. Trust. Knowing deep down in her bones that, somehow, everything was going to be all right.

Even if it brought back a whole gob of painful memories to hear her bosses planning some big party thing to raise a bunch of money for a place like the one that saved her, it was worth it.

Who knew what other girl might be out there, just like her, just waiting for a place like Miss J's? Waiting to be blessed?

Downstairs, she could hear some guy banging on someone's door.

"I'm gon' kill you, Tasha. Lemme in!" he yelled over and over, over and over.

Finally, he just gave up, slinking out into the night or whatever corner he'd rolled out from.

At least tonight, Tasha was safe. Laney was safe.

Lissa was safe.

Laney pulled out her Bible and turned to the place she'd opened so many times she probably didn't even need the bookmark still, though there it was. The streetlight cast just enough glow so she could read the pages.

"So do not fear, for I am with you; do not be dismayed, for I am your God. I will strengthen you and help you; I will uphold you with my righteous right hand." She'd underlined the passage twice, circled all the "I will"s several times, tucked the verse deep in her heart so she'd never forget. Not that she could afford a tattoo, but when she could, that's the one she'd get. Big and bold, so everyone could see.

Isaiah 41:10, from the NIV translation, the black one with the gold-edged pages Miss J gave her that very first night on the cot in her back room, before all her paperwork was done and Laney still went by "Lee" and jumped at almost every sound.

But Miss J, she gave Laney her new name and her new way, pointed her toward Jesus, and sent her off right.

She still might jump every so often, still might feel that weird itch deep down in her bones when a man looked at her just so, the itch that made her want to run clear out in the middle of nowhere and never talk to anyone ever again, the itch that made her want to punch and scream and kick and holler, put up a barricade between her and Lissa and the rest of the whole blasted world.

"But even horses get the willies now and then, sweet one," Miss

J always said. "Even me. Best remember that, now. No one has the right to take away your peace. Never again."

Never again.

Laney breathed it in and out once more, there in her bed. *Never* . . . breathe in . . . *again* . . . breathe out.

Never again.

CHAPTER 12

Natalie

On Thursday afternoon, Natalie stood at the front counter of Sunstrokes, reading the *Dahlia Weekly*. Right on the front page was a picture of her, Finn, and Rebecca, the publisher, along with Pastor Dave, Rev Bryant from Dahlia Community Church, and Cheyenne Tillman from the Salon on Main, all arm-in-arm on Wayne DeLuc's property.

"A place for women in crisis," the headline read, talking about the churches' plans for the property and the ways the community planned to help, including a big "Independence Day" celebration the Saturday before July 4, with a silent auction, door prizes, paint sessions, haircuts, coffee, pastries, and more, with all proceeds going to the Tikvah House.

Rebecca especially loved the idea of an Independence Day event helping women gain some of their own independence after a life, as she wrote in her editorial, "Shackled by the oppression of poverty, systemic racism, domestic abuse, and more."

"I'm impressed," Ashley said, clanking her diet soda can against Natalie's own while Laney led the kids' art class in the back.

Behind them, the twins were busy creating soccer ball art with a dozen other elementary-age kids, including Laney's Lissa.

"I knew it'd get good press, what with Helen Chastain's connection to the paper, but this is phenomenal. Can you imagine all the good this is going to do for people?" Natalie gazed at the newspaper.

"And you know Cheyenne's story, right?"

"The hairdresser?"

Ash nodded. "Yeah, she's been really open about her own struggles. Her dad was a big-time alcoholic, died of liver disease I think, and she had her own battle with sobriety before she got her life together and went to beauty school down in Columbia. Apparently she's been running the AA over in Aberville for, what, sixteen years now?"

"I knew the AA thing, but not the full story. Good for her."

Ash shook her head. "The best part about all this is the truth-telling. Everyone thinks Dahlia's this squeaky clean wholesome little town where nothing ever goes wrong and everyone's perfect. Nope—we're just a bunch of imperfect people trying our best to live right."

Natalie gave her sister a grin. "Except you. Everyone knows you're perfect."

Ashley swatted at her, and they giggled.

"All you need is one more set of twins. Then we'll know for sure."

"Oh, if you only knew." Ashley sighed.

"Knew what?"

"Matt and I have been trying for another baby—what, maybe four years now? Nothing. These two might be it for us."

Ash thumbed back at the kids, a shadow momentarily crossing her pretty face.

"Oh, Ash, I'm so sorry!"

"I know we're blessed to have them, and I shouldn't fuss. But, well, you know I've always wanted a big family. Matt has five sisters and a brother, and I'd love to have a houseful." She shrugged. "I have a doctor appointment next week just to make sure everything's working right, and then I guess we'll call it quits sooner or later. Though we are thinking of adoption, maybe fostering."

Natalie hugged her sister. "I'll be praying for you."

Ash blinked back tears. "Thanks."

"Oh, I almost forgot." Natalie reached under the counter, pulled out a violet flyer. "Open Paint Night here, this Friday. Only fifteen bucks, unless you're a Motts, which makes it free." She winked at Ash. "Think Matt will hang with the kiddos? Mom might even come."

Ash dropped her jaw exaggeratedly, and they laughed.

"It'll do her good to get out of the house once in a while," Ash said. "Daddy can be . . ."

"A stick in the mud?" Nat made a face. "But yeah, she's bringing a couple ladies from her Bible study. Invite whoever you can. The more the merrier."

She even stuck a flyer under one of Finn's windshield wipers with a personal note inviting him to come.

"Hayley coming too?" Ash sipped her soda.

"No, she said she has a date."

"Let me guess. Ben Smathers?"

Nat yawned. "Probably."

"Well, at least one of us will make Mom's dreams come true."

"Speaking of Hay, have you noticed she's been a bit . . .?"

Ash scrunched her nose. "Yeah. I've been wondering when the sassy teen years would hit. I almost thought she'd make it through, the only one of us even-keeled. I think breaking her foot pushed her over the moodiness cliff."

"Glad it's not just me who's noticing."

"Mom's had it up to here with her. Dad, too." Ash shook her head, then peered over at the kids, hard at work. "Speaking of Dad,

I don't know what he's fussing about, always after you to get a marketing job. From what I see, you're doing great."

I wish. Natalie took a breath. "I'm doing . . . okay. People are coming in, mostly kids. I'm keeping my rates super low, too low, really. And the camps help a ton. But summer only lasts so long. It's hard to draw in the adults, come up with things to keep it sustainable."

"You will." Ash reached over and gave her arm a squeeze. "I know you. And hey, the Open Paint Night? That's a great idea. It's not like there's much to do around here in the evenings, anyway."

The next afternoon, Natalie popped over once more to the hardware shop, the insurance place, and the coffee shop, reminding everyone about Open Paint Night.

"I'm making my husband come with me," the insurance agent, a short-haired woman named Deb, told her. "We haven't had a date in ages."

She left Joe Mama's for last, figuring the extra shot of caffeine would help carry her through till night.

But Finn shook his head when she reminded him. "I can't."

"Come on. Even introverts need a little social time."

He rolled his eyes at her but laughed. "What makes you think I don't get enough social time working here all day?"

She giggled in spite of herself. "Touché. Well, if you change your mind, I hope you come."

She meant it, too. Natalie was surprised to realize she was genuinely disappointed Finn wouldn't be there.

But at least Laney would be, and Lissa, too. And Ash, and even Mom.

"Hey, Lissy-girl." Natalie ruffled the kid's hair when she got back to the art shop, handing Laney one of two coffee cups.

"Figured you could use some pep," Natalie told Laney, who smiled in surprise.

"Thanks."

Just before six thirty, Nat was eating a sandwich and gazing out at the slow roll of Friday evening traffic when she noticed Finn climb out of his black truck and pop the hood. He fiddled with stuff a moment, and she watched. Finally, she put her sandwich down and poked her head out the door.

"Need a jump?"

"Yeah, left my interior light on. But I must have left my jumper cables at home in the garage."

"I've got a set. Hang on."

Natalie slipped back inside to grab her keys from her purse, then backed her car out so it was in front of Finn's truck.

"One condition." She crossed her arms and gave him a hard stare.

"Uh, okay?"

"I jump your truck, you come to my paint party. Just a half hour, but you make an appearance."

He laughed at this. "You're serious?"

"Completely." Her lips quivered, but she managed to keep a straight face.

He laughed again. "Fine. I'll come to your party. But only cause you're forcing me."

Natalie fisted the air in a mock cheer. "Yes!"

He kept his word, following her back to the art shop where Laney and Lissa and now Ash were finishing setting out palettes, water cups, and canvasses for the thirteen people who said they'd come.

Natalie caught Laney's eye, then motioned to Lissa, who'd been busy scurrying back and forth from the sink to the tables with the water cups.

"You are a terrific helper, Lissa. Thank you! I want to give you a tip." Natalie said, reaching into her pocket and pulling out a five-dollar bill.

She placed the bill in the girl's hands, and Lissa cradled it like it was gold.

"Mama, can I keep it?" Lissa looked at Laney, her little face lit with joy and possibility.

Natalie remembered being that young, so excited even for the tiniest amount of cash that came her way.

"Absolutely you may," Laney nodded, tucking the cash deep in Lissa's SpongeBob backpack, which the girl was still wearing.

"We should probably do more, just in case." Ash surveyed the room. "I have a feeling . . ."

Her feeling was right. By seven thirty, two-dozen adults and a handful of teens lined the tables, laughing and chatting while picking out their designs.

"I hope you don't mind the last-minute addition. My neighbors wanted to come, too, and I figured two extras wouldn't hurt anything," one lady with silver-streaked hair told Natalie.

Her words were echoed by at least seven others, who brought older kids, sisters, neighbors, and spouses.

"The more the merrier," Natalie assured them all, and meant it.

Finn stood between Deb the insurance agent and Natalie's mom, peering with confusion at the canvas.

"So, just mimic this?" He pointed to the sample in front of him, a beach scene with a rowboat stuck in the sand.

Natalie came from behind, pointing at the numbers on the painting. "See this, the number one? That's your base color. And two, down here?" She pointed. "That's the sand, your bottom base. You can use your pencil, too. No one will see it after the paint's on."

She watched as he lightly traced a thin line with the pencil, then dipped a brush in the blue.

"Here goes nothing." Finn laughed and swept a bold wash of paint across the canvas.

"Never thought I'd see you getting creative," Deb elbowed him. "It's fun, isn't it?"

Finn caught Natalie's eye. "It is fun."

Natalie grinned, watching her mom and Ash start on theirs. Mom was doing a vivid pink tulip, while Ash picked a big mossy oak, its arms cascading gently to the lawn below.

Across the room, Laney showed a group of older women how to get started. The women giggled and teased each other, clearly having a good time.

She noticed how Laney always seemed to have one eye on Lissa, helping the women, then circling back to the girl, then to the women, and back again.

Like a mama bear, Natalie thought, wondering if every mom did this. There was something about Laney, though, the protectively fierce way she seemed to almost guard the child, that struck her as different. More intense, somehow. Like she was watching, waiting, for something bad to happen.

Laney caught her eye and gave her a cheery thumbs-up, and Natalie smiled in return.

Hours later, when it was all over and all the paper-plate palettes were in the trash, the water cups dumped in the sink, and all the people gone, toting their canvases proudly home, Natalie looked around, happy. Lissa dozed in the corner on a pile of fluffy pillows, her SpongeBob backpack beneath her head. Ash and Laney were straightening the tables and pushing in chairs, Natalie was at the sink rinsing brushes, and Finn was over near the front, sweeping.

"You don't have to stay and help, Finn," Natalie called over.

Finn just waved. "It's late, and my mom would turn in her grave knowing I took off, letting you ladies close up this late at night."

Natalie grinned. "This is Dahlia, you know, not some big city."

Finn shrugged and kept sweeping.

Laney looked at her watch, then over at Natalie. "You sure you can still drop us off? It's not crazy-far, but . . ."

"I can run y'all home if you want," Finn volunteered.

But Natalie saw the momentary panic in Laney's eyes, the way she almost seemed to freeze in slow motion. *No.* Not a word spilled from her lips, but Natalie could read her loud and clear.

"No, I got it." Natalie waved a hand. "I could use a drive to clear my head after all this, anyhow."

Laney looked visibly relieved, and Finn didn't even seem to notice the exchange, just kept on sweeping.

On the drive to Laney's, Natalie glanced back at the little girl sleeping peacefully in the backseat, then over at Laney.

"You're a really good mom," she said, turning at the light, the soft tick of the car's blinker wrapping around them like a comforting, steady rhythm.

Laney shrugged. "She's my world."

Natalie wanted to ask a million questions—is her dad around? Why Dahlia? Why the panic about Finn?—but she kept her mouth shut. Laney's wall stood a mile high, and Nat felt it distinctly.

"Up here, on the right." Laney pointed.

Natalie pulled up at a rundown-looking apartment building. One flickering streetlamp lit the entryway and a battered sign, with peeling paint. "Zion Apartments," it read, only the Z was so scarred it almost looked like "Lion Apartments."

"Need a hand? I can carry the car seat."

Laney shook her head, lifting Lissa out and unlatching the seat from the back of Natalie's SUV.

"Here you go, sweet girl. Stand for Mommy just a moment," Laney murmured to the girl, who did as she was told.

"See you tomorrow," Laney said. The flickering light from the streetlamp glinted off the stud in her nose, sending sparkles into the night. "Thanks for the ride."

Natalie watched the pair walk up the path to the building, Lissa holding tight to her mom's left hand, and Laney hoisting the car seat in her right.

When Natalie got home and settled in bed, she pulled out her sketchpad and flipped through to the latest portrait she'd started of Stacey, intending to work more on shading before she fell asleep.

But instead, she flipped to a clean page and found herself sketching Laney—deep, dark eyes, intense eyes. Fierce eyes.

Eyes that had clearly seen way, way too much. Too much for any one soul to handle.

CHAPTER 13

Laney

LANEY WATCHED NATALIE DRIVE OFF, then climbed the stairs to their apartment.

"Carry me, Mama," Lissa murmured.

"Just a few more steps, baby."

On the second-floor landing, some guy stood outside, the door open to his unit. Smoke wafted from the cigarette in his fingers, and he slowly looked Laney up and down.

Laney lifted Lissa to her hip, kept her eyes down and kept climbing, didn't stop until they reached their own floor and were safe inside their apartment, the lock twisted tight.

She settled Lissa in her bed, then paced the small space, restless. Finally, she pushed one of the kitchen chairs in front of the door, tilted it so if anyone tried to open the door, the chair would jam it closed. Just in case.

Not like there was any real danger. Still, it made her feel better.

Laney perched at the tiny kitchen table and fiddled with her house keys, the small metal cross from Miss J pressing deep into her palm. *Is it going to be like this forever? With every guy I encounter?*

Miss J said maybe so, said it was perfectly fine to go the rest of her whole life alone, no man, nobody by her side.

"You just gotta guard yourself, sugar. Forget two steps ahead—stay five steps ahead. Don't let life's emergencies tempt you to use again, or go back to The Life again, even just once. Cause there's no such thing as 'just once,' not for you, not no more. You stay as far away and as far removed as you can. You remember that, sugar."

Miss J knew what she was talking about. Somehow, though, she'd gone on. Married a good man, had four kids. Even widowed and all her kids grown, she'd found a way to make things right by helping other women, women like she'd once been.

"We Ladies of the Night, we know what it's like to be desperate, to do what we hafta do for food and a place to sleep, for protection. That's why you always gotta stay far, far ahead. Play the game, don't let the game play you."

Laney brewed a cup of tea and sat back down. She cradled the mug in her hands, the heat of the chipped ceramic searing into her palms.

Ethan had played her, played her good. She'd die before that ever happened again—to her, or to Lissa.

Laney closed her eyes, remembering that night, back in Zeb's bar. The High Roller, he'd called it. Mama used to work there, and Chrissy, and all the other girls. Her aunties, Mama called them, only they weren't really aunties.

Once Mama died, they stopped being nice to her, even Chrissy. Chrissy wanted dibs on Zeb, only Zeb didn't like her. Didn't ever seem to want anyone, like anyone, but Mama. After Mama died, Zeb checked out. Went from keeping Laney out of the bar, period, case closed, to turning a blind eye.

That summer she'd started wearing Mama's clothes and stuffing her bra, digging through Mama's makeup drawer when Zeb wasn't home—most nights, really. With Mama dead and gone, why would he want to be home, with her, surrounded by ghosts and memories of what was and what would never be?

Ethan wasn't much older back then, at least not to her. He seemed to believe her claim that she was seventeen, not thirteen. And he'd been good to her, sweet. Brought her pretty things when he'd come into the bar, defended her when that jerk trucker wouldn't keep his paws off her. He was the one who'd first told her the other bar girls weren't her friends, after all. Didn't even like her. He'd hear them talking about her, putting her down, wishing she'd just go, get out of there, set Zeb free. Not like Zeb was her dad, anyway, just her Mama's boyfriend. And with Mama gone, what was he now, anyway?

It wasn't long before Ethan started showing up every night, sitting with her, making her feel special.

That night, the Fourth of July, Zeb had that big metal band and everyone was out in the streets watching the fireworks. That was the night Ethan finally let her have one of his happy pills. That was what he called them. He'd always told her she was too good for that, but she'd wanted it by then, wanted whatever he had just to please him. Make him proud. Make him think she could keep up with him, his friends, the girls in his crew.

She could keep up. Always had.

That was the night he'd first kissed her.

It wasn't long after that before she was crashing at his place, before she left Zeb's behind without much of a glance backwards.

Left her childhood and her dreams far behind.

The pills took her after that, made it all seem okay. It didn't seem to matter when Ethan went from sweet to firm to controlling to the enemy, when first one girl then another started crashing there with them. Pretty soon it was just her and the girls, Ethan drifting in and out.

Once—months, maybe years later—she'd woken up at a truck stop in Virginia and didn't even know how she'd gotten there or where she was going. None of it mattered, though.

It all ended in one catastrophically brilliant decision she'd made in a flip second at a red light. One moment she and Shaylene were driving to the Charleston airport, brand-new carry-ons in the trunk and orders to meet Ethan's boss Ray and his right hand, Mick, at the ticket counter. The next second she was telling Shaylene to get rid of anything in her pockets cause it was all going down. Now.

"Ohmanohmanohmanohman." Shaylene's hands had been shaking as she'd fished the baggie from the pocket of her skintight low-rise jeans, crammed it deep under the seat. "Did you leave the blinker off on purpose? What the heck, Lee?"

Lee. Her old name. Short for Kayley, but who cared. Not her, not Ethan, no one.

Flashing blue lights. "Out of the car," the cop ordered as he'd eyed them, taking in Shaylene's skintight jeans and Laney's own halter top and short skirt.

"Hands on the hood."

"She's got nothing to do with this. I was just giving her a ride home," Laney'd said, loud enough for the female cop to hear.

"I don't even know her name," Shaylene whined. "Please. I got a kid at home."

"You got drugs in the car?" The male cop asked.

"It's all mine." Laney had choked the words out. "I'm Kayley Barrett. If you run me, you'll find two warrants. Car's under my boyfriend's name. Ethan Sansone."

"Sansone, huh."

Of course he'd recognized the name. Most of them did. Dirtbags, that's what the cops were trained to weed out, lock up. Put behind bars to keep the rest of the city safe.

Safe from people like Ethan.

People like her.

Instead of feeling terrified, a warm blanket of soothing calm settled over her, like clean towels fresh from the dryer, crisp and pure and perfect.

She wasn't going back.

The female cop read her rights as Laney closed her eyes, leaned her forehead against the hot metal of the car.

She was getting out. Out of The Life.

And this time, it was for good.

It was a week later in the Columbia detention center that she'd found out she was pregnant. She'd had no idea.

Miss J had vouched for her, didn't even know her back then, but vouched for her anyway. Let her move to Sunrise House, helped her work the deal with prosecutors so Ethan and Ray and Mick and their partners in Jersey went down, locked up tight. Drug charges, trafficking. It was the youngest girl Cece that really did them in. Cece wasn't any younger than Laney'd been when she first left with Ethan all those years ago, not that anyone knew. By that point Laney was twenty or twenty-one, old enough that no one cared. But Cece was fifteen barely, and her parents pressed charges to the max once they got her back.

Ethan went down hard. And now Laney had a new life, a new name, a new look. She'd probably packed on twenty pounds at Miss J's house, too, not that anyone could tell. She'd been bone-skinny before then. Now she just looked . . . average. Regular. But for the purple streaks and nose stud, she looked like any other woman her age.

But she had to do the purple streaks, the short hair, the piercings. Part of the armor. At least that's what Miss J had said when she took one look at Laney the day she came home from the drugstore with the boxes of hair dye and the clippers.

"You do you, girl." Miss J had laughed, but it was a good laugh. A hearty laugh. The kind of laugh that was fully, one hundred percent with her, every step of the way. "You do you."

That's exactly what Laney had been doing ever since—her version of "you," not Miss J's. Not Ethan's or Zeb's or even Mama's. All traces of Lee, of Kayley, now gone, locked up tight with Ethan and everyone else.

Locked up for good.

And that's where they'll stay.

Laney put the empty mug in the sink and padded down the hallway to her room. Lissa had flipped onto her belly, hugging her stuffed dog like he was her best friend in the whole wide world.

Laney slipped between the sheets and picked up her Bible, flipping past Isaiah to the chapter she was on now. James, and being doers of the word, not just hearers.

Doers.

She read awhile, the flickering streetlamp finally lulling her to sleep. She dreamed of Miss J's house, only now it was right here in Dahlia. Cece was there, and Mama. Lissa, too.

And somehow, it was all okay.

CHAPTER 14

Natalie

Natalie peered at the kid in front of her, making sure she heard him right. He was about fourteen going on forty, she decided, an old soul in a teenager's body, and he stood there in the midst of the summer camp pointing out the classrooms.

"So when they show up, in about fifteen minutes, we'll do the welcome stuff, then the songs, and then groups." Devon motioned to the room he'd assigned her, which was all set up with canvasses, paint, water, and plastic tablecloths. "You're sure this is enough space for you?"

Natalie eyed the kid. He wore a bright yellow Camp Dahlia shirt, the words "director" in all caps across the back. His dark skin made the yellow shirt seem extra bright, and his close-cropped hair and vivid neon-green sunglasses reminded her of some eighties movie come to life right before her eyes.

"More than enough." She shrugged. "How many kids again?"

"Forty-seven all together, but you'll get fifteen at a time, rotating in shifts. Oh, and don't worry. Marla's your helper this morning. She's my Bonus Mom, and she's amazing, so you don't have to worry about a thing."

Bonus Mom? Natalie knew only a little about Devon, the adopted son of Rev Bryant from Dahlia Community Church and his gorgeous wife, Marla, but whatever he was selling, she figured she had no choice but to buy. *This kid will be the mayor one day.*

About that she had no doubts whatsoever.

"Who's got that awesome?" she heard Devon call from the stage in the front room twenty minutes later, followed by a roaring from the crowd, "We've got that awesome!"

"Who's gonna shine?"

"We're gonna shine!"

Marla took Natalie's arm, pointing at the stage. "You can't argue with his positivity. Those kids just lap it all up."

"You're telling me. You do realize he's going to run for mayor in, what, four years?" Nat blinked, awestruck.

Marla waved a hand. "Please. He's focused on president."

The women laughed.

After the welcome, Natalie and Marla were slammed all morning through lunch. She was there for art camp at Camp Dahlia, an idea she'd posed to young Devon even before Sunstrokes opened. Of course he was all in, though he'd insisted on her bringing the camp to them, not the other way around.

"It's really a logistical nightmare, if you follow," he'd told Natalie, the words rolling from his mouth as if kids his age used phrases like "logistical nightmare" all day long. "Way easier if you come here."

Of course, he was right. Just watch and learn, she decided. Some people were just born to lead, and Devon? There was no doubt about that.

At one, Natalie packed up her paints, rinsing the brushes so everything would be fresh for tomorrow.

Marla, who'd been helping Devon and the other camp directors line up the kids for lunch, joined her to finish sweeping.

"By the way, I'm thrilled you're helping with the fundraiser for Tikvah House. Helen's a close friend of mine," Marla said, dumping the dust pan in the trash. "What that lady sets her mind to, shoo. Look out, world!"

"Her granddaughter seems like she's about the same."

Marla laughed. "Oh, she is. Anyone tell you that's how Helen and Rev and I got so close? Rebecca and our Devon struck up a good friendship a couple years ago when she first moved here. In fact, she's the one who helped us figure out the bad situation he was living in, helped us start the adoption process and get his Memaw all moved into that retirement place."

"You're kidding me. No, I had no idea."

"The Chastains and the Bryants? We're like this." Marla held up two crossed fingers. "'Course, now that Rebecca's married to Josh Jamison, I guess you could say the Chastains, the Bryants, *and* the Jamisons."

Natalie giggled, drying the rest of the brushes and setting everything out, ready for tomorrow.

She looked at Marla. "You've been here a long time, and you probably see a lot, given your work with the church. Do you really think the Tikvah House will make an impact? Here in Dahlia, that is."

"Yeah, I sure do." Marla nodded sadly. "Not that the only women we serve will come from this community. Helen's vision is to bring in women from all over South Carolina, maybe one day even beyond. But Dahlia does have its share of hardship. And of course, you probably know Finn understands a good deal about some of that."

Natalie cocked her head. Actually, she didn't know, but she didn't want to admit that to Marla. Instead she just shrugged and gathered up the towels.

"See you tomorrow. Thanks for the help," Natalie said as she grabbed her keys and the dirty towels and headed for her SUV.

Driving toward Sunstrokes, she swung by the house first to grab an iced tea and a sandwich, see if maybe Hayley wanted to tag along.

Natalie felt for her kid sister. Hayley had always been a good kid—strong student, competitive, a good athlete. She'd run with the same nice group of girls since kindergarten, and all of them had gone through confirmation together at church and everything. But now, the injury had seemed to strike some inner turmoil in Hayley that Natalie hadn't seen before, flip some switch, something.

"Hay?" she called, tossing her car keys on the kitchen counter and jogging up the stairs. Mom wasn't home, probably off doing that garden tour thing with her friends. It's all she'd talked about the last few days.

She could hear Hayley banging around in her room, her voice raised.

"Just shut up, Chelsey. You don't think about anybody but yourself anymore. You and Zoe. Y'all can just shove it. Go to the pool. See if I care."

Whoa. Natalie heard a loud slam and a clatter, like Hay had thrown her phone or a shoe or something across the room, then what sounded like a frustrated yell.

She knew Hayley wouldn't want for her to have heard all that. Quietly, she crept back down the stairs to the kitchen door. Then she opened and shut it loudly, stomping through the house, and banged up the stairs.

"Hay!" Natalie yelled, knocking loudly on Hayley's door. "I'm home for a sec. Can you come help me out with something?"

A furious-eyed Hayley appeared at her door a moment later. "What?"

"Excuse me." Natalie held up both her hands and took a step

back. "Just wanted to see if you want to ride over to Sunstrokes with me, help out a few hours."

Hayley jutted her chin. "Don't you have your helper that you hired?"

Natalie looked at her. If Hayley'd been crying, it didn't show. Then again, she'd been wearing a lot more makeup than normal lately.

"Yeah, but it doesn't mean I can't use more help. Look, you don't have to. But I could use a hand. And I'll pay."

Hayley glared at her a long moment. Finally she shrugged. "Fine."

The short drive to the art shop was quiet.

When they got there, Laney was busy finishing up the afternoon class, and Natalie got Hayley to work in the back, pouring out paint from the huge jugs into the more manageable bottles. It was way cheaper to buy the paint in bulk, but the big containers were cumbersome. Still, Natalie got Hayley situated, her foot propped up and the big containers all set out on the table.

"If the label-maker runs out of tape, just use a permanent marker. I'm not picky."

Hayley nodded in acknowledgment, and Natalie retreated up front.

An hour later, she checked on Hayley.

"Nice job." Natalie was impressed.

Hayley lifted her chin. "That's the last one."

"I see that. Thanks. Think you might be able to give me a hand with some of the samples?"

Most of the classes Natalie and Laney led were the group participation kind, where they demonstrated a step and the class followed along, then another and another, until finally the canvas was done, each one with its own unique stamp of individuality. But tonight she was hosting another Open Paint, where people got to pick their own designs, and those needed to be labeled ahead of time so she wouldn't be jumping all over the place, spread so thin no one was having a good time.

"It's like grown-up paint-by-numbers," she'd explained last week to Laney, and Natalie had to admit the description was apt.

Hayley helped her finish up until Mom swung by from the garden tour to bring her home.

"Thanks again, Hay." Natalie gave her thirty dollars for the three hours of work.

Hayley just shoved it into her pocket and mumbled a thanks.

After they'd gone, Laney came up beside her. "Your sister—is she okay?"

Lissa was coloring in the back, so Natalie kept her voice down.

"I think she's just . . . really depressed. One broken leg and her whole summer's shot, her whole social life, everything. She's lucky she'll be able to rejoin track in the fall so long as she stays off her foot for the summer. And at least she goes out with her boyfriend from time to time."

Laney frowned. "Boyfriend?"

Natalie wagged her head from side to side. "Ben Smathers. He's the sweetest guy, and we've know him forever. In fact, if I know my mom she's probably working behind the scenes trying to arrange their marriage. Kidding!" she said to Laney's shocked expression.

"She just seems, I don't know. Troubled." Laney pushed up from the table. "Anyway, sure you don't need help tonight?"

"I'm good. You and Lissa catch a ride with Cha Cha before she heads back for the day."

"Works for me."

Natalie was outside saying goodbye as they pulled away in Cha Cha's brown clunker when she saw Finn locking up at Joe Mama's for the day.

Marla's words about Finn from earlier echoed.

She put a hand up to wave when he noticed her watching, gave a wave in return as he backed his black truck out of the drive and headed north, toward wherever it was he lived.

She really knew very little about Finn McCafferty, she realized. Loner in high school, loner today. Worked at the gas station, hung out with maybe one or two close guy friends. No girlfriend or wife that she could see, and his only family tie a mom who'd passed away right after graduation. She knew he went to the Methodist church, he'd mentioned that the day they all did that photo for the newspaper. But other than that, that was all she knew.

And yet he was a nice guy. Likeable. Kind.

The kind of person who didn't want them all closing up late at night alone because his mom would expect that.

Yet somehow the kind of guy who'd cause his employee to freeze in panic at the prospect of a ride home.

She wasn't sure if that said something about him, or Laney, or both of them.

Natalie watched Finn drive off, his brake lights glowing soft in the fading afternoon. She wanted to know more about him. A lot more, she realized.

Not in a romantic way, of course. After everything with Tucker, romance was the last thing she wanted in her life—maybe ever. But there was something about Finn, some kindred spirit she recognized. Something that called to her, made her want to reach out. Know him. Call him "friend."

Stupid, of course. Natalie Motts didn't have guy friends. She'd always had a string of guys who fawned at her feet, boys who'd pretend to be pals in case she decided to throw caution to the proverbial wind and say yes when they'd finally get the nerve up to ask her out. That's how it had always been.

Stacey'd always envied that. Not Natalie, though. Who needed admirers? She'd just wanted connection. People. Good people,

people she could laugh with, play with, share life with.

Come to think of it, Stacey had envied a lot of things about Natalie. After she died, Natalie found out just how deep that went.

Yet she was supposed to have been her best friend. Supposed to.

A single car turned into the parking lot, followed by another. Natalie shook herself—the party was here.

She straightened her lightweight summer dress and plastered on the Motts Megawatt.

Showtime.

After camp the next day, Natalie checked her phone. Three missed calls, and a text—all from Ashley.

Her sister picked up on the first ring.

"Can you meet me?" Ashley sounded like she was crying.

Natalie's heart thudded. "Of course. Where?"

"Gigi's, by the hospital."

It was a good thirty-minute drive, and by the time Natalie arrived, Ash was far more composed, but her eyes were red.

Natalie slid into the booth across from her and squeezed Ashley's hands.

"I'm here. What's going on?"

Ash's face looked almost crumpled, but when she spoke her voice was steady. "I know I should be telling Matt first, but he's got that big meeting with corporate that I told him not to cancel. But if I don't get it off my chest, I'm gonna explode."

Natalie's chest was tight as Ashley told her all of it—the tumor, probably benign. The partial hysterectomy her doctor wanted to do, pronto. Not having more kids was the least Ash had to worry about.

"Dr. Warner thinks it's not cancer, but she doesn't know for certain. But there's enough 'other stuff' going on that makes her want to take it all out, ASAP." Ash sniffled. "I'm only thirty-two. A partial hysterectomy doesn't mean full-on menopause, but it's not going to be fun. And poor Matt—he wants more kids so freaking bad."

Ashley's eyes, already welling with tears, spilled over now, hot liquid coursing down her cheeks.

"He wants you alive and okay even more than he wants kids." Natalie's words were soft, but she meant them with every ounce of her being.

Ash wiped at her face. "I know."

"Does Mom know?"

"No!" Ashley's eyes blazed. "And you can't tell her. At least not yet. I mean it, Natalie. She—she flips out. Like, crazy-woman style. Thinks she's being all helpful, but I just . . . can't. Remember when the twins were born and Petey had to be in the NICU for a few days? I swear I thought I was going to tear my eyelashes out, she drove me that bonkers. I can't deal with her knowing."

"Okay." Natalie squeezed Ashley's hands, forced herself to think.

The server came over but seemed to notice what was going on, so she just left their waters and tiptoed off.

"Do you . . . think maybe the twins can come do paint stuff at your shop tonight?" Ashley dabbed at the corner of her eye with a wadded-up tissue. "So I can tell Matt alone, without having to, you know. Worry."

"Oh, girl, of course. In fact, maybe they can sleep over with Auntie Nat tonight."

She grinned, imagining Paisley. At the last family dinner, on Saturday, Paisley'd shyly requested to do her makeup and hair. Natalie still had a few hot pink sparkles in her hair at church the next morning.

Ash shook her head quicky. "No, no, I need my babies with me tonight. Just a couple hours. I . . . just need a little time. A little alone time."

Natalie reached out and touched her sister's nose, like they used to do when they were kids.

"You got it, Ash-ash." She used her baby name for her sister, hoping it would prompt a giggle.

It did. Ashley sniffled, but her grin held.

"I am going to tell Mom, you know." Ash sighed. "Just not today. Or tomorrow."

They laughed.

"Thanks, sis. I am so—grateful. So incredibly grateful you're home."

Natalie swallowed past the lump in her throat. "Me, too. And oh, do I mean that."

She did, too.

Driving back to Dahlia, headed to get the twins from the friend's house where they'd been playing, she realized for the first time that Dahlia really did feel like home again.

And Tucker, and Stacey, and Nashville felt far, far away. Like she'd dreamed it all.

Maybe she had. Maybe it had all been one foggy, overblown nightmare, and she was finally waking up. For good.

CHAPTER 15

Natalie

A WEEK LATER, Natalie and Finn sat with Cheyenne Tillman on one end of the table in the church meeting room, listening as Rebecca Chastain shared plans about the upcoming Independence Festival fundraiser for Tikvah House.

"The mayor told me yesterday we can definitely use the village square, and the gazebo, so that's set. And the newspaper will cover promotion and signage. Nat, are you going to need one or two tents for the paint classes?"

"Two would be better, as long as I can get Laney to help. I'll firm it up with her tomorrow."

Cheyenne raised a hand. "Three of my girls volunteered their services, too, so we can have four haircuts going at a time. But we don't need much space. Maybe one tent for us."

Finn shrugged. "Put me wherever. Whatever you need. I'll have iced coffee, and pastries, and if we can figure out a way to get the frother in, we can make cappuccinos and lattes, too. It is July, though, so maybe a coffee milkshake might be better."

Rev glanced over. "Would you be opposed to a food-truck-style thing? I've got a friend in Charlotte who just closed his barbecue place. Said he's willing to loan out the food truck so long as he can have it back by end of July."

Finn grinned. "Fantastic!"

Bobby Smathers cleared his throat. "Tiff and I can help with the silent auction."

Tiff piped up, "And my brother, James? He's been working at this inflatables rental place in Alabama, near my late mama's family. He said they might be willing to donate a bouncy house for the day, or see if one of their partners nearby can help."

Helen Chastain stood and looked around the room, her eyes moist. "This . . . this is like the old days. Seeing Dahlia come together like this does my heart proud."

"Mine, too, Miss Helen." Pastor Dave gazed up at her. "Mine, too."

After the meeting, Natalie and Finn walked out to their cars. It was a pretty evening, not too humid. Across the way at the recreation center, she could hear the shouts and cheers of families watching their kids play soccer.

"Two more weeks," she said as they walked, shaking her head. "It's a good thing the church decided to chip in funds for our supplies. I mean, I would have done it without, but the extra helps cover costs. This thing is growing by the day!"

"Got that right." Finn peered up like he was calculating. "Yeah, between the coffee alone and now the milk and ice cream, we're going to need some serious stock if we want to have enough to keep the whole town happy."

She paused as they approached her SUV. "I never asked—why are you doing all this? I mean, I'm just fired up because of the church and community part. I interned at a shelter for abused women my sophomore year in college, when I still thought I was going into law instead of marketing. I'm tired of churches doing all these internal things, building buildings, that sort of stuff. Helping outside our own walls? Now *that* gets me going. But you, what's your draw?"

Finn shrugged. "Old Man Wayne was good to us after my dad took off. He gave my mom free produce, brought her eggs twice a week, really did what he could to help out. Felt like my dad did my mom a real injustice. He wasn't wrong."

They stayed quiet for a moment, and Natalie looked up at him. "I didn't know your dad took off. I mean, I knew it was just you and your mom, but I guess that's really all I knew. Maybe . . . well, it sounds like maybe I should have asked."

Finn made a face. "I probably wouldn't have told you back then. Had a chip on my shoulder so big it took years to knock off. But yeah. My dad was a first-rate jerk. Used to push Mom around, give her black eyes, even broke her nose once, before he finally took off for good. I'm glad for it, and so was Mom. But it sure wasn't easy."

Natalie frowned, trying to picture it. She'd known Finn since, what, elementary school? This was the first she'd heard of it.

"We kept it pretty quiet," Finn said, looking over at her. "It's not like you would've known."

"Still, I wish I would have. Wish I could have . . . helped in some way. The old me, I was all wrapped up in my own world, all cheerleading and choir and all that nonsense. But the shelter I volunteered at? Really opened my eyes."

"I think we all need our eyes opened." Finn said it softly, but she could hear a hint of pain behind his words. "Guess that's why I care. Old Man Wayne, he was a good guy. He cared, and he and Miz Cherry would've loved to know their property was going to help women like my mom, women who need a fresh start. Truth be told, my mom sure could have used a place like that. Maybe if she'd had one, she wouldn't have gotten stuck with my dad, thinking she had no other options."

"I bet you miss her." Natalie cast a look at him, realizing how little she'd understood all these years.

"Sure do." He tossed his keys in the air, then clicked the unlock button. "See you tomorrow."

She waved, noticing he waited until she pulled out of the church parking lot before heading out himself.

When she got home, Mom was in the kitchen setting the coffee for tomorrow.

"Leftovers are in the fridge if you want some, Nat honey."

"Thanks, Mom." Natalie kissed her mom on the cheek before opening the fridge and grabbing what looked like chicken divan in Tupperware.

She helped Mom load the rest of the dishes in the dishwasher while her food heated up.

"Did you know Finn McCafferty's dad was a horrible human being?"

Mom sighed. "Good riddance is all I have to say. That man was trouble with a capital T. Did I ever tell you he once had words with your father?"

"Daddy? No!"

"Oh, yes. He was being ugly outside the diner one night, threatening his wife and all. Your dad offered for us to take her home, and Red McCafferty just about punched him a good one, accusing him of being sweet on his wife. I mean, I was right there, standing next to your father the whole time! The nerve."

The picture, of Daddy not only out to dinner with her mom but sticking his neck out for someone, wasn't something Nat had seen much of.

"I can't picture Daddy, well. Getting involved."

Mom sniffed. "Well, he certainly doesn't do it much. You know him, Mr. Caution and Care and all. But shove some injustice in front of his face? Your dad would rather get locked in the slammer than see some poor woman get her what-for by a no-good loser like Red McCafferty. Did I ever tell you how he used to take up for your Uncle Joey before Joey went off to war?"

Natalie blinked. "Nope."

"Oh, yeah. Daddy was no soldier, but when those boys started heading off to Vietnam and your Uncle Joey was all gung-ho to do his patriotic duty? He got picked on something fierce. That's when your dad started walking him home after football practice. Won my heart the way he stuck up for my kid brother, he did. Shame Joey never came back from the war. They would've made good pals."

Daddy, her daddy, standing up for people, standing up for injustice? Not just working his nine-to-five all day, coming home, and kicking his feet up in the recliner, but doing what was right, not just what was safe?

Natalie frowned. What changed in him? What happened that stuck him in that blasted chair all evening and weekend long, yammering on about what was wrong in the world instead of stepping up and really doing something about it?

Mom yawned and set the dishwasher to run, then pressed the auto-start function on the coffeemaker.

"Night-night, sweetheart. See you in the morning. I'm heading to Ashley's tomorrow to watch the twins while she and Matt go meet with the surgeon."

"Love you, Mom."

In bed that night, Natalie tried to picture her father as a young man. She'd seen pictures—Daddy and his horn-rimmed glasses, looking like he'd never seen a day of fun in his whole life. Mr. Serious, Mr. Cautious, Mr. Responsible, Mr. Accountant—and now, Mr. Great Defender Against Injustice?

Half of her wanted to march across the hall and see if he'd be willing to help with the Independence Festival, help with Tikvah House. But she knew what his answer would be: Never give something away for free. It's the same philosophy she borrowed and used to her advantage at Armstrong Communications.

Yet she'd changed.

Or had she? The old Nat would have written off Daddy as a change-phobic unmovable force, never even asked him. In truth, she'd have been afraid to ask him.

Wasn't this still the case? Convincing herself she shouldn't even bother to ask Daddy to join the festival team because she assumed he'd say no—that, in fact, it was safer not to ask him?

Her bedside clock said it was almost ten thirty. Tomorrow. She'd think on it tomorrow.

No, she corrected herself—she'd ask him tomorrow. The worst he could say was no.

It turned out "no" wasn't the worst thing he could say.

"You've got to be kidding me. Free tax returns? Do you have any idea what goes into that sort of thing?"

Natalie clutched the phone, grateful she didn't go in person to see him. Somehow, the distance was easier.

"It doesn't have to be tax returns—"

"No. One hundred percent, unequivocally no. Not just that, but what business do you have even getting involved with this operation? You want people to think you're some battered woman, that this is the reason why my daughter called off her fancy white wedding?"

It felt like a punch. Her words wouldn't come. She stood there, frozen, her hand on the phone. He knew the truth of what happened, about Tucker and Stacey, knew she'd lost everything, every last thing. And yet he'd say such a thing?

A pounding from deep within her started, and her voice didn't even sound like her own when she finally gathered the strength to speak.

"I didn't 'call off my wedding.'"

"That's not what I meant . . ."

"But it is what I meant. And I don't care if some gossip-hungry neighbor thinks maybe I'm involved with Tikvah House because I'm a victim of intimate partner violence or any other reason. I know the truth."

"No, that's—"

"—let me finish."

He stayed quiet, and Natalie took a breath.

"I know the truth. *You* know the truth. I'm helping Tikvah House because it's the right thing to do. It's good for Dahlia. And because I care—that's it." Her words were clipped, short, and she could feel her cheeks grow hot with anger. "If you don't want to help because you're too stingy to donate your company's services, fine. But with all due respect, Daddy, don't for a second insinuate that I shouldn't get involved because 'what would the neighbors think.' How dare you?"

He was dead quiet now, and she disconnected the call before she could say anything else.

The second it was done she wanted to throw up. Fiery tears welled behind her eyes, but she wouldn't let them come, couldn't let them come.

Her hands balled into fists . . .

And that's when she looked up to see Finn McCafferty standing outside her shop, staring at her.

One hand snaked to her mouth, and she was tempted to run to the back.

Instead she motioned him in.

Slowly, he opened the door, the cheerful bell almost a palpable jar to her senses.

They were quiet a moment. She couldn't even look at him.

". . . you . . . okay?" His words were hesitant.

She started to nod, wave it all away like it was nothing.

But instead she forced herself to breathe in and out, in and out.

"My . . . father . . . thinks I shouldn't be helping Tikvah House because people will get the 'wrong idea' about why I'm no longer living in Nashville or why I'm not happily married."

"Oh . . ."

"Exactly." She looked up with a tight-lipped grin. "And I'm *furious.*"

The silence between them grew, and she thought she'd said too much. In fact, she knew she'd said too much, and she opened her mouth to apologize when suddenly she was staring at him and him at her.

"Come on," he said. "Before you can change your mind."

"Wait—what?"

"You have any classes today?"

"Not till three—"

"Perfect." He slipped behind the counter, grabbed a piece of scrap paper and scrawled in red, "Family issue. Closed till two," and taped it to the door.

Then he grabbed her hand.

"The best part about owning your own business? Sometimes, just this. Doing whatever you want or need to do, just because you can. Grab your purse. I'm driving. Laney has a key, right?"

"Yeah, but . . ."

"Let's go."

Moments later, they were driving in his truck, headed west out of town.

"Where are we going?"

"You'll see."

She closed her eyes and leaned her head back, didn't budge when he said "wait here" and dashed inside the sandwich shop, returning to place a brown bag on the floorboard at her feet.

Finally, he stopped the car, jammed the emergency brake, and turned off the ignition.

She opened her eyes to see they were at the Wahca River.

He peered at her feet, and she shot him a look.

"Just checking to make sure you're not in heels. Which I should have done before we left, but well. Act first, think second."

She giggled, and they hopped out of the truck. He snagged the brown bag from the truck and a thin blanket from under the seat, then led them down the trailhead.

"I haven't been here in . . . years."

"Me either, till recently," he said.

She looked around as they walked. Above, the canopy of pine trees surrounded them like a soft, protective blanket. Taking a deep breath, she noticed the dark scent of soil and fish and river water, smiled at the memories of field trips and church outings and all the other stuff this place had come to represent.

Finn shrugged. "I'm no fisherman. Don't even like eating fish much. But this here? I reckon it's the most perfect picnic spot you'll find east of the Mississippi—Nashville included."

She laughed again and realized her stomach was no longer in knots and her fists no longer clenched. In fact, she felt almost . . . happy. Giddy.

Like a kid again.

"Finn, I think you just might be correct."

He spread the blanket beneath a tree and plopped down, motioning for her to join him.

Moments later, they were eating turkey subs and tossing stones in the river.

After a few minutes, he looked over at her. "Still mad at your dad?"

"Honestly, yeah. He was wrong, Finn. Had no right to say what he said. But . . . I'm no longer furious."

Finn nodded. "Good."

A moment passed, then another.

"You never asked." Her voice was soft.

"Asked what?"

"Why I moved back. I'm sure news travels. . ."

Finn shrugged. "I tend to tune out gossip."

"Same!" She sat up straight and popped a potato chip into her mouth. "I hate talk, which is part of the reason why I moved back home—figured it would be easier to start over here than back in Nashville, where everywhere I went reminded me of the past."

"Is it?"

"Easier? In some ways. But in a lot of ways, no. Starting over is starting over—hard any way you try to do it."

"I'm inclined to agree."

They were quiet a moment more, and she decided she liked that. Most of her friendships, particularly with females, were conversation-driven. Tucker was a talker, too, come to think of it. But with Finn, the silences felt normal. Natural. Like she could breathe and just be herself, and he could be him.

That was a good thing.

She drew her knees to her chest and wrapped her arms around her legs.

"I came back because my whole world got wrecked. I was engaged to the boss's son at work, planning a summer wedding. But one night I was out late—I'd been working this big client, really doing heavy schmoozing, no holds barred, the works, and I had to miss a big party I knew he really wanted to go to. Turns out he took my best friend, Stacey. She was like a sister to me. They had too much to drink and crashed his Corvette, flipped it right in front of the Parthenon in Centennial Park. Killed them both instantly. I—found out later they'd been having a fling for months, and nobody told me."

He stayed quiet, just listening.

"So I tucked my tail between my legs and headed home. Figured I'd regroup and see what I'd do next. Only . . ."

"You were shattered."

"Yep." *Shattered.* A good word.

"Marketing didn't feel right anymore. Mom kept begging me to go into teaching, but it's just not my thing. But art. Now, art's my thing."

"This I can see."

She glanced over to see him smiling at her.

"No, seriously," he said. "That's as clear as the hand in front of my face. Watching you the other night at the paint party—"

"—the party you didn't even want to go to . . ."

"That one indeed. But watching you, it was, well, a sight for sore eyes, my mom would've said. Getting to see someone do what she's clearly always wanted to do. The joy on your face—it's infectious. Did you notice how everyone had a good time that night?"

"Well, they seemed to . . ."

"Really, truly, everyone. The soccer moms, the church ladies, the couples, everyone."

She thought a moment, realized he was right. They did have fun.

"That's because of you, Nat. You made it fun. You're bringing that joy into their lives. And it's because you're doing what feels right to do, and showing them how it's done."

Her cheeks flushed, and when she swallowed, her throat felt thick. "I honestly think that might be the nicest thing anyone's ever said to me."

"It's the truth."

They were silent a few minutes more, the only sound between them the crunch of potato chips and the plop of a stone in the river.

"Personally, I think your dad was wrong to say what he said. I'm glad you moved back, and it's nobody's business why you're helping Tikvah House. You're helping, and that's a good thing."

"Thanks, Finn."

She was back long before two, and the proverbial sky hadn't fallen. Finn was right.

When Laney arrived and settled Lissa in the back with her snack and some crayons, Natalie motioned her up front.

"Would you be willing to help at the festival, the one for Tikvah House? I can't imagine we'll have any business here that day, and of course I'll pay you. They're thinking they can supply two tents, and I was thinking you can lead a session in one and I can do a session in the other, and we can swap back and forth and help each other."

Laney hesitated. "What about Lissa? I'd have to bring her, and I don't know what that will look like."

She started to suggest Ashley would watch Lissa with the twins, but realized she probably couldn't. They had an unbelievably quick opening on the surgery schedule, with Ash's partial hysterectomy scheduled for next Tuesday, but she'd need a good two or three weeks to recuperate, not to mention whatever the biopsy results might reveal. Even watching her own kids would possibly require help.

"Bringing her would be great, and it doesn't have to be the whole day, either."

But Laney still looked doubtful. "Let me think a little if you don't mind?"

Natalie was puzzled but tried her best not to show it. "Of course! No problem at all."

Laney seemed off all afternoon, and when Cha Cha showed up to get them at six, her goodbye was quick.

"See you tomorrow," Nat said like it was nothing.

After all, she wasn't the only one who had bad days. For all she knew, something had happened at home, or in Laney's family.

Finn stopped by when he closed up. She had one small evening class, but they were occupied with an easy section, so she smiled and approached the counter.

"Thanks again for this morning. I had no idea how much I needed that."

He smiled. "We should do it again. This weekend I was thinking of driving into Aberville or even Charlotte to get some things for the festival."

"I need to do the same. We could take my SUV—it's got tons of room if we find anything."

He nodded. "How about tomorrow night? After you close up?"

It was the first Friday night she had no paint parties booked, and for certain the big-box store in Aberville was open late. She ordered most of her supplies online, but some things it was better to put eyes on.

"Perfect." The second she said it, her nerves gathered like a tumbleweed in the desert.

He just smiled. "I'm looking forward to it."

And deep down, she knew the truth: She was, too.

CHAPTER 16

Laney

ALL LANEY WANTED to do was go home, bury her head in her pillow, and cry. Instead, she was in the fast-food playground watching Lissa slide down the giant bubble slide for the fourteenth time and pretending everything was a-okay.

But oh, was it ever not okay.

Because Ethan was out. Like, out of jail for good, out.

And it took every last ounce of faith in her bones not to pack everything they owned in a suitcase, beg Cha Cha to drive them to Columbia, and hop on a train north, never to return.

God, help me.

Lay low. That's what she needed to do. Just lay low, pretend he wasn't going to look for her in every fleabag motel from here to Atlanta and back again, just to do one thing.

Make her pay.

It's what he'd said a thousand times before—don't you ever cross me, ever rat me out, ever. You'll wish you never saw the light of day.

She hadn't meant to. Fully intended to just suck it up when she got busted, do her time, whatever she needed to do. She didn't even care if she spent the rest of her life in the slammer if it meant getting away from him. After that last binge, and she'd heard him talking, heard his plans to sell her and Shaylene and some of the older ones to the Jersey crew, that was it. The final straw in what had been a decade of blurred living and pain.

Back then, she didn't know God other than that he was some pie-in-the-sky father figure, looking down from way up high at her and all the other people on this planet, little ants scurrying around in oblivion. But she'd known she'd wanted out. Known anything had to be better than this, even jail. Even death.

But then . . . the pregnancy. Seeing the baby inside her on that ultrasound machine there in the clinic. Hearing the heartbeat, and much later, feeling her kick.

It changed—everything, really. Her whole life.

Took her from nothing to live for to something . . . someone. Someone's mama.

And when they'd told her they could wipe her record and set her up with a clean slate and a new name and a fresh start in exchange for her testimony, she didn't even need to sleep on it.

"I'm in," she'd said.

They'd promised he'd never get out, that none of them would.

So how was Ethan now walking around free?

"Look at me, Mama!" Lissa shrieked with delight. Now she was upside down at the top, her tiny sock feet all twisted up in the jungle gym cords as she wiggled her hands around.

Some other kid shoved her, and Lissa plopped down on her hands and knees and stared at him a moment, as if all the possible reactions were zipping through her mind like a tiny ball gone loose in a pinball machine.

Finally, she just hugged the kid. "You must be sad," Laney heard her say. "It's okay. You can have a turn."

Laney's heart clutched. She'd have just cried, or maybe punched the boy. Not Lissa.

If it was one thing she was doing right in this world, it was Lissa. She was the only thing that mattered.

Not Ethan, not the ghosts of her past, not even what could happen.

Just her girl.

Lissa zipped down the slide and slipped into the booth next to Laney.

"Getting sleepy."

"And pretty stinky, too." Laney kissed Lissa's head. "Let's walk home and get you in the bath. Sound good?"

It was only half a mile to their apartment, and Laney carried Lissa piggyback-style most of the way.

At the corner, she saw some young guys and braced herself for the catcalls and whistles. But these guys were respectful, or maybe they'd just noticed the little kid on her back. Whatever the reason, she was relieved.

Lissa perked up for the bath, and they played mermaid with some dollar-store toys until they both had wrinkles on their fingertips and the water'd gone cool.

"Ready for bed, sweet one?"

She tucked her in, and Lissa led prayer time, adding at the end, "And God please bless the mad-sad boy from the playground and help him make friends. Amen."

"Amen," Laney repeated, tucking the covers around Lissa tight. "You have a good heart, Alissa Jane. You're a good person."

"You're a good person, too, Mama."

She was fast asleep before Laney even made it to the bedroom door.

In the kitchen, Laney pulled the letter from the junk drawer, read it again.

It was just a courtesy notification, and everything was still intact. He didn't know her new name, didn't know she had a kid or even that she was still living in South Carolina. Still, it was like someone had stuck a zillion ice cubes way down deep in her core, and there was no way she'd ever get warm again.

Even though it was almost nine, she dialed Miss J again.

No answer.

She'd called her three times today. Yesterday, too.

Was she hurt? Sick?

Dead?

It's been months since you last talked to her, anyway. Almost a year, she reminded herself.

Miss J was busy, and besides, she certainly wasn't waiting around for one of a hundred girls she'd helped over the years to keep in touch. She had other girls to help, other Laneys and Lissas.

Still, Laney couldn't shake the bad feeling deep in her belly, so deep she could almost feel it in her toes.

It's why she didn't want to volunteer at Nat's big festival thing, why she barely even wanted to show her face at the coffee shop or Sunstrokes.

Not that Ethan would ever come strolling through a town like Dahlia and buy a latte or take a painting class like some normal human being. Who was she kidding? He'd only ever breeze by looking for the nearest bathroom off the interstate, and Dahlia wasn't anywhere near the interstate. In fact, you had to pretty much go out of your way to get to Dahlia in the first place, or happen to stop through if you were taking the back roads someplace bigger, like Charlotte.

It was part of the reason why she'd picked Dahlia in the first place.

You're fine. Everything's fine. He's not gonna find you.

But telling herself a thing and believing that thing weren't always one and the same.

Even though it was summer, she couldn't get warm enough, and she dug around in the closet until she found her softest sweatshirt. Then, pulling on her thickest socks, she washed her face and hopped in bed.

Jesus, please don't let Ethan find us. Please keep Lissa and me safe. She dug her thumbnail into her palm in a crisscross just to seal the prayer.

Her dreams were a tumble of chaos and fear, black water rising in the black, black night.

CHAPTER 17

Natalie

On Friday morning, Natalie waited till both her parents had left the house before she tiptoed downstairs, grabbed some whole wheat toast and whatever coffee was left in the urn, and retreated back upstairs to her bedroom.

She heard flirtatious laughter from Hayley's room. Surprised her sister was awake already, Natalie stepped a bit closer to the door, listening. Just in case.

"Oh, stop. You know I'm not like those girls," Hayley was telling someone. She'd dropped her voice an octave lower, like she was trying to sound sophisticated to whoever was on the other side of the phone call.

Probably Ben Smathers, Natalie told herself and started to slip back into her own room. The last thing Hay needed was her big sister involved in her high school romance.

But then she heard Hayley laugh again, that low, extra-flirty laugh. "Jared, stop."

Natalie blinked. *Guess it's not Ben after all.*

She slipped inside her room and shut the door, forcing herself to forget about Hayley's love life. She had enough going on today to worry about—not to mention the tiff with Daddy. She'd intentionally lingered extra late at the shop last night, organizing and straightening up and cleaning, finally coming home so late both Mom and Daddy were already in bed, and Hayley, too. She'd love to just keep on avoiding everyone, if she had it her way.

But sooner or later . . .

Natalie crossed her legs and sat in the center of her bed, pulling her blue-striped notebook from her purse. Dahlia was nowhere near Nashville, so the kind of fundraisers she used to go to wouldn't be the sort of thing she needed to recreate here, which was actually a relief.

What was harder was making it somehow more meaningful and attractive to people who already knew everybody anyway, and probably had already started contributing at church. What would make them give more, help more, care more?

Stories. That was always the magic ticket when it came to selling anything. Tell a story, paint a picture, stoke a fire so someone wanted it, needed it, felt it so close to their heart they could identify with it.

That's why the video Pastor Dave played in church had grabbed her so hard, made her want to help. Because the lady in the video reminded her of the girl at the Nashville shelter. Anita. The one who'd left the program two days in and wound up dead a week later. Her boyfriend had killed her in a fit of rage, and that was that. No more Anita.

It made Natalie sick, that men could do that. That people could do that, period. Hurt others, over and over—and just get away with it.

Anita hadn't liked the shelter. Felt like a hospital, she'd said. But a place like Tikvah House, it could help women like Anita, or Effie from the video. Women on the run, or even women just starting over.

Women like Natalie. The difference was Natalie happened to have a good family and a cushy house and lots of money in savings when her life fell apart. She had education and resources and privilege, not to mention a place to call home.

Not every woman had such a place.

A wave of guilt pricked her, and she remembered the exchange from yesterday with her father. He'd been wrong, yes—but so had she. They'd both said things they probably didn't mean, both hurt each other with their words.

Natalie drained her coffee and took a last bite of toast, then flipped open her notebook to a fresh page.

> *Daddy, I'm sorry for what I said on the phone. I was hurt and thought you were being insensitive to my situation, but I shouldn't have gotten so angry. I'm grateful to you and Mom for giving me a home when I needed you most. I hope you can forgive me. Love, Natalie*

She folded the paper and put a little heart and "Daddy" on the front. She'd leave it on his recliner, where he'd see it when he got home from work.

Then she started her list for tonight.

That afternoon, her heart thudded and her tummy dropped the closer it got to seven. Why someone started calling them "butterflies" was beyond her. More like locusts, or piranhas.

Finally, it was closing time. She locked up her shop and glanced toward Joe Mama's.

Finn was walking toward her.

Her stomach gave another slow, slow tumble, but she forced

herself to smile.

He smiled back.

"Still okay with taking my car?" she asked lightly.

"As long as you let me pay for dinner."

She grinned. "Deal."

They listened to music all the way to Aberville, surprised they liked many of the same bands. She even shocked herself by belting out one of the tunes loud and proud. *It's like I've known him forever.*

Strike that, she giggled to herself—she practically had. Rather, it was like they'd been friends forever. And that felt strangely, blissfully good.

In Aberville, they picked an Italian place on the main drag, which had the best lasagna she'd eaten in ages, and by nine they were goofing off and poking each other in the aisles of Walmart.

In the garden section, she showed him what she'd been thinking.

"Maybe it's corny, but instead of canvases, I was thinking stones. You know, like the woman in the Gospel of John, who's about to get stoned but Jesus says only a person without sin can throw the first stone? And no one's without sin, so she doesn't die. She gets her fresh start. I mean, she's got to stop sinning, too, but she gets to start over. So I was thinking we could all paint 'hope,' or 'Tikvah,' which is the Hebrew word for hope, on the rocks."

"Symbolizing the fresh start we all get," Finn said thoughtfully.

"Exactly!"

"Like, the connection between us and the people Tikvah House is going to be able to help."

Natalie picked up a bag of landscape stones, felt their surface through the packaging. Now that she was there, actually touching the stones, the idea felt even more right. She closed her eyes a moment, thought about the idea.

"I love it, Nat. Really."

She opened her eyes and smiled into his. "I was thinking I could even print up little cards with the Bible story, maybe put at the bottom, 'Tikvah equals hope,' something like that."

"I bet Rebecca at the paper can help with that."

"Oh, good thinking!"

She grabbed a few bags of the stones, enough so there was more than plenty, not only for the festival but for kid art camps she'd be doing the rest of the summer, and put them in their cart.

"Now let me show you my idea, which is probably completely off-the-wall, but I can't let it go."

She was intrigued, and he tugged her over, deeper into the garden section.

"So, obviously this has nothing to do with coffee," he said, snagging a paper packet of heirloom tomato seeds from one of the cardboard kiosks. "But I was thinking—with each cup, or each pastry, someone gets a pack of seeds. They're paying a little more for the item, but they're getting more, too. And when they get home, they can plant the seeds . . ."

". . . just like we're also planting the seeds of hope at Tikvah," she finished.

"Yes! So it's like hidden seeds, seeds we're planting now that will one day become something far more than what it is now. But it's also paying homage to Old Man Wayne, his farm and his garden, all the good he did there over the years."

Unexpected tears sprang to her eyes, and she wanted to hug him. Instead, she just clutched her chest and did a little happy wiggle.

"That is absolutely perfect," she gushed.

He chuckled and looked at her. "Do that again."

"What?"

"That little . . . dance thing you just did."

She bent over, laughing, and swatted him, and he held up his hands in mock defense.

They were still laughing and teasing thirty minutes later when they pushed the cart out of the store and loaded the bags of stones and seeds into her SUV.

"I think we need ice cream now," Finn said. "This night can't end without ice cream."

"You are reading my mind."

She steered the car through the parking lot and down past another plaza. This one had some seedy bar in the center, but at the end was an ice cream place open till at least eleven on Fridays. She was cruising by, edging past the bar . . .

And slammed on the brakes hard.

Finn shot her a look. "You okay?"

Natalie's eyes went wide. "No."

Right in front of her, in the shortest tiger-print skirt she'd ever laid eyes on, with so much makeup plastered on she was almost unrecognizable, was the one person Natalie never thought she'd be seeing at a place like this.

Hayley. Cast, crutches, and all.

CHAPTER 18

Natalie

Hayley didn't seem to notice Natalie stop the car in the middle of the parking lot and storm right up to the door.

She just kept on twirling her hair with some fruity-looking beverage in her hand, talking to a man far, far too old for her.

Hayley didn't see Natalie, but the guy sure did.

"Hayley Suzanne." Natalie knew she sounded like Mom, but she didn't care.

Hayley whirled around, her mouth a perfect O of horror. "Nat!"

The guy narrowed his eyes at Natalie and slinked an arm around Hayley's waist. "You okay, babe?"

Natalie gripped Hayley's wrist, one hand on the crutches. The drink tumbled to the ground.

"Hey, watch it!" yelled a woman behind them.

"She's underage. Get in the car, Hayley. You're coming with me."

Finn was at her side now, and together they guided a woozy, clearly inebriated Hayley to the car and strapped her in.

She peered up to see whether the guy was going to give them any trouble, but he'd disappeared. *Good riddance.*

"Can you drive?" Natalie looked at Finn.

Her hands shook, and she didn't know whether from shock or anger. No matter. The only thing that mattered was getting Hayley out of there and safely home, pronto.

The car was dead silent as Finn navigated the thirty-plus minutes back to Dahlia. When they finally stopped, in the Sunstrokes plaza where Finn's truck was still parked, Natalie's jaw was clenched so tight she almost didn't hear Hayley's weak moan from the backseat.

Just in time, they got the girl unbuckled and watched her get sick on the pavement.

"Here." Finn pulled a napkin from his pocket.

Natalie wiped at Hayley's face.

"Don't take me home, please, Natty," Hayley slurred. "Mom thinks I'm at Zoe's."

"Lying to Mom, too. Great."

"Please." Hayley was crying now.

Finn eyed Natalie and they both grimaced.

"Raincheck on the ice cream?" she murmured.

"Definitely."

When she was convinced Hayley wouldn't get sick all over her car, Natalie drove them home, Finn waiting until they safely pulled out before he headed in the opposite direction.

The house was dark when they arrived, and they crept up the stairs to Hayley's room. Natalie wanted to yell at the top of her lungs, shake some common sense into her little sister. What was she doing, out with that older guy? Didn't she know she could get hurt, or far worse?

In the bathroom, she scrubbed every trace of makeup from Hayley's face, then helped her change into thin cotton jammies.

Natalie snagged the tiger skirt and low-cut blouse from the floor, and the single high heel, jamming them all into the bathroom trash bag, which she tied up tight and stuck by her own bedroom door till she could take it out in the morning.

By now, Hayley was sound asleep on top of the covers, one arm thrown limply over her face like she used to sleep as a little kid, before Natalie left for college.

Idiot. She wanted to wake Hayley up, make her realize how bad tonight could have gone, how dangerous a situation she put herself in. But it was no use.

And who's that . . . that man she was with, anyway?

Instead, she covered Hayley with a cozy blanket from the edge of her bed, turned out her lamp, and tiptoed back to her own bedroom.

Thank you, Lord, for letting me find her before things got too out of hand, Natalie prayed before falling into a deep, deep sleep.

In the morning, Hayley tapped at her door, entering before Natalie could answer.

Hayley's face was puffy, her hair a tangled mess, but other than that, she looked like the kid sister she'd been the day before.

Natalie just looked at her. "What were you thinking?"

"I wasn't," Hayley said in a small voice.

"You got that right." Natalie shook her head. "You could have gotten killed. Raped. Kidnapped."

Hayley looked at her fingernails, fiddling with the jagged edges.

"I've just been so . . . lonely, and bored. I didn't think it was a big thing. I promise you, Nat. I'll never do it again."

"When Mom finds out, I don't think you'll ever be allowed out of the house again, so I think that's the least of our worries."

"Please, don't tell her, Nat! She's been so worried about Ash, and the twins. I lied and said I was sleeping at Zoe's, but I know now I was wrong. That guy, he's way too old for me. I thought he was my age, but he's not."

"No kidding he's not." Natalie's heart tugged as fresh tears welled in Hayley's blue eyes. "How did you meet him, anyway?"

"Just online. He said he went to Aberville High, promised to pick me up for this awesome all-night party everyone's been talking about. We started drinking and . . . I don't really remember the rest."

"You met some guy online and decided to go out with him not knowing a single thing about him? Don't you watch the news, Hayley?"

Hayley buried her face in her hands. "It was so, so stupid, I know. Please, Nat. Don't tell Mom. She's worried enough right now. The last thing she needs is to be worried about me, too."

Natalie stayed quiet a long time. "Do you promise me you will never, ever do that again?"

"I promise, Nat. I give you my word."

Hayley held out her pinky like they used to do years ago, and they shook.

Then she looked at Natalie and groaned. "You were out on a date when you found me, weren't you."

"It wasn't a date. Just a friend thing. With Finn, from the coffee shop."

"From Joe Mama's?" Hayley buried her face in her hands again. "I can never show my face there again!"

Natalie giggled in spite of herself. "I'm sure he's seen his share of teenage crazy."

Hayley headed off to shower, and Natalie got dressed for work.

But downstairs, Daddy stopped her on her way out the door.

"I got your note," he said gruffly. He looked awkward there in the kitchen, and far older than she remembered, surrounded by all the yellow and white. "I'm sorry, too."

Natalie set her purse down and wrapped him in a hug.

"I love you, Daddy."

"See you tonight at dinner."

It turned out to be the busiest Saturday Natalie'd had since Sunstrokes opened, and she was especially grateful today for Laney. Between the two of them, they barely had time to wolf down lunch.

Which was exactly what she was doing when Shelly and her daughter, Brianne, walked in.

Shelly's pregnant belly was even bigger than it had been a month ago.

"Are you sure you're not going to give birth right here in my shop?" Natalie teased.

"Eat those words." Shelly laughed. "I'm looking for some of your at-home kits for Brianne here, and also wondering if you do birthday parties." She winked at Natalie. "I'm thinking big sister here could use an extra-special celebration when her day rolls around."

"Absolutely." Natalie slid out the calendar, penciling in the date and giving Shelly the rates. "We'll need a deposit to make it official, but I've got you down."

Shelly considered. "Can I just pay for the whole thing now? I have no idea where my brain's going to be come September. Sound good, cutie?" She gazed down at her daughter, who seemed far more enthusiastic than when they first walked in.

"Thanks, Mama!"

As they prepared to leave, Shelly leaned in. "By the way, thank you so much for all you're doing for that Tikvah place. You ask me, this is exactly the sort of thing our churches need to be doing."

Rev Bryant's wife, Marla, and their son Devon walked in for some posterboard and markers.

"We're doing a week on hope themes at the camp," Devon said

over his shoulder as he bounded toward the back, one hand up in a friendly wave.

Marla smiled at Nat and sank against the counter.

"Still staying out of his way?" Nat smirked.

"You bet." Marla's laugh was warm. "Let me know if you need a hand with the festival stuff. I decided I'm joining the Tikvah Board. Oh, and Helen Chastain and I are starting training nights at Dahlia First for volunteers. You know, generating excitement but also being practical."

"They say it takes a village . . ."

"You've got that right."

Finn stopped by twice, but both times she was slammed with customers. She waved, a tickle of . . . friendliness? Excitement? . . . fluttering up within. She didn't know quite what kind of label to slap on her feelings just yet.

After work, he leaned against his truck, waiting for her.

"Any chance you want to cash in that ice cream raincheck tonight?" He gave an exaggeratedly goofy grin, and she giggled.

"I can't. It's family dinner night." She wrinkled her nose in apology. "Every Saturday."

He made a face. "After last night, I imagine that will be especially interesting."

Natalie huffed out a breath. "That child is mortified. Oh, and if she avoids your coffee shop until college? Please don't take it personally."

"Did you end up telling your mom?"

She leaned against the truck next to him. She almost bumped his arm—it would have been so easy, so comfortable to brush against him. Already it felt too familiar between them, and yet she couldn't seem to help herself. Or at least, didn't want to.

Slow it down. Let this, whatever it is, happen at its own pace.

"Against my better judgment, no. Hayley swears she'll never,

ever pull a stunt like that again, and I believe her. But she did make a good point—Mom's stressed enough with all the stuff Ashley's going through."

"Surgery's Tuesday?"

"Yeah."

It felt good to have a . . . friend again—someone who genuinely cared, who knew what was going on, who asked questions and knew stuff about her life.

She looked over at him. "What about you? Going to satisfy that ice cream craving without me?"

"Probably just frozen pizza and a movie from the comfort of my own home. It's an introvert's dream night."

She giggled again and, this time, elbowed him. "Depends on the frozen pizza."

Her elbow buzzed with warmth when she pulled away.

She clicked the lock on her SUV and eased her tired body off the truck. "Goodnight, Finn."

"Goodnight, Natalie."

The way he said it, her full name like that, in just that exact tone of voice, made her gaze at him an extra-long time, and smile.

CHAPTER 19

Laney

LANEY CRADLED THE PHONE against her shoulder as she stood in her kitchen that Sunday.

"Miss J's . . . in the hospital?"

The woman on the other end of the line, from Sunrise House, sounded rushed but sympathetic.

"A heart attack. Nothing too awful. She'll be released today to rehab for the next week or two. I'm stepping up while she's gone, but hopefully she'll be back soon. Any chance you feel like coming down to help? You sound like someone who knows the ropes, if you catch my drift."

"I was there eighteen months, and I wish I could, but I've got two jobs here, not to mention my kid. I can't." Laney grabbed a pen. "Will they let her have visitors?"

She scribbled down the information, then fingered the paper a moment, unsure what to do next. It's not like she had a car, not like she could drive herself all the way to Columbia. Besides, did you even visit someone so soon after a heart attack?

When she hung up, Lissa was at her knees. "Can we go to the playground?"

"After church. Come on, let's get you changed into something pretty. Mrs. Bailey will be here soon."

Mrs. Bailey from church was waiting in her Buick when Laney and Lissa walked out. Her daughter, Marchelle, helped Laney buckle in the car seat and they were off, driving the four miles to Dahlia Community Church.

Lissa wiggled in the pew, but no one seemed to mind. This was one of the things Laney loved about the church—it felt real, like real people went there. Real concerns. Real issues. And they helped each other, too. Like Mrs. Bailey—Laney didn't even know her, really, or Marchelle. But when Rev's wife, Marla, had learned Laney didn't have a car and lived in the apartments on the edge of town, all it took was a word to Mrs. Bailey who lived nearby, and that was that. Now she had a ride every Sunday as long as she liked.

During prayer time, Rev asked for any concerns, and a smattering of people offered the names of family and friends with struggles.

Laney surprised herself by piping up for the first time. "Can you please pray for my friend, Miss Jessamine? She's recovering from a heart issue."

They all prayed fervently, then came the sermon and the singing.

After church, most everyone headed downstairs for lunch, including Laney and Lissa and the Baileys. Today was a Southern feast—fried chicken, collard greens, lima beans, and mac and cheese, the good baked-in-the-oven kind.

"Did you cook all this, Miss Marla?" Lissa asked the pastor's wife.

Marla laughed long and loud, tapping Lissa on her nose like she was the most precious kid in the whole world.

"Oh, does Rev *wish* his wife could cook this good. Nope, sugar pie, I didn't. But let's enjoy it together, shall we?"

Laney loved Marla, with her flowy, jewel-colored clothes and infectious, full-body laugh. It was the kind of laugh that started way down deep and traveled up and out, like singing, only better.

Laney recognized a few people she'd seen earlier in the week at Sunstrokes or Joe Mama's, and a handful came by to say hi and chat, ask how her summer was going. It made her feel like she had . . . people, somehow. Like she wasn't some loner misfit, the misfit she'd been all her life.

After a while, Rev made his way over, a huge plate of food in his hands and a big grin on his face.

They all talked and laughed a long while, and Rev and Marla's son Devon pulled out a deck of cards and taught Lissa to play Go Fish.

When everyone was occupied, Rev leaned close to Laney, his voice soft.

"Your friend with the prayer request." He paused, like he was weighing his words. "That's not Jessamine . . . Jackson, is it?"

In an instant, Laney's throat went dry.

He knows!

It was as if the whole room flickered, like the streetlight outside her bedroom window, and suddenly she was exposed, her past wide open like a paperback novel someone forgot to bring home, pages flipping in the breeze for all to see.

A million things zipped through her mind—*he knows I'm one of Miss J's girls. Or maybe he thinks I've worked with Miss J. Or maybe I'm an advocate, or an ally, or a . . .*

But at the end, it all boiled down to one truth. He knew. Now, her pastor *knew.*

The look on her face must have said it all, because Rev held up a hand, his eyes soft.

"Forgive me, and I don't mean to pry. I just don't know many Jessamines, and for some reason, God laid it on my heart to ask. I've known her a long, long time, back when I was in seminary in

Columbia. I won't say a word, and I'll be praying."

Rev cleared his plate and patted his stomach. As if on cue, people started throwing away plates or standing up for seconds, talking about Ethel Frady's pound cake and whether they had room for the tiniest of slices.

Lissa curled up in her lap, like somehow she knew her mama wanted to be a thousand miles away from here.

Laney linked her arms around the girl tight and rested her chin on Lissa's soft hair. It still smelled like grape bubble gum from her bath the night before, comforting and sweet. Pure.

Just breathe, she told herself. *In and out. You got this.*

That afternoon, she pushed Lissa on the swings at the school playground. This fall, Lissa would be old enough to go here. If they were still in Dahlia, that is.

Laney peered at the brick building, so much like all the elementary schools she went to when she was a kid. Before Zeb, she and Mama moved around a ton, but that last time, her fifth-grade year, that was when everything started to feel right. When she and Mama slowed down and came to a full stop, maybe for the first time ever.

When Mama got pregnant, that was when Laney let herself imagine what life could be. A real life, with a house, a daddy in Zeb. Her and Zeb and Mama and the baby.

Baby Henry. She'd named him that even though Mama didn't have any names picked out, didn't even want to know if he was a boy or a girl, wanted to be surprised at the birth.

But he'd come early, way too early.

Lissa dashed over to the sandbox. Someone had left a toy truck in there, and a shovel, and she busied herself pouring sand into the back of the truck and pushing it around, making *beepbeepbeep* noises like it was backing out with a heavy load.

Laney took a seat on the bench. She knew the memories were coming, wanted to push them back, but she couldn't seem to stop them from rolling in like a thundercloud.

Seventh grade, summertime. Zeb had gone out of town, and she and Mama had been home in the little apartment above the bar, watching scary movies and eating popcorn.

Then the blood, and Mama falling. The music from the TV blared loud as she'd gaped at Mama, there in the bathroom, her stretchy PJ pants still half off. A puddle had left a flood, soaking Mama's neon-green socks.

"You're bleeding!"

"I hit my head," Mama had murmured as she'd started to sit up, clutching her temple, a wad of toilet paper pressed tight against her head.

Mama blinked all drowsy-like and peered over at the puddle, then seemed to take it all in.

One puffy-fingered hand flew to her mouth. "That's not . . . baby, my water broke. We need to get to the hospital."

Henry was coming—now.

They'd let her in, the nurses and doctor, mostly 'cause Mama insisted.

"No heartbeat detected," the younger, heavyset nurse had said, her eyes on the ER doctor, an older skinny lady.

"Mrs. Barrett, I'm Dr. Hammond." The doctor spoke clear and crisp, like her teacher before a standardized test. "There's something going on with your baby. We need you to push as hard as you can. Do you understand?"

Mama'd locked eyes with the doctor and nodded.

"Push! Come on!" The nurse sounded mad, but her face looked worried.

"We're gonna need sedation," the doctor said.

"I can do it!" Mama's face was drenched with sweat, and her yellow nightshirt was still spotted with blood from the fall in the bathroom.

Come on, Mama. Come on, Henry. She'd crossed her fingers as tight as she could, both hands, and clenched her jaw.

Mama sounded like a cow as she bellowed loud, a sharp painful cry at the end.

"It's out," someone said.

"Oh, dear," said another. "Get that one out of here."

Someone pushed Laney back, out the door, but she could see them swoop a bundle of blankets from between Mama's legs and off to some table on the side, several people bent over the blankets while the nurse held Mama down, put what must have been an oxygen mask to her face.

That bundle of blankets must be the baby, only there was no crying to be heard.

No tiny legs and arms kicking like in the movies.

Just a bunch of people, gathered around a table, poking and prodding and whatever else they were doing.

A gentle hand rested on her shoulder then, and she looked up to see an old woman, some nurse or tech from the front.

"Come on with me, sweetheart. Your mama's gonna be occupied awhile."

"What about my brother? What about the baby?"

The old lady just shook her head. "I'm sure everything will be just fine. Let's get you settled out here."

But everything wasn't just fine. By the time someone came to fetch her and take her back to Mama it was close to one in the morning.

"What about the baby?" she'd asked, trying to keep up with the woman as she led her back through the double doors and down the long corridors, left and right so many times Laney lost track.

The woman didn't answer, just stopped outside the door to a small hospital room.

Mama was alone in the bed, the lights low.

"Mama?" She'd crept toward the bed. Where was the baby?

Something was wrong.

Mama's face looked normal again, not puffy-pink like before, but her eyes were sunken in, and she'd looked like she'd been crying.

Mama held out her arms. "He's . . . gone." Her voice was barely a whisper.

She tried to tug back, ask Mama what she meant, but Mama's arms tightened around her, pinning her close to her chest and the scratchy, bleach-smelling hospital sheet. *Gone?*

"Stillborn. Dead in the womb." Mama's voice sounded like she was underwater almost. "They said he died earlier this morning, maybe yesterday. That's why I kept having all that pain, but I guess I didn't understand. Go figure."

Mama tried to laugh, but it came out somewhere between a bark and a cough, and then she was crying, long low wails like nothing Laney had ever heard before.

"I should call Zeb."

"Don't bother. He won't answer." She didn't say it bitterly, only tired. Resigned.

"Mama, where is he?"

She waved a hand all fluttery, like some pageant lady. "Just . . . business."

A knock on the door came then, and a younger, heavy nurse poked her head in.

"Mrs. Barrett?"

Laney backed toward the far edge of the room. Invisible.

The nurse changed out the bag of what looked like water by

Mama's bedside and checked what seemed to be an enormous diaper between Mama's legs.

"Do you think you're ready to see him?" The nurse's voice was gentle. Him.

"I thought he . . ." Mama looked confused.

The nurse seemed to understand what Mama was saying.

"Your baby did . . . pass away . . . in the womb, but we find it's helpful after situations like this for mothers to see their child, say a proper goodbye. Is there a husband we can call?"

Mama's lips thinned. "He's out of town. Can't reach him."

The nurse returned a few minutes later with another nurse and a small bundle of blankets.

The look on Mama's face about broke Laney's heart.

"Oh," Mama said, a hand barely touching her lips as the other accepted the baby they rested in her arms.

The other nurse motioned to Laney, there in the corner. "Come say goodbye to your little brother."

Her brother. Henry.

Mama's face was as white as those porcelain dolls on display in the library. Eyes wide, she appeared to be studying his face. Memorizing it.

"Like you . . ." she murmured, casting a quick glance at Laney.

After that, Mama checked out. Zeb gave her pills to feel better, and soon that's all Mama wanted.

A year later, she was dead, too. Overdose, they told Laney.

But Laney knew the truth. Mama'd died of a broken heart, died that same day, there in the hospital with her baby brother.

Died, right along with all of Laney's own dreams.

Until Lissa. That's when she started to dream again.

"Mama . . ."

Laney blinked, and Lissa was there now, before her. She'd rested both her tiny hands on either side of Laney's face, and she pressed her forehead in close.

"You're a sad mama today," Lissa said.

Laney sniffled back the tears, but one trickled down her cheek anyway, unbidden.

"I . . . was thinking about my own mama."

Lissa's mouth made a tiny O. "Mama's mama?"

"Mama's mama." She clutched the girl tight, pulled her up onto her lap, and rocked her, right there on the park bench, the memories swirling around hard and fast.

"It's going to be okay, Mama," Lissa said finally.

Laney breathed out a laugh and kissed her girl on her hair once more. "You're so right, baby girl. It sure is."

As they walked back to the apartment, Laney could see the moon begin to rise, even though it was still daylight.

Make a wish . . .

She closed her eyes a moment, paused. Rev might know, or suspect. But she and Lissa were safe. Secure. Far, far away from Ethan, and Zeb, and all the ghosts and goblins.

Help us be okay, God. Please. Help us be okay.

CHAPTER 20

Natalie

On Monday after supper, Natalie sat cross-legged in her bedroom, the scrapbook she'd bought for Ashley open before her. It was just a little something she was putting together to give her sister before the surgery tomorrow, old pictures of the two of them as kids, but she knew it would make Ash smile.

Supposedly the surgery wouldn't be too bad—at least, that's what Ash had told them all, and Matt hadn't said any different. No lifting for a long while, but thankfully the kids were too big for carrying.

Mom was a wreck disguised as manic energy. She'd been cleaning at Ashley's the last two days, had even enlisted Hayley to help here and there.

Of course, Natalie was the calm one. As the middle child, calm and peaceable had been her hallmark traits most of her life. Even before Hayley was born, come to think of it. Ash was the go-getter, the class president, the do-every-club-and-then-some kid. Even now, she was the best stay-at-home mom Natalie'd ever imagined. Natalie always swore she'd won Homecoming Queen only because Ashley had first. Well, that and because she'd been dating Bobby

Smathers all through high school. By the time college application season rolled around, she and Bobby had both known they were through, but it had just been easier to stay together till graduation. Why break up and disappoint everyone?

A giggle wormed into her chest as she plucked another old photo from the box. Her and Ash, probably seven and ten, red-popsicle stains across their lips and down the front of their matching Fourth of July T-shirts. That one was going in the scrapbook for sure. She smeared a glue stick across the back and pressed it diagonally across the top left of the page. "Lipstick queens," she scrawled in bold black permanent marker just below the picture.

Another one went below, both of them fishing with Paw-Paw before he'd passed away. She snagged one of them hunting for Easter eggs at the church, then another in the matching Christmas outfits Mom made them wear till Ash was sixteen and finally refused. Daddy had actually taken Ash's side, which of course meant it was settled. Nat could probably count on one hand the times Daddy had taken a side and settled a matter when it came to Mom and her girls, but when he did, that was that.

Natalie almost gasped when she came to one from Ashley's wedding day—she looked so much like Mom that Natalie sat stunned a moment. There they all were, Ash, Mom, and Natalie, with Hayley as the flower girl, her honey-brown locks all curled in skinny ringlets. Natalie wore the deep blue maid-of-honor gown Ash loved so much, and Ash's smile was so radiant she could've been an angel.

Is an angel, really. All her life, she'd looked up to Ashley, the golden child, with her straight-As and her solos in choir, even wanted to be her, as if that were possible. Ash didn't ever seem to notice, just struck out into the world as the oldest daughter should, never looking back, never noticing Natalie staring after her in the shadows, all envious as Ash paved the way, blazed the trail, climbed the mountain, every single cliché she could think of, all for the rest of them. For her and Hayley, showing them how it was done.

Natalie's hand rested upon another photo of her, smiling and proud at the birth of the twins. Ash was there in the bed, all rosy-cheeked and gleaming as if she'd just been dancing instead of squeezing out two kids.

My big sissy, she whispered to herself, looking at Ashley's beaming face, the babies cradled in her arms as Natalie leaned in for the requisite say-cheese photo grin.

She couldn't wait till the surgery was over and done with, when Ash could get back to regular life again. She'd talked about going back to teaching when the twins were old enough—maybe now she could.

Natalie fumbled through the box for one more photo, closing her hand on what felt like a card. She pulled it out, then sank back, stunned.

It was a save-the-date card. *Her* save-the-date card, in fact. June 7, for her and Tucker's wedding, right here in Dahlia.

Hot tears sprang unbidden, and for a moment Natalie couldn't help herself. Her hands shook as she pried open the card, pulled out the little photo inside. Her and Tucker, at his granddad's farm over in Knoxville. She remembered that day so clearly, how happy they'd been, how he'd taken her on the bay mare up the ridge to the top, looked out a long, long time over the mountains in the distance, talking about what could be—what would be, he'd promised.

Had it all been a lie, even then? When had things turned off course?

And why . . . why Stacey? Of all people, why her? Natalie's best friend. Had he zeroed in on Stace, charmed her like some conquest, like the clients at work, some game to play? Had Stacey thrown herself at him? Or had they been . . . in love? Had it all happened on accident?

The worst was she'd never know. Never. Not now, not next year, not ever.

You arrogant, pompous, idiot monster, she seethed as she gazed at the photo, tears pooling until they spilled over and down her cheeks. Hot tears. Angry tears.

She thought she'd destroyed every one of those blasted wedding cards, but somehow one had wound up in her photo box.

She peered at the photo hard, looked deep into his confident, smiling face, all rugged and slightly stubbly but filled with levity, like he had no problems whatsoever in all the universe. Even his smile wasn't the posed smile plastered across her own face, hers so conscious of the photographer and his cues to help them get "just the right angle." It was like Tucker knew every angle was the right angle, every photo would be just fine, just like everything always turned out for him.

It's not that I'm bitter, really.

A hard lump formed in her throat even behind the tears. *Who am I kidding?* She crumpled the photo tight in her hands, the pointy corner poking hard into the flesh of her palm.

Perhaps the actual worst wasn't the not knowing, but the not being able to confront. What she'd give to roar the accusations and the condemnations in his face, in Stacey's, to jab her finger at them and make them feel like the worst people in the world for what they'd done to her, to all of them. Now they were blissfully off in the never-never . . . where—heaven? She didn't even want to think about that, where the two of them were now. It was far easier just to know they were gone, sleeping peacefully off in who-knew-where, away from her wrath and her pain and the guilt of all they'd done.

All they'd done to her.

Her whole life, over.

At the funeral, his parents had been kind, but she'd seen something behind their eyes, wondered if they knew or had known. Had Tucker been planning to call things off? Had Stacey been a fling? Or had they been just as surprised as Natalie herself?

Natalie's assistant Bella had been all blubbering and puffy-faced, full of all the right things to say, but Natalie saw the pity behind her eyes. Bella knew—everyone knew—she'd been a colossal fool. And Natalie herself, of course, was the very last to know.

Her cell phone buzzed as she clenched the balled-up photo tight. It was a message from Finn, she saw, and squeezed her eyes shut in response.

She wasn't even sure she liked Finn that way or not, or if it was just the male attention that felt so good after everything.

You have no business messing with that guy or any guy, Natalie Annabelle Motts. You're too raw, too wounded, and it's way, way too soon. What's it been—a year? She'd almost lost count, and that was a good thing. But deep down she knew she'd be scarred for life. What was that term they used for stuff so broken they couldn't be resold? Damaged goods? Yeah, that was her.

She glanced at Finn's message. He was letting her know he'd be praying for Ashley and to holler if she needed anything.

It was sweet, and tempting. It would be so easy to text back, let things evolve. But then there'd be a date, and then that requisite got-to-put-the-brakes-on conversation, because there was no way in the world she should be dating someone a year after her fiancé died, no matter how cute and funny and thoughtful Finn was, and no matter how good and warm she felt inside when she was around him.

And who was she kidding, thinking she could be actual friends with a guy. She'd noticed the way Finn had started looking at her—probably the same way she'd been looking at him.

A thunderclap pierced the night air outside the window and she shivered, thinking instantly of Ashley. *She'll be fine.* It wasn't even a major surgery, really, though it was major to Ash, and to her.

That night, she fell asleep listening to the sound of rain on the roof, praying to God everything really would be okay.

Only God didn't exactly cooperate.

CHAPTER 21

Natalie

THE NEXT MORNING, Natalie and her mom met Ashley and Matt at the hospital. Natalie gave her the scrapbook and a gift certificate to the day spa in Charlotte for when she'd recovered, and by the time the anesthesiologist got there and Natalie headed over to open Sunstrokes, everything seemed fine. Routine. Normal.

Yet she couldn't calm that odd little twinge in her belly, the one that meant her worries were starting to bubble up like boiled water.

Not five minutes after she'd turned the closed sign to open, her cell phone rang.

Matt. "I need your calm."

He sounded like he was joking, but she could hear the worry in his voice.

Natalie gripped the phone. "What's going on?"

"Doctor found . . . something, and now they've got to do a total hysterectomy, plus a biopsy. Your mom doesn't know yet, so it would be great if you got back before they're done—"

". . . so Mom doesn't flip out. Got it. Oh, Matt. You okay?"

"Yeah, yeah, I'm fine," he said, all breezy-like.

Natalie saw through it but played along. "Be right over."

Even if it was *something*-something, Ashley was going to be all right. Natalie knew this. It wasn't like she was having brain surgery, or heart surgery, and it was all routine, supposedly. At least, that's what everyone kept saying. But knowing it couldn't stop the quivers from running through her belly as she slung her purse strap over her shoulder and popped into Joe Mama's.

Laney was at the counter.

Natalie breathed a sigh of relief when she saw her. "Any chance Finn will let you hop over to the art shop awhile? Complications with my sister's surgery, and it looks like I have to be at the hospital, maybe all day."

Finn walked out from the back then, and she could tell he'd heard.

"Of course," he said, looking at Laney. His eyes penetrated Nat's, and she saw the worry.

Laney nodded. "Don't you worry about a thing. I can stay all day, even close up if needed."

Natalie gave them both a tight smile. "Thanks."

Finn looked like he was going to say more, but she was out the door and behind the wheel of her SUV before he could even get the words out.

By the time she arrived back at the hospital, she'd put her game face on. And it was a good thing.

"They're taking a long time." Mom was grumpy, which meant she was worried.

"Well, we wouldn't want the speedy version, would we?" Natalie pecked her mom on the cheek and slid past to where Matt slumped in the corner, staring at his cell phone like it held the meaning of life.

"Thanks," he mouthed.

She smiled her best comforting smile.

Dr. Warner sat down with them briefly when she finished the

surgery, before they were allowed to go back and see Ashley.

"The surgery was far more invasive than I'd anticipated. The tumor has grown, too, something I never like. Just to be safe, we took it all out—the uterus, cervix, ovaries, fallopian tubes."

Matt looked somber. "Is the recovery time still about the same?"

Dr. Warner shook her head. "At least four to six weeks, possibly longer. But for now, she's okay, and the surgery went well, with no complications. We should have the biopsy results within a week or two, hopefully sooner."

Mom's eyes were wide. "Is it . . . does it look like. . .?"

"Cancer? I'm afraid it does. But I believe we got it all out. That's the best news. And Ashley's young and healthy. That's also on her side."

Mom clutched her cross necklace, and Natalie squeezed her hand.

Matt shook the doctor's hand, and she ducked back out the door.

When they'd all gathered around Ashley's bed, Natalie wasn't surprised to see her sister was the cheeriest one of them all.

"I'll be fine, Mom. And Nat, that spa? Maybe we can go my birthday weekend."

"I'm ready when you are," Natalie said, wiggling Ash's bright pink sock toe, which poked out from under the bedsheets.

Matt was at her side, gently stroking her hair.

That night after she closed the shop, Natalie rushed home in time to help tuck the twins into the sofa bed in Daddy's home office. Mom was reading from *The Complete Tales of Winnie the Pooh*, and Nat saw it was the same tattered copy she and Ash used to read when they were little, the same one she used to read Hayley before Natalie left for college.

Peter had the covers pulled up to his chin.

"Auntie Nat, Grammy says we get to stay here all week while Daddy's staying with Mommy in the hospital!"

He looked excited, not scared, and for some reason this made all the tiny butterflies gathered in Natalie's tummy settle down and stay quiet.

"And we get to go to the pool tomorrow," Paisley told her brother, her grin fierce. "Can you come, too, Aunt Nat?"

"Not tomorrow, sweetie, but maybe Grammy can bring you two by my shop for some popsicles and painting after."

Natalie's eyes sparkled as the twins high-fived each other and excitedly clamored on about some pool game they planned to play until Mom quieted them down.

They kissed the kids goodnight, switched on the nightlight, and slipped out of the room.

In the kitchen, Mom sagged into a chair at the table. "Thank God they're taking it well."

"I think Peter considers everything an adventure." Nat popped open the plastic tub of grocery-store cookies, passed one over to her mom.

"And Paisley, too, as long as she gets to be in charge." Mom took a bite and winked at her. "Reminds me of someone I know."

"Me? Ash was always in charge."

"She was just the oldest. You? You've always been the boss. Remember the summer you started that dance club with all the neighbor kids?"

Natalie giggled and reached for another cookie. "I forgot about that! I made us all audition to get in, even though everyone was accepted, just to make sure everyone was serious about it. And that dance finale!"

"You kids put flyers in every mailbox up and down this street, practically commanding the neighbors to come. You even got

Daddy to help set up chairs in the backyard, and he did it, too."

Natalie shook her head remembering all the work they'd put in—the costumes and the sparkles and the rehearsals, over and over till everything was just perfect. "I sure was bossy."

"Not bossy." Mom held up a finger. "A *leader*. There's a difference."

Natalie just laughed again. "I'm not sure the neighbor kids saw it that way."

Mom closed the cookie bin with a snap and gazed over at her. "You're a good girl, Nat. I'm glad you're home."

For some reason, Natalie's eyes felt wet, and she reached over for a quick hug. "I'm glad I'm home, too, Mom."

When she climbed the stairs to go to bed, she saw another text from Finn.

"I didn't get a chance to see you today, but I hope Ashley is feeling better. Stop by in the morning if you can."

She started to respond but stopped herself.

Just stop this, Nat. You have no business leading him on.

Instead, she just put the phone on the charger and lugged the canvas of Ashley out of her closet, working on her sister's golden hair and pert chin long into the night.

"Am I being a pest?"

Finn stood at the front door of Sunstrokes with a to-go cup in his hand late the next morning.

She intentionally didn't go by Joe Mama's before work, hoping he'd eventually get the message to back off a little.

But hearing his words sent a little stab in her heart. "No, no! It's just—I'm just busy is all. My sister, and the shop, and, well. . . you know."

Finn just looked at her like he knew what she was doing but had the decency not to call her out on it.

"Okay. Well, I thought you could use a pick-me-up." He quickly passed over the coffee, then backed up so he was by the door again. *Boundaries, check.* "Is Ashley doing all right?"

She plastered on her polite smile and waved a hand almost dismissively. "Hanging in there. She might come home tomorrow. Friday latest."

"Keep us posted." Finn looked like he wanted to say more.

"Thanks for the coffee." Natalie moved toward the tables, setting up for the class she'd lead in an hour.

"Anytime."

He gave a quick wave and was gone.

It's for the best. Nip it in the bud now before things get complicated.

Still, all the energy she'd had moments ago was now completely gone, and all she wanted to do was hole up in the back and put her head down. She contemplated closing up for an hour and doing just that, but she couldn't. She really did have to set up for the class, and today was Laney's day off. Still, the look on his face, those sad dark eyes, the way he'd darted back toward the front door . . . she could tell she'd hurt him.

She switched on music and popped in her ear buds, cranking up the volume loud so it would drown out all her thoughts.

It was Friday before she saw him again. This time she made herself pop into Joe Mama's, steeling her spine as she ordered a latte from Laney and made small talk.

Finn looked over and gave a half-distant wave from the back as she waited for her order, and she plastered on her own distant smile and gave a polite wave right back.

Then she was gone again, out the door to her shop, staying as busy as she could so she couldn't think.

After all, she couldn't afford to have her heart broken again—or break someone else's.

CHAPTER 22

Laney

On Sunday, instead of going to church, Laney and Alissa were in the car with Cha Cha's friend Fergie, driving to Columbia.

"This it?" Fergie asked when they arrived, peering up at the brick-and-glass hospital.

"Yeah, but not the main entrance. Pull around the side to the long-term care wing." Laney pointed, and Fergie's tiny light blue car zipped around the bend and up to a circular driveway.

"Pick you up at three sharp, right?" Fergie asked when they hopped out.

Laney started to unbuckle the car seat from the back, but Fergie stopped her.

"You can leave the kid's seat with me, I mean, unless you really *want* to lug it around with you all day. It's not goin' nowhere."

Laney wasn't sure she trusted Fergie completely, but Cha Cha vouched for her, and she hadn't paid Fergie all the gas money yet anyway, so it was probably safe enough.

If not, I guess we have bigger problems to worry about—like how to get home, for starters. Trust might be something Laney always had to work on, but that suited her just fine. She curled a protective arm around Alissa.

"See you at three."

Alissa waved at Fergie, who tooted her horn and drove off. Then she grabbed her mom's hand and the two of them walked inside the air-conditioned hospital.

"Are you gonna tell me the soo-prise now, Mommy?" Lissa asked, dancing around as they walked to the counter.

Laney winked at her. "Soon."

At the counter, she was told how to find Jessamine Jackson, and they took the long hall down to the elevators and all the way up to the twelfth floor.

"Miss J!" Lissa squealed when they opened the hospital door.

It had been a good ten months, maybe eleven, since Laney'd last laid eyes on Miss J. Her eyes were still just as warm, and her laugh just as sweet, like honey and warm brown sugar. But there in the bed, it seemed like she'd aged a decade at least.

"Well, ain't you a sight for sore eyes. Come give me some sugar."

Miss J opened her arms, and Lissa almost flew right in, Laney a close second.

"Why are you in the hopsickle, Miss J?" Lissa asked.

Laney met Miss J's eyes. "I didn't tell her much."

Miss J patted the girl's hair and planted a loud smooch on her cheek. "Aw, don't you worry none about Miss J. I'm just fine. Had a little trouble with my heart, so they're resting me up and getting me well again so I can get right on back to work."

"Okay, Miss J." Lissa smiled and snuggled right into the woman's arms there in the hospital bed, and Laney's heart swelled to see the two of them, there together like that.

"I sure have missed you." Laney sank into the chair next to the bed.

"Well, you just tell Miss J everything. I want to hear it all."

And she did—told her about Joe Mama's, and Sunstrokes, and

Cha Cha and Dahlia Community Church, and the rent hike, and even about Tikvah House and the upcoming festival, now just one week away.

"Mmm, mm. Now *that* does my heart extra-good," Miss J said when she heard about the women's center. "But I bet it gave you a bit of a reality check, am I right?"

Laney shrugged, embarrassed now to admit her initial reaction. "Yeah, guess it felt like my underpants were showing."

"I feel you. And now?"

"I don't know." Laney frowned, considering. "I guess I'm . . . kind of excited. To think I'm living in a community that cares this much, and that maybe some more women can get the help they need."

Miss J looked at her a long moment. "You know, sugar plum, maybe that's what the Lord has in store for you next."

"What, you think Lissa and I need to move back into a place like Sunrise?" Laney blinked, surprised. She wouldn't trade her time there for, well, anything. But she'd worked hard to get a home of their own, get her credit established so she could get utilities turned on and start building her place in the world. Did Miss J want her to go backward, or worse, think she couldn't handle it?

"No, no, no, sugar, that's not what I mean at all." Miss J chuckled and reached over to squeeze Laney's hand. "I mean, maybe the Good Lord wants you to step up and help at that place. Volunteer. Shoo, maybe even run the place."

". . . Me? Run it?"

"Why not you?" Miss J looked her straight in the eyes, that no-nonsense look Laney had seen a hundred times before.

"I don't know. I'm not really a leadership kind of person." Laney looked down, studying her hands. Truth be told, she'd always been more of a follower than a leader, had been since she was a kid.

"Hmph. Think Moses was a leadership person? Didn't he try

to pawn the job off on his brother? How about David, a lowly shepherd? God equips the called, sugar. Haven't I told you that a thousand times? And haven't you been able to step up in ways you never thought you could, being a mama?"

Laney made a face, and they both laughed.

It was true, though—she hadn't known Thing One about motherhood, but she'd tried hard, and prayed for help, and hadn't let pride stop her from asking questions when she didn't know something. So far when it came to Lissa, so good, but that was one person. *No way I could handle a whole houseful, or even want to.*

Laney waved a hand. "Anyway, enough about me. How are you? What sort of things are they having you do here?"

"Torture, plain torture." Miss J grinned. "Physical therapy every day, and they're making me 'take it easy,' something my girls keep reminding me about every hour."

"Well, good thing we do, Mama, or maybe you wouldn't be here still," came a voice from the door.

Laney turned to see one of Miss J's daughters, still in her church dress.

"Oh, goodness, it's the PT police come to make sure I'm doing my exercises," Miss J teased.

"Hi, Mama." The woman swept in and gave her mom a hug, then wiggled her fingers at Lissa, who was still cuddled up in the bed with Miss J.

"I'm Rosa," the woman said to Laney. "I think we've met before?"

"Laney." Laney held out her hand and they shook. "Good to see you again. And good to see your mom is doing well."

Rosa fanned herself. "Well, she gave us quite a scare, let me tell you. And don't let her get going on getting her fanny back to work. We've already started advertising for a new director."

Miss J swatted in her daughter's direction. "You can get all the new directors you want, but you can't keep me from my Sunrise

House. Those girls are just as much my daughters as you and your sisters."

"Yeah, yeah," Rosa said, but there was kindness in her voice.

Smiling softly, Laney watched the interchange. One day, that could be her and Lissa, God willing. *Would* be her and Lissa, she corrected herself internally. At least if she had any say in the matter.

Rosa dragged over another chair from the corner and sat, dropping her purse on the ground. "Feels like a furnace out there. You're lucky you're all pampered in this air-conditioning. I still need to brave the shops this afternoon."

Miss J caught Laney's eye. "Rosa here's getting married at the end of the year, so she's been out looking at wedding dresses."

"Never thought I'd be tying the knot in my forties, or really, getting married period," Rosa told Laney with a grin. "But I finally found a man who can keep up with me and doesn't mind the long hours I have to put in for work."

"Well, he is an attorney like you, so I imagine he understands it. And I also imagine God himself had his hand in all this," Miss J said.

"On that, Mama, I can agree on all counts."

"Congratulations," Laney said.

"Ooh, do you get to wear a princess dress?" Lissa piped up from the bed. "All white and sparkly?"

"Maybe." Rosa smiled, scrolling through her phone to show them the dresses she'd looked at yesterday. "Though I love this cream one here. Look at that bodice."

"I want to wear a white sparkling fluffy dress and have pink hair and real earrings with real holes in my ears," Lissa told them, her face lit like sunshine.

They all laughed, and Rosa tweaked Lissa's nose like her mom did earlier.

"And that will be absolutely lovely," she told the girl.

Later, driving back to Dahlia with Fergie, Laney leaned her head back against the car seat. Fergie's windows were open to let the breeze in, and it felt so good against her skin. She'd have loved to doze off like Lissa in the backseat, but of course she wouldn't.

Whatever Fergie had playing on the car radio had a pounding drumbeat, almost tribal-like, and Laney gazed out the window at the cars whizzing by on the other side of the line, her eyes half-closed as she thought about all she and Miss J had discussed. The drumbeats were slow and steady, like her heartbeat, and she let herself relax into the music, at least as much as she could.

Volunteering at Tikvah House, that was something that hadn't occurred to her before today. Miss J had always been a strong proponent of "paying it forward," taking a bit of what you'd been given and passing on some of that goodness someplace else. To someone else.

Helping women like she'd once been, women starting over, that was as good an example of paying it forward as Laney could imagine.

Laney imagined herself there, sitting down in some room, maybe teaching a group of women how to do basic stuff, like schedule doctor appointments or apply for utility assistance, stuff she hadn't known without someone else's help. Maybe she could help out once a week or so. Helping didn't mean anyone could guess her own past. *I mean, no one looks at that gray-haired Helen Chastain lady and thinks she was in The Life.*

Laney crossed her arms against her chest. Even if the idea of stepping foot inside Tikvah made her feel exposed, like she was in her birthday suit at a party, she knew it was the right thing to do. *Even if I have to push myself.*

What was that Scripture, the one Rev preached about a couple weeks ago, about how freely we've been given things, so freely we should be giving to other people? It was something Jesus had told his disciples—that, and how everyone would know they were Christians by the way they loved and treated other people.

Laney might be new at this whole religion thing, but that was the point, wasn't it? It wasn't about hogging it all to yourself but about sharing it with the world.

It was about sharing it with all the other Laneys out there, Laneys who didn't have a Miss J in their corner cheering them on.

Laney saw the "welcome to Dahlia" sign up ahead and swallowed, dread pooling in her belly as she remembered the other thing she'd told Miss J, about Ethan getting out. Rosa had taken Lissa down to get ice cream from the hospital cafeteria, and Laney had blurted it when the door was closed and it was just them. She'd felt the hot tears pressing against her eyelids, threatening to spill, but they didn't. She'd managed to hold them back.

Still, Miss J had heard the pain in Laney's voice. She'd wriggled up on her pillows in the hospital bed and looked Laney dead in the eye.

"There's not a way he can find you, baby girl. Don't even let that get under your skin. Not one inch."

Miss J is right. Laney swallowed past a lump as Fergie navigated the streets of this town she now called home, dropping her and Lissa off at the front of their apartment complex.

The fear might be there, always. That was something Laney had to live with, figure out, walk through.

But rationally, logically, she knew—they were safe here in Dahlia. Safe and sound.

She hoped to God it was the truth.

CHAPTER 23

Natalie

NATALIE CLUTCHED THE PHONE. "It's definitely cancer?"

Ashley sounded tired.

"They caught it early, just shy of Stage Two, thank God. There's a cancer care place in Charlotte Dr. Warner likes a lot, and she went to med school with the gynecological oncologist there. I've got an appointment Thursday."

"That's fast."

"Well, Dr. Warner promised to pull all the strings she had. As far as I'm concerned, let's get this party started ASAP so we can put it all behind us."

Some party. But Natalie forced a laugh. "That's the spirit."

At family dinner Saturday, Ashley chatted away like everything was fine, though Natalie couldn't help but see how extra-tender Matt was with her, pulling out her chair at the dinner table and keeping the kids occupied.

Daddy jabbed at a piece of steak and chewed thoughtfully. "It's normal they can start this whole . . . procedure so quick?" He waved a hand.

Natalie eyed him, amused. As far as she could tell, she'd gone her entire teenage years without him mentioning anything female-related, even when all three of the Motts ladies had their time of the month simultaneously. It was as if even the idea of it embarrassed him.

She caught Hayley's eye and cast her a grin, but her kid sister flicked her gaze away, shoveling down green beans like she had somewhere else to be.

Natalie got a glimpse of Hayley's nails, noticing for the first time they were no longer the bare, nibbled-down fingertips she normally sported. Instead, they were an icy blue, long and glossy, and filed into sharp points.

Mom put a hand on Daddy's arm. "The quicker the better in cases like this. Ashley, remind me again of the plan they crafted for you? Five rounds of chemotherapy, and twenty-five doses of radiation?"

Ash nodded. "Plus some internal radiation. The whole thing will take about five or six weeks, then they'll assess how my body responded."

Matt cleared his throat. "Mary Lynn, thanks again for being okay with driving Ash every day."

Mom waved a hand. "Between your job and the twins, you've got your hands full. And Nat here's got the shop. I've got nothing but time till mid-August, when school starts up again."

Natalie stabbed a green bean. "Hayley, your nails look good."

Hayley shrugged like it was nothing, though Natalie saw her flick her hand just so, admiring them.

"A friend treated me."

A car horn tooted in the driveway. Hayley looked like she'd just been liberated from prison.

"That's Jasmine." Hayley started to stand, reaching for the crutches leaning against the wall behind her.

"Not so fast." Mom frowned. "It's family dinner night. And

who's Jasmine?"

"But—" Hayley's face twisted like she'd eaten something sour.

"No buts." Mom straightened the napkin on her lap.

"Oh, Mary Lynn, just let her go." Daddy sighed. "Kid's been doing nothing all summer but sitting there, looking miserable."

Mom opened her mouth like she was about to object, but then closed it again.

Hayley hobbled over and planted a kiss on Daddy's cheek. "We're just going to the movies. I won't be too late."

She was out the door and in the waiting car before anyone else could say a word.

A girl was driving, but Natalie couldn't see who. The car was a newish one, a shiny red zippy thing with a loud motor, and the tires squealed as the driver backed out and peeled away.

"What? I've dealt with my share of moody teens." Daddy shrugged. "And you two were no exception. Better to give you a little freedom. Besides, what's going to happen in Dahlia?"

Mom tried to make Ashley sit at the kitchen table during dishes.

But Ashley just scoffed and elbowed her way in. "You can treat me like an invalid when I start getting all tired from chemo. For now? Let's just be normal, okay?"

She picked up a handful of bubbles from the sink and blew one at Mom, and they all giggled.

It felt good to laugh together, all of them. Mom's face, which had been pinched with worry most of the week, looked relaxed again and almost happy. And Ash herself, sunny as always, seemed to have picked the most optimistic of all colors to wear that night, a vivid, cheerful yellow that made it seem she had no cares in the world.

A shiver of dread snaked down Natalie's spine, and she shoved it away. *Just leave it alone.*

But deep down, she was scared. And even if no one else was going to admit it, she was—at least to herself.

After everyone had left and Mom and Daddy had gone up to bed, Natalie laced up her sneakers and went out for a nighttime run. *Please God, please God.* The words echoed through her head as her shoes slapped the sidewalk.

Ashley was young, and healthy. They'd caught it early. But Natalie'd heard the stories, knew how quickly cancer could claim someone. *Please not Ash*, she begged in her mind.

She ran a different way tonight, toward Main Street and past the village square and gazebo. Someone left their sprinklers on, and the drizzle of water cast a wet sheen beneath the streetlights, reminding her of tears.

She swallowed back her own tears as if in response. But the lump wouldn't go away, and finally she eased her run to a fast walk and then a stroll.

It's all right, baby girl. Natalie felt more than heard the words in her head, and she closed her eyes a moment, grateful. Whether it was God speaking the words to her or her own mind trying to calm itself down, she didn't much care.

When she reached the gazebo, she climbed the short flight of steps and took a seat in one of the swings, kicking back so she glided. The summer air felt good on her skin, almost dewy, and she stayed a long while, letting her heartbeat slip back to normal.

A dog yipped in the distance, and for a moment she thought it was a young girl. Maybe Hayley. But another dog barked something in reply, and the night settled down once more.

Natalie swung awhile, thinking of Ashley and Hayley, of Mom and Daddy. Hayley had been full of attitude these last few weeks. After the incident at the bar, Natalie'd thought things would get better, but Hayley had only gotten more moody and withdrawn. At least she hadn't been going out drinking—hopefully. But Hayley hadn't left before Natalie'd looked her up and down. In spite of the crazy-long nails, her sister wore baggy shorts and an old T-shirt, and she didn't have a stitch of makeup on. Natalie would bet money Hayley wasn't going out on the town looking like that. Still, she also would have bet money she'd never find her little sister boozing it up in some sleazy strip mall like she'd been the night Natalie and Finn had seen her.

Finn. Natalie winced at the name she'd tried to avoid all week, and almost succeeded. Until now.

The texts had stopped, and the friendly little pop-ins. She'd almost managed to avoid looking for his black truck in the parking lot, at least most days. Another week or two, and it'd be like it never happened. Not that anything had actually happened.

Still, she couldn't help but imagine the promise of what could have been.

On the street, Natalie heard giggles and saw a group of teens walk by. She recognized Hayley's friends Zoe and Chelsey, and a couple of boys, all bouncing a basketball while walking somebody's fluffy white dog.

She checked her watch, then stood and headed back toward her house. For a moment, she wished she could call Finn, and the thought threatened to overwhelm.

You're just lonely. She knew it was true. When she'd lost Tucker and Stacy, she'd lost her whole world. And even though she had Ashley now, it wasn't quite the same.

Tomorrow she'd sign up for one of those Bible studies Pastor Dave was always pushing at church, and maybe some other volunteer thing. With Mom taking Ash to Charlotte every day, maybe she could pick up the slack with the back-to-school collection Mom was organizing, or maybe do something with Tikvah House.

Helen Chastain and Marla had that big training thing going on in the fellowship hall a few nights a week. She might as well get involved.

Maybe she'd even invite Hayley to join her. It would give the girl something to do besides sit around and mope. What did she have, three or four more weeks in the cast? At least she could stay busy.

But when Natalie got home, Hayley wasn't back from the movies yet. Her bed was still made, all purple ruffles and that tattered old teddy bear plopped in the middle like a centerpiece. Magoo, Natalie remembered. A wave of memories passed over her as she remembered little Hayley clinging to her as she headed back to Nashville, then older Hayley begging for Natalie to fix her hair or paint her toenails. When was the last time they'd done anything like that, Natalie wondered, looking around the room at the mixture of childhood and woman all swirled into one. Posters and fake vines decorated the wall behind her bed, and one high heel poked out from beneath the dresser, while in the corner sat a basket of stuffed animals and old favorite dolls, now forgotten.

In the morning I'll invite her, Natalie told herself.

But in the morning, Hayley was still in bed when they left for church.

"Stomach bug." Mom scrunched up her nose as they locked the house and slipped into the car.

Daddy was already behind the wheel, a long-suffering look on his face, like he'd been waiting half his life for people to get ready and out the door.

Natalie gazed at her little sister's window, saw the curtains move a hair. Like Hayley was just waiting for them to leave.

"Sure you can't join?" she texted her sister.

But the text stayed unread all the way through the service.

After worship, Natalie slipped through the crowd and found

Helen Chastain chatting with a few other older women.

Helen waved when she walked up, a toothy smile lighting her soft, wrinkled face. Her steel gray curls bobbed beneath a cute little summer hat.

"Still good to meet Tuesday about the fundraiser? I can't believe it's this weekend."

Natalie nodded. "Absolutely."

"You're the art shop girl," one of Helen's friends said, reaching out to adjust the collar on Natalie's shirt.

"Woman, not girl." Her other friend, a tall white-haired lady with lime-green eyeglasses, swatted her, then smiled at Natalie. "You have a cute place! My grandsons and I were in the other day. The elephants?"

Natalie remembered her and the two little boys. They'd done one of the lunchtime classes and ended up staying through the afternoon.

"It was the best afternoon we've had in ages."

"You really are doing a wonderful job. Such a good addition to Dahlia," the other lady said.

Natalie felt her cheeks flush with the praise. "Thank you." She looked at Helen. "You're doing some trainings for the Tikvah House, aren't you? I was thinking I might want to get more involved."

The lime-green glasses lady elbowed Helen. "See? Told you people would want to."

Helen looked into Natalie's eyes with interest. "We're trying to develop some life-building skills for the women when they come. Practical things, like resume-writing, or help studying for the GED. Jane here is working on a literacy class, too."

"Reading?"

Jane adjusted her glasses. "I taught high-school English forty-five years before I retired, and I'm always surprised at how many adults still don't have the skills they need."

Natalie considered. "I have a degree in marketing, and I can definitely help with the career stuff. But I'm not so sure I know the first thing about teaching."

Jane winked. "It's more like tutoring. And you'd be surprised at how much fun it is."

Helen patted Natalie's arm. "Monday and Wednesday evenings we do trainings in the fellowship hall. Come, and bring a friend. We'll get you plugged in."

Natalie found her parents, and for the rest of the afternoon, the idea swirled in her brain. Plugged in. It sounded exactly like what she needed—an outlet for her time.

An outlet to keep her mind off Tucker, and Ashley.

And Finn.

CHAPTER 24

Laney

For days after the visit to Miss J, Laney thought about Tikvah House. She dreamed about Tikvah House.

And finally, just to get herself to stop thinking about it, she gave in and told Natalie she'd help at the festival.

"Oh, good!" Natalie looked surprised but happy. "And I was thinking—can we put Lissa to work, too? She's a great helper. She can work with the little kids, show them how to do stuff."

Laney considered. It wasn't a bad idea. Besides, she'd realized Lissa was far better behaved when she had a job. Laney'd been giving her chores at home just to keep her occupied after the camp counselors told her they'd made her an honorary junior counselor. August, and the start of kindergarten, couldn't come soon enough.

Today, Laney was alone at the shop. The remains of her iced coffee sat pooling condensation on the front counter as a dozen elementary-aged girls excitedly painted their vision of princesses on canvasses. Moms and a couple dads and grandmas clustered in the back, chatting as their kids played with color.

"Good job!" she told one girl, who'd painted a unicorn's horn on her princess's head and what looked like butterfly wings trailing from a long bubble-gum pink gown. She grinned as she noticed the girl also painted purple and black combat boots for footwear. *My kind of princess*, Laney thought.

The door tinkled as someone walked in. It was a teenager in crutches, and she scowled as she approached the counter, scanning the room. Hayley.

Laney smiled. "Looking for Nat?"

The girl narrowed her eyes at Laney, looking her up and down with a "well, duh, who else would I be looking for" expression on her face.

"She's over at the fundraiser meeting for Tikvah House," Laney said, then added at the girl's blank stare, "you know, the women's crisis center?"

The girl sniffed. "Just tell her Hayley came by. Our mom sent a bunch of junk for the school packs."

She set down a tote bag, and Laney saw it was filled with spiral notebooks and boxes of pencils.

Before Laney could say okay, Hayley was out the door again, hobbling toward a red car blaring loud hip hop. She climbed into the passenger side, and the driver took off, tires squealing as they went.

Well, fine then. Laney stared after them, watched the car take a turn far too fast and bump over the curb, then go barreling off toward the west side of town.

She turned her attention back to the kids, and by the time Natalie finally got back from her meeting, the last kid had left with her dad and Laney was rinsing out brushes in the back.

Natalie looked pretty in a pink cotton T-shirt dress, her long blond hair pulled back in a loose ponytail, and for a moment Laney felt like a reject, all gawky and clumsy and stupid in comparison.

But Natalie's enthusiasm was contagious, and Laney found herself sucked in to the plans she explained about the fundraiser.

"I showed you the stones, right?" Natalie stopped mid-sentence.

Laney grinned. "Yeah, and I love the idea. Plus, we can use up those cheapy brushes you've been wanting to get rid of. They'll do just fine painting on a rough surface like the stones, especially if we're using dark colors."

"Like navy, or red?" Natalie said.

"Exactly!"

Natalie disappeared to the back and returned with one of the bags of stones, then snagged two from the bag.

"Here, let's practice." She handed one to Laney, grabbing them two brushes and a little of the red and navy acrylic.

"Hope," Laney scrawled in bright red upon the stone's surface. As she painted, she thought about the word, one that meant far more to her now than she'd ever expected.

Inspired, she added a deep blue circle in the center of the O in hope, and for a moment she peered at it, gazing at the single point of dark color surrounded by all that bright, cheerful red. *Isn't that how hope is sometimes—so much more obvious when compared to the darkness you've been in?*

Natalie glanced over. "I like that contrast," she said.

Laney remembered the bag Natalie's sister left earlier, and Natalie perked up at the mention.

"Good! I'm going by the church later, so I'll bring it then." Natalie cast a thoughtful look toward Laney. "Would you be interested in coming, too? It's a Bible study on the books of Samuel."

Laney thought of Lissa and started to decline.

But Natalie held up a finger. "Before you decide, they have free childcare, and a light dinner, too. And I'd be happy to take you both home after."

Laney glanced down at the stone in her hand, gazing once more at the word "hope." She hadn't done a group Bible study since she left Sunrise House—no time, honestly, and without a car it hadn't exactly been convenient. But she'd been wanting to, and here it was, an opportunity just falling into her lap, and from one of her bosses, no less. What had Miss J always said, like manna from heaven?

She looked at Natalie, expecting her to be waiting for an answer, but Natalie was focused on finishing her own stone as if whatever Laney said was fine by her, as if plenty of room to make her own decisions was perfectly normal in Natalie's world. Probably was.

But for Laney, it was a new thing, all these choices. And it felt . . . good, she decided.

"I think I will," she said softly. "If you're sure you don't mind giving us a lift."

They closed the shop right at seven and got the car seat all buckled into Natalie's silver SUV.

"For you, Mama." Lissa held out a blue construction-paper flower.

Laney took it and planted a smooch on Lissa's hair. "Thanks, sweet one."

Dinner at the church was simple—wrapped sandwiches and some chips on the side, and Lissa waved happily from the colorful carpet in the kids' wing, where the two teachers had them settled, munching while they listened to a Bible story.

It was mostly ladies in the Bible study classroom, with a smattering of older men and, to Laney's surprise, Finn.

His eyes were mostly on Natalie as they walked in and found seats. "Twice in one day."

He tried to say it all casual, but Laney could see through the act. He liked Natalie, a whole lot. But either something happened between them or Natalie was just about as avoidant of men as Laney herself, because Natalie clammed up like a silly teen whenever she saw him now, or else put on that showy howya-doin' thing she did, as if her smile and confidence could keep him at bay. A shield of sorts. Finn was a nice guy, and coming from Laney, that was saying a lot. She'd be willing to bet Natalie liked him back, only Natalie didn't quite know what to do with those feelings.

"How about that," Natalie murmured back at him with a small wave, then steered her and Laney over to empty seats across the room.

"Twice?" Laney whispered.

"He was at that fundraiser meeting I went to earlier today. For Tikvah House."

"Ohhh."

The teacher, a skinny, tall gray-haired lady with bright green glasses, was good at what she did, and soon they jumped into the chapter for the day and were deep in discussion.

Laney was too shy to answer any of the questions, but Natalie launched right in. Laney wished she had that kind of confidence, that she could be the kind of person able to stand up in front of a room of people and talk about, well, anything. But even before The Life, she'd been shy, reserved. Now? Forget it.

After, the teacher flagged Nat down.

"Did you think about the tutoring thing?"

Natalie sighed and shook her head. "I did, but my shop doesn't close till seven. I can't."

The teacher made a face. "I get that." She looked at Laney, adjusting her glasses. "How about you—are you interested in tutoring?"

Laney's eyes widened. She thought Laney needed tutoring? "Ah, no, I don't think I need help with anything like that. I'm done with school."

The woman laughed good-naturedly. "No, I mean *you* serving as a tutor. For people who need a little help learning to read and such."

"Oh!" Laney's cheeks flushed. A tutor? Her? "Well, I guess I'll think about it. I'm not sure I have the time."

The teacher smiled at her.

As they drove home, Natalie looked over. "Thanks for going with me."

Lissa was already asleep in the car seat, her little Sponge Bob backpack cuddled in her arms like a stuffed animal.

"I think I finally figured out I don't really like going to places like that, places with lots of people, alone. It's easier with someone—with a friend." Natalie gave her a smile.

Laney blinked at the word "friend" and smiled. That's how it felt, she realized, almost like she and Natalie were friends. She hadn't had a friend in, well. Ages. The Life made friendship almost impossible. Everyone was out for herself, had to be, or you'd get eaten alive and swallowed whole. Come to think of it, she couldn't remember the last time she'd had a friend her own age. Miss J was her friend, but she was also a lot more like a mom. And Ethan? She'd thought he was her friend, but friends don't do what Ethan did to her. No way, no how.

"Much easier with a friend. You grew up here. I imagine you'd have a ton of friends from high school still."

"They all moved away, like I did." They drove in silence a moment before Natalie murmured, "I had a best friend. Stacey. We were roommates in Nashville, had been since college. She died about a year ago. Since then, well . . ."

A soft mist of rain started then, and Natalie flicked on the wipers as she rounded the corner, heading toward Laney's apartment.

"I know what you mean." Laney's words were almost a whisper.

She remembered Carla now, Carla with her long raven-black hair and skinny choker necklace. Carla who'd been as close to a best friend as Laney'd ever had before she OD'd on something Ethan gave her.

They'd had no choice but to leave her body outside the hospital, drive off before anyone could spot them.

Years had passed since that night, but the memory still made Laney want to cry.

They pulled up at the apartment, and Laney gently lifted Lissa from the car seat, then unlatched the seat from the SUV.

"Thanks for the ride, Nat." Laney hoisted Lissa up higher onto her hip, the car seat heavy in her other hand.

"See you tomorrow."

Laney watched Nat's headlights disappear into the night, two bright points of red that reminded her of the stone she'd painted earlier. Hope.

A future.

A friend.

Then she turned, set Lissa down to walk, and they headed inside for the night.

She could feel the eyes of the guys on her, a cluster congregated at the edge of the apartment complex, smoking and guzzling cans of beer. Laughing.

Maybe laughing at her, or about what they'd want to do with her. To her.

In her experience, that's all men cared about, really. What they could do to her.

She hurried Lissa up the short flight of stairs to their tiny apartment, got the girl stripped out of her play clothes and into a quick bath, then tucked her all snuggly into bed. Warm and safe.

"Goodnight, bunny bear." Laney nuzzled Lissa's nose with her own.

Lissa nuzzled back. "Nighty-night, mama bear."

Laney watched her daughter for a long time after she fell asleep. *Did I do the right thing, bringing her here? Would it be better if I moved back someplace, like Sunrise House?*

Outside the window, behind the slit of sheet, she could see the small playground at the edge of the apartment's property, and the laundromat beyond, and the rows of older houses. Beyond that, she knew, was the elementary school, and then an old gas station, and eventually way, way down was the church—her church. Dahlia Community Church.

A movement outside the window caught her eye, and she looked out to see two guys beneath one of the streetlights, talking to some girl, who shoved right past them. Her body language was like armor, Laney thought suddenly, and she peered at them a few minutes. Waiting for the boys to pounce.

But they didn't, and the girl just kept on walking. She had long soft hair, and for a minute she reminded Laney of Nat's sister, the one with the major attitude who'd given Laney the side eye and looked at Laney like she was some piece of garbage. It wasn't the sister, Laney knew that. This girl had different hair, curly, and besides, she wasn't limping around on a broken foot. Still, they shared the same "back off" demeanor. The same kind of shield.

When she'd passed, the boys turned their attention to something else, something they found in the street. Some can or box of some sort.

She watched the boys a long time, until finally they drifted off again down the street and Laney flicked out the bedside lamp and turned her gaze elsewhere.

Climbing beneath the cotton sheets, she pulled the blanket up to her chin and slid down, fishing her Bible from the bedside table.

"No one who hopes in you will ever be put to shame, but shame will come on those who are treacherous without cause," Laney read from Psalm 25.

Treacherous without cause. She could think of a lot of people like this.

But as for her, and Lissa? Laney pictured the hope stone, wishing for a moment she'd brought it home with her instead of leaving it up on display at Sunstrokes.

"We hope in you, God," Laney whispered. "Don't let us be put to shame."

When she slept, her dreams were filled with boys, only instead of kicking a cardboard box beneath the streetlights, they were kicking her, over and over. And all she could do was hang on and wait.

CHAPTER 25

Natalie

ON THE DAY OF THE Tikvah House Independence Day Festival, Natalie surveyed the packed town square, her face a broad grin.

"It's a beautiful thing, isn't it?" Rebecca Jamison from the newspaper nudged her, both of them watching what looked like every man, woman, and child in Dahlia all gathered for what could be a picture-perfect scene from a Hallmark movie. Near the gazebo, Finn's borrowed food truck served up coffee milkshakes and baked goods, and a stage stood smack in the center of all the hubbub, with a cover band down from Charlotte who was a client of Ashley's husband, Matt. They were singing "Brown-Eyed Girl," and a few couples and a throng of little kids danced in front of the stage.

Behind her, Natalie's tent was filled with people painting landscape stones and laughing, Laney and little Lissa setting out extra cups of paint for each table. Cheyenne's haircut tent was just as packed.

"Make sure you come Thursday for Open Paint Night, all right?" Natalie heard Laney tell a pair of women as they carefully packed up their creations, each friend marveling at the other's artwork. So far they had twenty people signed up for Thursday's event, and all their kid class flyers were gone.

Across, on the other side of the gazebo, Camp Dahlia had set up some of their camp games, and Natalie saw Devon leading a group of kids in cornhole, ladderball, and what looked like some giant Connect Four contraption.

Rebecca's husband, a broad-shouldered guy named Josh, came up with a bottle of water for his wife and passed one to Natalie, too.

"I think this needs to be an annual Dahlia tradition," Josh said, tugging Rebecca's ponytail, and she laced an arm around his waist.

"Granny says they used to do just this kind of thing every year back when she was young. Fizzled out ages ago, but why not? It's a lot of work, but well worth it. It's good to see Dahlia come together for an important cause."

Natalie took a long swig of water, wiping her brow. It was hot but not horrible, and the tents helped a ton. And they certainly couldn't have asked for better weather—not a cloud in the sky. In the distance she could see Tiff snapping photos, and the band paused to let the mayor announce just one more hour remained to make bids on the silent auction.

Natalie blinked. Two o'clock already? She ducked back under the tent to help people with their stones, and the afternoon blazed by in a swirl of busy levity.

Around four, they all gathered in front of the stage as Rev Bryant and Pastor Dave took turns announcing the silent auction winners. Natalie stood near her parents, Matt, and the twins, surprised Daddy had actually come. She knew he didn't like crowds, and small talk even less, but he seemed happy enough. Mom apparently convinced him to wear a Tikvah House T-shirt, and he looked even more uncomfortable than usual, but he was there.

"They need some chairs next year, Mary Lynn," he grumbled, and Mom just patted his hand, watching as one lucky winner danced up to the stage for the Smathers Grocery gift basket she'd just won.

Rev Bryant cleared his throat. "Next, the winner of one free tax return from our good friends at Motts Accounting . . . Paula Stover! Come on up to claim your prize."

Natalie's mouth hung open as she risked a glance at her father. Motts Accounting? Her . . . own dad? Maybe he hadn't offered a tax-help tent, but donating a tax return—well, donating anything—was big, especially for him. And she'd had no idea.

Daddy just grinned back at her like he'd pulled a fast one. "Guess your old man's not the stingy jerk you think he is."

Speechless, all she could do was hug him. And to her astonishment, he hugged her back, a real hug, right there in front of everyone.

"Even curmudgeons can show a soft side when it comes to a good cause," Daddy whispered into her ear before he pulled back and gave her a wink.

Natalie could feel her throat grow tight as her eyes filled with tears.

By six, the crowd had mostly cleared. Matt and the twins headed home to check on Ashley, and Mom and Daddy took off right after the auction, Mom in some huff over Hayley and why she'd never showed.

"I don't know what's getting into that girl," Mom murmured under her breath, her lips thin. "It's like she doesn't care one whit about anything anymore!"

Daddy just jingled the car keys, his telltale cue for his wife to hurry it up—he'd peopled far too long.

Nat helped Cheyenne stack her salon chairs in the back of her Tahoe, then noticed Laney struggling to lug two giant trash bags as tall as she was toward the dumpster.

"I've got these. Can you and Lissa try to break down those tables?"

Laney handed over the bags with a grateful look.

But when Nat went to toss the first bag in the dumpster, the tie broke, and half a dozen empty paint cups tumbled out.

"Ah, man!" She dropped to her knees in the grass, gathering them as best she could into the bag, when she noticed someone else kneeling beside her, helping her hold the broken bag upright.

Finn.

Her hand brushed his ever so slightly as she shoved the cups deep in the bag, and she could feel her cheeks grow hot as she jerked back, grabbing a few more paper towels from the ground that she missed.

"Thanks," she murmured.

"Don't mention it." He met her eyes briefly before slinging the trash bag up and into the dumpster with the rest.

That's when she noticed a big glob of bright blue paint on his wrist.

"Oh, Finn, here." She grabbed the paint towel from where it was tucked into the waistband of her shorts and wiped at the paint, trying not to look at him as she did.

She took a step back when she was done. "So was your food truck as packed as our tent? We were slammed all day! Poor Laney's sure to need a few days off after this, and probably the rest of us, too."

She was babbling, she knew it, but she couldn't help it. If only he didn't make her feel so nervous, like he was judging her as some silly airhead. *That's not fair—he's never treated you that way.* Still, he was just so . . . so quiet while she yammered on, her voice filling the tension between them like she could knock it down with sheer willpower alone.

He just shrugged in response as they walked back to the square. "Super busy. Helen says we might have cleared thirty."

"Thousand?" Natalie stopped, her eyes widening. "That's a lot of money for one town festival."

"And that's just the silent auction alone."

"Wow." And just like that, her words ran out.

They walked in silence back to the stage, then she veered off toward her tent.

"See you." She gave a half wave.

He did the same, and then he was gone.

Thirty thousand dollars, Natalie marveled as she helped Laney tear down the rest of the folding tables and lug them to her SUV. That's what one of the silent auctions her church in Nashville would have pulled in, and they were a huge congregation. To think her tiny hometown of Dahlia, South Carolina, right smack in the center of nowheresville, could pull in that kind of cash with one dinky town festival . . .

Well, it wasn't exactly dinky, and they did put in a gob of hard work, she told herself. Not to mention, it was the first festival Dahlia'd hosted in eons.

Still, it boded well for Tikvah's fundraising potential—and the heartstrings it clearly tugged for the throng of people who came out today. Sheesh, even Daddy made it.

Natalie looked up to see Laney watching her, the girl's mouth twisted in a grin.

"You're a million miles away."

Natalie laughed as she realized she'd been staring into space instead of clicking the lock on her silver SUV.

"Oops," she said, the chirp of the car sounding as the door automatically lifted and they loaded the tables in.

She and Laney slowly walked back to grab the rest of their things, Lissa running ahead of them, bubbles from her bubble wand trailing behind her as she went. Her little-kid giggle was infectious, and Natalie sighed as she could feel her body relax after the long day.

"I'm just staggered, I guess," she told Laney. "We brought in a ton of money today. I used to do marketing in Nashville for, like, ten years before I moved back home. It just . . . I don't know, makes me think of the massive amount of potential this place is going to have."

"The house?" Laney asked.

"Yeah! I mean, I was hooked the second I saw the video at church. To think of all those women, all running from who knows what. Drugs, prison time, abusive marriages, all getting the chance for a reset, a do-over?" Natalie huffed out a breath, picturing the woman from the video. What was it she'd said, a new life? New hope? "And to think we can do that for people right here in Dahlia. What an opportunity."

She glanced over at Laney, who'd gone quiet. *She's got to be tired*, Nat told herself. Originally she'd planned to let Laney and Lissa head out after the auction closed, but the day ended up being far busier than any of them anticipated.

They gathered the few remaining items from under the tent, then loaded them into the SUV.

"Here." Natalie slipped extra cash into Laney's hands as they buckled into the car.

Laney tried to protest, but Nat insisted. "You worked your tail off. You, too, peanut." Nat looked over her shoulder toward Lissa, who clutched her SpongeBob backpack happily in the car seat. "Thanks for the help."

"Anytime." Laney murmured, then gazed out the window as they drove the few miles to her apartment complex.

Nat watched them walk inside the building from the parking lot, Lissa holding tight to her mom's hand as Laney shifted the car seat so it was up high, on her hip.

Two guys stood outside the building, and Natalie could see them give Laney a slow once-over as she and the girl hurried past. One of the guys jostled the other, and they laughed as Laney and

Lissa disappeared into the shadows of the building, eyes on them the whole time.

Natalie just shook her head and shifted the SUV into drive, cruising the long way back toward home.

A grant. The thought came unbidden, but when it did, she couldn't let it go. Surely Tikvah House would be a strong candidate for a sizeable grant—and not just from the churches. Stacey used to do fundraising for that animal shelter before she got that big job for Nashville Animal Advocacy. They were getting grants all the time from big family foundations and other corporate sponsors. Come to think of it, The Armstrong Group even did a matching gift that one Christmas. Surely a women's crisis center would be far more grant-worthy than an animal shelter, wouldn't it?

The wheels in her mind were spinning so fast she was almost to Nico's Gas and Go at the edge of town before she realized she'd driven clear past her house and almost to the site.

Only a few cars were at the pumps as she idled by, turning onto the dirt pull-off and easing her car into park in front of a lone mailbox. DeLuc, it read. Inside, she could see some dusty postcard in the bottom half of the mailbox, where the newspapers were supposed to go.

She turned off the vehicle and sat there, the car door cracked to let in the hint of breeze. Quiet in the warm afternoon light, she looked out over the fields of green grass. In the distance, the setting sun cast long rays of golden light. At one time, she knew, the place was bustling with farmworkers and crops of every kind imaginable—soybeans and cotton, maybe even tobacco, squashes and tomatoes and more. Now the land was lush and overgrown.

Not too far from the road, she could see the DeLuc farmhouse, a white clapboard style two-story structure with a big wraparound porch. She didn't know Old Man Wayne or his wife, Miz Cherry, but everyone knew of them, of course. The house was falling apart—they'd lived in the retirement place the last few years before their death, and the house had fallen into disrepair. But the decaying house painted a vivid picture in her mind.

She imagined them, collecting a basket of vegetables and giving them to young Finn and his mom, looking out for them when no one else even had a clue they should.

Now, their old house and property would live on with something even better . . . a legacy of helping women get a new start in life, a reboot after who knew what kind of madness they'd escaped from.

Nat didn't even realize she'd gotten out of the car until the woosh of a tractor-trailer driving by sent a wave of dust past her.

For an instant, she was there at the house, at least in her mind—there on the porch, talking to a woman. There, sitting in the living room giving a talk about basic finances. In the garden now, showing some ladies and their kids how to plant seeds and pat them down deep into the soil, just right.

Where's this coming from? She shook her head to clear the vision.

As she did, she could feel her phone vibrate in her back pocket.

"Should we hold dinner?" It was a text from Mom.

Quickly she jabbed out her reply—on the way—and slid back into the car, shifting the SUV into drive and pulling back out onto the road, doing a U-turn and heading back toward downtown Dahlia.

CHAPTER 26

Natalie

At Bible study Tuesday, Natalie pulled Helen Chastain aside and explained her idea.

"A grant? That's a terrific idea." The older woman trained steel-gray eyes on her.

Around them, the room was abuzz with activity. The study leader, Jane, was setting up the television set in front of the room, where the group would watch a video before diving into the chapter. In the corner, Natalie saw Laney chatting with Bev, her co-worker from Joe Mama's. Finn hadn't come since that first night, but Bev brought her twin, Lucille, who taught physical education at the elementary school with Natalie's mom. They were laughing about something, Nat didn't know what, but she was happy to see Laney's cheeks flushed and bright.

Nat dug into her purse and passed Helen the folder of printouts. "Not just a grant, though—corporate sponsors, too. Matching gifts. I found these last night thanks to Google. And that's just this part of the state, over toward the beach and down in Charleston. I'm betting Greenville has a bunch, too."

Helen scanned the papers, her eyes lighting up. "This is good stuff!" She peered at Natalie. "You did marketing in Nashville before you moved back home, didn't you? Any chance you might be up for a director role? At Tikvah."

Natalie held up both hands but grinned. "I appreciate it, but not for me. I've got the art shop, and besides. I wouldn't know the first thing about running a nonprofit."

Helen just looked at her, her eyes appraising and calm. Thoughtful. "Just think about it. Oh, and don't forget. Saturday?"

"I'll be there," Nat said. Pastor Dave had announced the groundbreaking for Tikvah House at church on Sunday.

Helen gave her arm a quick squeeze. "Good."

Jane clapped her hands to signal the start of Bible study, her green glasses bumping with the motion, and people started to take their seats. Natalie slipped into the chair Laney saved for her, an older Latino woman on her other side, and the class began.

As the DVD played, Natalie settled into her chair, smiling faintly at Helen Chastain's suggestion. Director of Tikvah House? It was a compliment, certainly. Helen was sharp, not the kind of person who said things lightly, and from her, Natalie knew it was high praise.

But it was also just about the farthest thing from her mind. Sunstrokes was her priority, not running a women's crisis center. Still, it felt good to be asked. Like landing a deal in Nashville . . .

For an instant, Tucker's warm smile flashed in her mind. "Our secret sauce," he'd called her at first, and then later, "my secret sauce." She remembered the thrill of it, that word "my," like it was some big honor to be his—his girlfriend, his fiancée, his everything.

Only she really wasn't. A bitter laugh bubbled in her chest, and she squeezed her eyes shut, tried to will her mind back to the video.

The speaker on the video was talking about pride, and she blinked a moment, watching him. The word hit hard, and she wondered about that—was it Tucker she missed, or the pride of belonging to Armstrong's golden boy, the way people in the office went from waving hi to looks of admiration, of awe.

Of course, none of it mattered in the end. Pride boiled down to squat.

When she'd gotten the call from the police that awful, awful night, it had been Stacey they were calling about—Stacey, not Tucker. Stacey had listed Nat as emergency contact on all her medical forms. After all, they'd been roommates since college. Stacey hadn't talked with her own family in who knew how long, not since her dad married the secretary in his firm and her mom was half a world away in Eastern Europe, someplace Nat couldn't pronounce, doing youth ministry.

She hadn't even known Tucker and Stace were together that night. To think she'd even called his phone half a dozen times on the way to the morgue about Stace . . . only to find Tucker's mom and dad there, too. While Stace had listed Nat on her emergency forms, Tucker had not.

There, standing in the morgue's far-too-bright hallway, it all came together in slow motion. It wasn't just Stacey she'd lost.

The betrayal hit harder than the loss. The words stung as they registered in her mind there in the darkened room, with only the glow of the TV screen casting shadows on her classmates' faces. Not only the betrayal of Tucker and Stacey, but having to find out about her own fiancé secondhand, felt like a slap. Still did.

Her phone buzzed in her purse, and she peered at the glowing words in the darkened room. It was a text from Ashley.

"Lunch tomorrow? I'll bring the sandwiches."

"Definitely," Natalie typed in quickly, then hit send before shoving the phone deep inside her purse and turning her attention back to the video.

The next day, Natalie gave Ashley an extra-long hug when she arrived.

"I love you, too!" Ashley giggled as she pulled away, her bright pink lips a pop of color in her otherwise pale face.

But Natalie hung onto her sister's hands a moment, peering at her.

Ashley gazed back. "I'm still me, you know."

Natalie sighed. "I know, I know. And the hair's amazing." She motioned to Ashley's new wig, which Mom helped her pick out a couple days ago in Charlotte. Just a shade warmer than her regular color, the wig was a longish layered cut that Ashley wore pulled back in a low ponytail, managing to look both pretty and a good five years younger at once.

"You're just afraid I'm going to break or something." Ashley made a face. "Matt's been giving me the same look."

"Well, we do love you, dummy."

"Yeah, yeah." Ashley stuck out her tongue, but her tone was sweet. She lugged the brown paper sack onto the counter. "Here—turkey and provolone on whole wheat. Extra mayo—kidding," she said to Natalie's expression. "I'll never forget how much you despise mayonnaise."

Natalie pulled the extra bar stool to the counter for Ashley and they both dug in.

"OJ?" She nodded toward Ashley's drink bottle.

Ash shrugged. "Yeah, I've got to lay off the diet soda, maybe for good. Bad for the bones, especially with the chemo. At least round two wasn't as bad as they'd warned."

"Let's hope it stays that way." Natalie squeezed Ashley's hand.

Ashley held up the pack of chips. "But these? I don't care what anyone says. These are the picture of health."

"Just don't tell me they're making you give up coffee."

"No, coffee's actually good for you now. Antioxidants and all that stuff."

Nat sniffed. "Wish they could come up with the same rationale for strawberry shortcake."

Ash giggled. "Speaking of coffee, how's your friend?" She waved vaguely toward the wall.

"My—friend?"

Ash smirked. "Mr. Good Looking over at the coffee shop. Finn."

Nat felt her cheeks get warm. "Oh, gosh, Ash. He's not *that* kind of friend."

"Mm-hm . . ."

"No, really. Besides, we aren't even that close anymore."

"Anymore." Ashley's tone was smug.

"I mean, not that we were close, or anything, it's just . . ." Natalie threw her hands in the air and let out a frustrated laugh. "I know what you're doing, Miss Busybody."

"Benefits of being a big sister." Ashley sat up a little straighter in her seat and tightened her ponytail. "I just heard you two were maybe just possibly out on a little innocent date one night."

"Hayley. I'm going to kill her. And it wasn't a *date* date. It was more like a shopping run."

"Mm-hm. Though it was a surprise hearing it from her first."

Natalie rolled her eyes. "The only reason she knew about it in the first place is 'cause we accidentally ran into her. She tell you that?"

Ashley held up her hands, an innocent expression on her face. "I got no details. Seriously, we were just chatting about stuff when I came to get the kids from Mom the other day. She asked if you and Finn were still seeing each other, and I had to play like I knew what she was talking about. Which I didn't." She leveled a gaze at her. "So how'd you end up running into her?"

Natalie sighed. "We were driving through that plaza to grab some ice cream and saw her standing outside some bar all dolled up like some twenty-five-year-old. Come to find out she was supposed to be sleeping over Zoe's."

"Some bar?" Ashley's eyes widened. "Hayley? Don't tell me she was . . . ?"

"Yep. Drunk. Swore up and down it was her first time and last too. Begged me not to tell Mom, so I didn't."

"Well you could've told me."

"And let you in on my shopping trip with Finn, too?'

Ash raised her orange juice bottle. "Point taken."

They were quiet a moment, finishing their sandwiches and drinks.

Finally, Natalie scrunched up her nose. "Truth is, Finn and I were . . . talking. But then I realized this was stupid. Way stupid. I mean, come on. It wasn't too long ago I was sending out save-the-date cards for my wedding this summer. I have zero business talking to some guy."

The back of her throat got all scratchy, surprising her.

Ashley grabbed her hand. "Sissy, your whole life got ransacked. There's nothing wrong with making a friend."

"But Ash—" Her voice cracked on her sister's name, and she couldn't finish.

"Hey, hey." Ashley scooted closer, wrapping her arm around Natalie's shoulders. "What happened to you was wrong. Horribly, awfully wrong. But there is nothing wrong with talking to the cute owner of the coffee shop who you just happened to go to high school with. Who just happens to be single. Not. A. Thing."

Natalie couldn't help but laugh.

"Thanks, Ash." She sniffled, wiping a stray tear from her eyes.

"So, you guys going out again soon?"

Natalie rolled her eyes. "Nope, I killed that. Shut it down hard and fast. Poor guy probably thinks I'm crazy now."

"I bet he doesn't."

Natalie snorted. "How much you willing to bet?"

That night, Mom and Daddy were already upstairs by the time she got home from the shop, tired but happy. It had been a good day, with a small but fun painting party to cap it all off. Jane and Helen from church were celebrating their friend Martha's seventy-fifth birthday, and the place was filled with the most hilarious, fun-loving older women Natalie had ever met. The birthday lady herself was all festive in head-to-toe electric blue, and her friends made her wear a tiara.

That's the kind of lady I want to be when I'm her age, Natalie thought, picturing her, Ash, and Hayley all older and silly together, like they'd been as kids.

She heated up leftovers in the microwave, then rinsed and put her plate in the dishwasher, setting it to run before locking all the doors and tiptoeing upstairs.

At the landing, she saw Hayley's light on beneath her bedroom door.

Before she could stop herself, she tapped softly.

"What." Hayley's gaze was decidedly unenthusiastic when Natalie poked her head in.

"Heard you're getting your cast off early." Nat forced herself to keep her tone bright. Moody teenagers.

Hayley shrugged. "Tuesday."

"At least you'll have one cast-free week of summer to play before senior year starts."

Hayley turned her attention back to her phone. "Yippee."

Natalie watched her a moment, noticing the icy blue fingernails had been replaced with a vivid royal purple.

She slipped fully inside the room, shutting the door behind her.

"Hay-Hay, are you okay? Talk to me."

Hayley barked out a short laugh. "I'm fine. Why do you suddenly care so much all of a sudden?"

A pang hit. "Hayley, I—always care."

Natalie perched on the bed, reaching out a hand toward her sister.

But Hayley wriggled up on her pillows, moving out of her reach.

"I'm just . . . mad. My friends, my whole life. Everything's just—"

"I know this summer has been rotten. But Zoe and Chelsey love you! And Ben! And track's starting up again next week, too, right?"

"I'm dropping track."

Natalie blinked. "What?"

"All this down time made me realize I don't really like it all that much."

"But your scholarship!"

Hayley waved a hand. "Whatever. Like USC's some life-changer or something?"

Natalie watched her sister. The girl's face was cold, hard. Hurting.

The pendant at Hayley's throat caught her eye. It was pretty—her initial, H, in rose gold with what looked to be tiny diamond-like sparkles where the edges curled.

"That's pretty."

"What?"

Natalie pointed. "Your necklace."

Hayley clutched it almost defensively. "Jasmine gave it to me."

Natalie raised a brow. "Jasmine's a generous friend. Manicures, a necklace?"

"That's what friends do. Real friends."

Right. Natalie sighed. "Look. I know it seems dumb and far away now, but college is coming before you know it. You don't want to blow your chances or drop something you're this invested in."

Hayley cocked her head at her. "Did I *ask* you for advice?"

"Excuse me?" Natalie sat up, stung.

"Thanks, but no thanks. I'm my own person. I've got this. I think you have better things to worry about—like why you're still living at home at almost thirty freaking years old, for starters."

Nat rose from the bed, not sure whether it was anger or unshed tears stinging the back of her throat. She opened her mouth to speak but shut it firmly before she could say something she'd regret.

Do not stoop. You are not seventeen, and the last thing you need is to get into a shouting match with your kid sister.

Hands clenched, Nat moved toward the door.

Hayley just watched her go, a smug look on her face.

CHAPTER 27

Laney

It was after nine-thirty when Laney finally got to Joe Mama's Wednesday morning. She'd asked Cha Cha to drop her at the elementary school after their stop at camp, and now she was breathless after the three-block walk to Joe Mama's. Not from the walk—from what happened. She was now the proud mama of a Dahlia Elementary Duckbill.

"Alissa's enrolled in kindergarten!" she gushed to Bev as she washed her hands and tied on her apron, stowing her little black backpack beneath the counter. Tucked inside, she had all she'd needed for that morning—the birth certificate, proof of residency, and now the little "welcome to school" handbook the five-foot-nothing registration lady gave her, along with the list of back-to-school events.

She wanted to pinch herself. *This is really happening!*

Bev raised a brow. "How in the world is she old enough for kindergarten already? Didn't you just potty train her last week?"

Laney swatted at her. "Oh, please."

Bev laughed and slid a few raspberry scones from the tray she was carrying into the display case.

The bell over the door tinkled, and Laney looked up to see Natalie breeze in, her hair pulled into a high ponytail that made her look like some fashion model instead of a real-life, ordinary person. She carried a blue-and-white striped satchel.

"Here!" Natalie passed over a stack of cheerful yellow flyers.

Groundbreaking for Tikvah House this Saturday at eleven, Laney read.

"Already?"

"Apparently the festival generated so much interest they pushed things up a month. Well, that and the sudden hole cleared in the contractor's schedule after that gas station thing fell through."

Bev rolled her eyes. "The last thing we need is another gas station in this town."

"Think Finn will mind setting these out for people?" Natalie glanced toward the back.

Laney shrugged. "I'm sure he won't. I'll ask him when I see him."

Natalie looked like she wanted to say more, but she just closed her mouth and stacked the flyers on the counter, then fished in her purse for her wallet.

"Can I get a caramel latte? Oh, and did you get Lissa all registered?"

Laney grinned. "Yep. We have a kindergartener!"

Ten minutes after she'd gone, Finn rounded the corner.

"You ladies all set?" He poured a cup of coffee for himself and surveyed the crowd, which had died down for now, even though all the tables still had customers.

"These are a hit." Bev pointed to the raspberry scones as she headed toward the back. "My third batch this morning."

Finn gave a mock salute. "Adding more mix to the list. Check."

Laney slid a yellow flyer from the top of the stack, passing it to her boss.

"Nat dropped these off."

She wasn't sure if it was her imagination or if he suddenly stood up straighter at the name, but Finn was now poring over the paper like it was some top-secret document commanding his full attention.

"She wants to know if it's okay to leave these out for people, help spread the word?" Laney added.

Finn just waved a hand. "Sure, of course."

Laney watched him. "So, are you going?"

"Going where?"

She snorted. "Um, the groundbreaking?"

"No."

Laney's brow creased. "But I thought—"

Finn put the flyer back on the stack and drained his coffee, moving once more toward the back.

"Saturdays are busy." His tone was gruff.

But you took the whole Saturday off a few weeks ago for the festival, she wanted to say, biting her tongue before the words could escape.

"Mind if I go?"

He shrugged. "Suit yourself."

When he'd gone, she gazed after him, wondering.

That afternoon, Cha Cha was in a rare mood.

"What's eating you?" Laney asked as they navigated Main Street, then turned left at the end toward their side of town.

Lissa was in the back coloring busily in her welcome-to-school coloring book, another little gift from the elementary school.

Cha Cha's face darkened, and she pulled into the gas station. "Nothing. Just need some smokes. Want anything?"

Laney shook her head.

Cha Cha was out the door and inside faster than Laney could

blink.

"So, are you excited to meet your new teacher?"

"Yes. I hope it's a girl."

Laney giggled. She'd never known a guy kindergarten teacher, though she was sure some existed.

"Why a girl?"

"Mans are scary. Girl ladies are the nice ones."

"Men," Laney gently corrected, then looked at her daughter. "Where'd you get that idea?"

Alissa shrugged, picking up a red crayon now. Laney watched her color the schoolhouse a vivid red, her small hands working fast and sure.

"Lissa, honey." Laney frowned. "Why do you think men are scary?"

Lissa glanced up, a matter-of-fact look on her face. "You don't like them."

"I mean, some are okay. Like—like Rev Bryant, from church. And Mr. Finn, from mommy's work. It's not that I don't like men, baby girl. Just . . ."

"I know, Mama. We have to be careful."

Lissa said the word slowly, so it almost sounded like cayer-fool.

Laney reached back and tucked a stray lock of hair from where it came loose from her daughter's pigtails, sliding it behind Lissa's ear.

Cha Cha was back now, slamming the door and jamming the car into gear.

"Jerks," Cha Cha muttered, frowning at the pickup truck pulling out just behind her. Two high school or college-age guys were in the cab, windows down and loud music blaring.

"You okay?" Laney eyed her.

"Those two bought the last packs of my brand. One more stop."

They headed to the convenience store past the apartments, and

Cha Cha ran inside once more. Lissa dozed in her car seat, and Laney people-watched. This gas station was a lot more rundown than the last, and there was a throng of guys at the end, chatting with two young women.

Laney peered closer, noticing one of the guys leaning against a bright red car. He was talking to a girl on crutches like he was some puffed-up rooster, and she was laughing at whatever he was saying, her way-too-short shorts an odd contrast with the cast.

Nat's sister, Laney realized, watching the girl flip her hair. She knew what she was doing, or at least thought she did. The other girl with her rested one hip provocatively against the car's hood.

They were way too young for these guys, Laney realized, and before she could think, she'd rolled down Cha Cha's car window and shouted over.

"Hayley. Hayley!"

She had to say it a few times before Nat's little sister looked her way.

"Do I know you?" The girl's tone was bored, distant.

"You need a ride?"

"Excuse me?"

Laney sighed. "I work for Natalie. At the art shop."

The guy talking to Hayley put an arm possessively around the girl's waist. Laney could see Hayley's shirt ride up a little, exposing her flat belly, and now she noticed big flashy earrings dangling from her ears. Glittery turquoise eyeliner was caked on the girl so bold it looked like she was dressing up for Halloween, or the stage, or both.

"She's got a ride," he said, before uttering a string of curse words Laney hadn't heard in what felt like eons.

Hayley jutted her chin and turned away, back toward her group of friends, but not before the guy smacked her rear possessively.

Cha Cha breezed out of the gas station, a carton in one hand

and a grin on her face.

"Now we're talkin'," she said, sliding into the driver's seat. "Let's roll."

Hayley's group didn't even glance their way as Cha Cha's tires peeled out of the parking lot and back toward Laney's apartment.

A shiver ran down Laney's spine as she watched them grow smaller and smaller in the distance behind them.

CHAPTER 28

Natalie

On Saturday at the groundbreaking, Natalie stood near Laney and Alissa, not too far from the front, where Rebecca from the newspaper was busy showing her granny, Helen Chastain, how to cut the ribbon when the time came.

A couple of other people Natalie knew—Pastor Dave, Mr. Perez from church, Rev Bryant and his wife, Marla, and Cheyenne Tillman—stood near the front. Helen was all dressed up in a floral skirt-suit and coordinating rose-colored heels. So far, there was no sign of Finn. Not that she should care.

There were a good number of people gathered, which made Natalie happy. Even her mom came, along with a few of her Bible study friends, even though she was slammed prepping for back to school.

"I wish we could build the new contemporary space, too, but this will be a good thing," Mom murmured grudgingly, and Natalie put an arm around her shoulders.

"Oh, you know you love meeting at Louree Kinley's," she teased.

Tiff was there, snapping pictures of the crowd with the big black Nikon slung around her neck, and Bobby Smathers gave Natalie a wave from across the way. She waved back.

"Isn't Finn coming?" Natalie whispered to Laney as Pastor Dave ushered Helen and the others toward the big red ribbon hung between two wooden posts hammered deep in the earth of what had once been Wayne DeLuc's farm.

She hadn't seen him since the festival, though truth be told, since her talk with Ashley last week, she'd be lying if she didn't admit she'd tried to run in to him at Joe Mama's a few times. Yet every time she'd popped in, he'd been scarce.

"No, he said he had to work all day." Laney shrugged.

A glimmer of disappointment shimmied through her. "Oh, of course."

Natalie pretended to focus on the pastor, who called everyone to bow their heads in prayer.

"Friends, thank y'all so much for coming today," Pastor Dave said after the prayer. "You know Tikvah House has been a passion of mine for months now, and none of this could have happened without the people standing beside me. Helen, Eduardo, Reverend Bryant?" he gestured.

Rev stepped forward. "We're thrilled to partner on Tikvah House, which is truly a community effort. You know how much money we've raised since the festival, and this week we just got a surprise matching gift from Wennerman Incorporated. They're matching dollar for dollar on every penny donated thus far."

Cheers went up, and Helen and Eduardo together lifted the oversized scissors.

"Today, we celebrate the official groundbreaking on Tikvah House," Helen Chastain cried.

They cut the ribbon as Tiff snapped picture after picture. Then, the four grabbed brand-new shovels placed nearby and, one by one, dug them into the dirt.

"Let the building begin!" Pastor Dave said with a laugh. "Now come. You're all invited back to our fellowship hall for cake."

"Cake!" Lissa squealed to her mom, and Laney shushed her, laughing.

She hopped on her tiptoes, clutching a little stuffed bunny rabbit, her sweet smile infectious and free.

Back at the church, Natalie pulled Helen aside. "That's outstanding about the matching gift."

"Well, your mention the other day about the grants got some wheels turning." Helen pointed to her head. "Did I tell you we're hoping to repurpose some of the original wood planks from their farmhouse in the new structure? I wish we could salvage the whole thing, but the structure isn't sound enough. But with the repurposing, there are a gob of historical grants out there, not to mention ones for women's and children's health and wellness."

"Sounds like maybe you need to be the director at Tikvah."

Helen shook her head. "Not me. Seriously, though. We're going to start advertising in the paper next month. If you're interested or know of anyone who might be, don't hesitate."

Natalie surprised herself by giving Helen a quick hug. The older lady laughed and squeezed back.

"It's good to have you home, dear. Now, how's your sister feeling?"

That night, Natalie pulled out her sketch pad for the first time in weeks. Flipping through, she gazed at her work. Stacey filled most of the pages, her dark hair and dark, dark eyes staring out at her like a ghost. But there were others in there, too. Ashley, and a few of Laney, and even one of Finn, though anybody paging through probably wouldn't recognize him. It was just the back of his head from that one day, when they'd had lunch at the Wahca

River. A soft beam of sunlight tousled his warm brown hair and, just barely, the hair on his forearm, which he'd rested on his Levi's as he watched the peaceful water flow.

Quickly, she flipped to a blank page and grabbed her charcoal pencil. She started with the eyes first, then the bridge of the nose. She was drawing Laney's daughter this time, unable to forget the girl's bright eyes and enthusiasm from this morning.

As she sketched, though, the lines grew darker, bolder, and soon she realized she wasn't drawing Lissa anymore but rather Hayley. Hayley, when she was Lissa's age, down to the tiny smattering of freckles on her cheeks and nose.

Hayley didn't have freckles anymore, or if she did, she covered them up with makeup. Still, it felt like just yesterday when she was coming home from college or those first few years at Armstrong, only to be greeted by a young Hayley, barreling into her like a cat on a chase, begging to sleep in her room for "girl time" or to tag along with her and Ashley shopping or whatever else they were doing.

"I'm old enough!" she'd insist in her little-kid voice.

Now she was, certainly, only she wasn't asking for sleepovers or shopping trips these days. No, these days Hayley didn't seem to want anything to do with her. Or with Ash, for that matter.

At least she'd helped Mom clean up after dinner earlier. Ashley'd looked extra-tired when she and Matt and the twins came over.

"It's to be expected," Ash had said. Some days were good, and some wore her out.

They'd caught the cancer early, and it hadn't spread. Prognosis was "excellent," the oncologist had told them.

"Lunch next week?" Natalie whispered when they were leaving.

"Hope so."

"I'll come to you."

"Well, in that case . . ." Ashley tried to smile.

Still, she couldn't shake the dread within her. *If anything happens to Ashley . . .*

A knock sounded just then on her bedroom door, and Natalie looked up from her sketch pad.

It was Mom. "Honey, I forgot. This came for you today."

Mom held out a small cream-colored envelope. As she handed it over, she glanced at the pad.

"That's Hayley," she observed.

Nat looked up. "Yeah. Gosh, she's grown up so fast."

Mom wrinkled her nose. "You're telling me."

"Were we all this . . . challenging?"

Mom smiled softly. "You especially."

"Gee, thanks."

When the door was closed, Natalie glanced at the envelope, then the return address. "Armstrong," it read, with a Nashville address.

Her heart did a slow flipflop before thudding.

Tucker's family.

Quickly, she opened the envelope to find a note from Tucker's mom.

> *Dearest Natalie,*
>
> *First, please know I've tried to write you so many, many times. I guess I didn't have the nerve before now. I just want you to know I'm so very sorry for what happened. From the bottom of my heart, I had no idea about anything with your friend, and neither did Tuck Sr. But I know Tucker loved you. And so did we. I'm not sure what was going on with him the night of the crash, and he'd been acting so oddly in the weeks leading up to his death. But I never dreamed anything like this. I want you to know we sincerely wish the very best for you. If there is ever anything at all we can do to help you, whether as a reference or personally, please do not hesitate to ask. You are a*

beautiful person inside and out. I only hope and pray you get the future happiness I know you deserve.

All kindness,

Catherine Armstrong

There was a lump in her throat by the time she'd finished reading, and for a moment she closed her eyes, expecting the tears to come like a waterfall.

When they didn't, Natalie opened her eyes, surprised at the peace settling over her.

She gazed back at the note, written in perfect penmanship on high-quality stationary, Catherine Armstrong's monogram embossed in gold on expensive-looking linen, a swoopy C and L flanking a large ornate A at the center. At the bottom, she saw Catherine had printed her phone number, too. Not that Natalie would ever actually call her. But knowing she'd reached out like this . . .

Somewhere deep inside, a crack she didn't know was there began to soften—to heal.

Natalie placed the notecard atop the sketchpad and stepped to her closet, reaching for the top shelf, and the box all the way in the back.

Inside the box, she shuffled all the way to the bottom and the manila envelope. Ready for "one day," whenever that would be.

Pictures of Tucker, of her and Tucker, even a few of her and Tucker and Stacey, along with whichever boyfriend Stacey had had at the time.

Pictures she hadn't been ready to look at . . .

Until now.

She sat on the floor, her back jammed up against the soft bed. Tears came as she pored through the photographs one by one—though not the devastated tears she'd cried in the early days. These were more like . . . sentimental tears, she realized. Tears of regret, but not anguish. Tears of memories, of days gone by.

Days she'd never have again.

One picture in particular—her and Stacey, both in jeans and fall sweaters standing at the top of some mountain peak—caught her eye. She remembered that day, almost felt it in her bones, like it was seared on her soul for eternity.

"I love you like a real sister," Stacey had told her that day. "Never forget that."

I forgive you. Natalie said it in her head at first, then she whispered it into the box. *I forgive you both. It hurt, and I might hurt forever. But I forgive you both.*

A wave of exhaustion suddenly crept over her, and she glanced at the clock. After eleven already?

She started to pile all the pictures back in the box, but at the last moment snagged the one of her and Stacey on the mountaintop. She set the box on top of the closet shelf once more, then turned to place the photo of her and Stacey front and center on her dresser.

She placed the notecard from Catherine next to it, a gentle smile playing at her lips.

That night, for the first time in ages, she dreamed of Stacey again. But this time it was a peaceful dream . . . a dream of joy, and laughter.

The old days, come to visit once more.

CHAPTER 29

Natalie

On Thursday, Natalie could almost feel the excitement pouring off Laney when she opened the door to Sunstrokes for her afternoon shift.

"I take it the first day of kindergarten went well?" Natalie asked, smiling.

Laney grinned. "She absolutely loved it! Literally fell asleep in bed talking my ear off about Mrs. Prince and the 'princelings,' which apparently is what all the kids call themselves. She even has a new best friend."

"I'm impressed."

"Same!" Laney laughed.

Natalie couldn't help but smile. She hadn't seen Laney this happy or relaxed since, well. Since ever.

"She wore her princess shirt today, of course."

"Like any good princeling should."

They laughed, and Natalie motioned Laney over. "We don't have anything major planned this afternoon, so I thought we might try out some of these new stencils till you go get Lissa from school. Make sure they'll work for open paint this weekend."

"Ooh, fun." Laney danced over.

Between customers, they both managed to finish their designs. Laney'd done a gorgeous fall-colored owl, its wings resplendent with shimmers of bronze. Natalie's was a vibrant sunflower, the center like a mosaic.

By late afternoon, Alissa was settled in the back with a snack doing her numbers sheet for school at one of the craft tables when Natalie's cell phone rang.

Mom.

"Of course I can pick up dinner on the way home. But you know I'm happy to cook, too." Natalie winked at Laney as she talked into the phone.

"Well, we never really did our back-to-school dinner. Tuesday was so crazy with getting Hayley's cast off and prep for the first day, and last night I was so beat I just couldn't. I ordered a big sheet of lasagna and a salad from the Italian place if you can just swing by."

"Absolutely."

"Hayley might be late, she's got some study thing, but everyone should be home by seven I'd think."

A study thing, already? They hung up, and Nat sighed.

"You know, I love that about your family," Laney said almost wistfully, looking over. "All the togetherness stuff you do, the big dinners and stuff. I want that for me and Alissa, one day. I want her to have what I didn't have."

"Didn't you do that growing up?"

Laney made a face. "I wish. But I aim to make things different for my girl."

The way she said it, all mama-bear-proud like that, made Natalie smile.

"You're good at this, Laney."

Laney blushed.

"You are. So get this—Hayley's got her cast off for exactly one day, and she's already going to be late for dinner."

Laney gave her a funny look. "Friends?"

"Some study thing."

Laney opened her mouth like she was debating whether to say something, then closed it. Finally, she blurted, "Did I tell you I saw her last week?"

Natalie shook her head. "No. Where?"

"At some gas station with some girl in a red flashy car and a mess of guys. Older guys."

Natalie frowned. "Jasmine?"

Laney shrugged. "I don't know her name, but the guys looked really . . . advanced, I guess you could say. You might want to keep tabs on her."

Natalie sighed. "I've tried, but she's having none of it. And frankly, the moods are killing me."

"I hear you there. She wasn't exactly Miss Congeniality. And, well . . ."

Laney bit her lower lip, like she was considering.

"You can tell me."

Laney sighed. "She was wearing a ton of makeup and super short shorts. And the other girl looked like she belonged in some lingerie catalogue."

"Yikes. I'll figure out a way to talk to her."

"That stuff can get. Well, bad. Really fast." Laney's cheeks pinked, and her brow creased at the center. "Trust me."

"Thanks."

That night, Hayley was already home when Natalie arrived with the bags of takeout, but any chance for small talk went out the window the second Mom arrived, and she disappeared to her bedroom to finish studying right after dinner.

"Too bad Ashley and Matt couldn't come," Daddy said, pushing back from the table and patting his belly.

"Well, the twins are a handful themselves this week with back-to-school and early bedtime." Mom stood to clear her plate. "Thank goodness she's on break for chemo another week."

"How are we going to handle that, with you back in school?" Nat joined her mom in the kitchen, carrying her own plate and the salad bowl. "I was thinking I could pitch in for driving next week. It's slowed down a lot at the shop now that school's back in session. Now my busiest times are evenings and weekends. It'd be easy for me to slip away, especially if Laney can cover here and there."

"I know Matt's doing the first session, but yeah, if you can, that would be great. Anne Marie and Louree offered to help, but you know Ashley'd rather have her own family."

"I can help on Thursday." Daddy's voice from the doorway surprised them both.

"You . . . can?" Mom blinked. "Well, sweetheart, that would be great."

Dad shrugged almost gruffly, setting his dinner plate in the sink. "I mean, I'm not chained to the office. I can drive my own daughter to the doctor when I'm needed."

Mom wrapped him in a hug.

"That would be wonderful, honey."

Natalie looked from one to the other. Daddy—carrying his own plate and offering to drive Ashley? Mom, actually hugging Daddy, calling him "sweetheart" and "honey"? They were the least physically affectionate people she knew, always had been.

"I guess I'm just realizing how much help she needs right now."

They were quiet a moment, the words almost tangible in the air around them.

"You're right, Daddy," Natalie said finally. "She does need help. And who better than us to pitch in when she needs it?"

"Exactly." His voice was stern but somehow tender.

And when she headed up to her room after dinner dishes were done and Mom was stationed at the table grading a stack of quizzes, Natalie surprised herself once more.

She leaned down and kissed the top of Daddy's head, then bounded up the stairs.

But that night Natalie's sleep, when it finally came, was fitful, filled with nightmares. Ashley in the ocean, drowning. Ashley, trapped in a burning house.

And finally, the last once, Stacey in the morgue—only this time when they pulled back the sheet, it wasn't Stacey but Ashley there in her place.

Dead and cold, gone forever.

No. Nat was drenched in sweat when she shook herself out of the dream. The clock read 2:05 a.m.

It's just a dream. She repeated it in her head over and over until she was convinced it was true, then glanced at her phone, just to make sure there were no late-night texts from Ashley, somehow calling for help. Her phone was silent—no missed texts or calls. All was well.

Still, she couldn't shake the dread seeping through her.

Dreams were the subconscious seeping through. She knew this, knew it even before the therapist she'd seen after the accident reminded her. Ashley was okay, the treatment was going well, and the dream wasn't some awful premonition. All it meant was that Natalie was worried about her sister in a big way—and probably tucked it down so deep inside it had no choice but to come out in a dream. Still, she couldn't escape the unsettled feelings the dream unearthed. Maybe a cup of chamomile would help.

Just a dream, just a dream. It echoed in her head as she tiptoed out of bed and down the hall, all the way down the stairs to the kitchen.

And there she came face to face with Hayley—one hand on the kitchen door.

CHAPTER 30

Natalie

Natalie gaped at her younger sister, taking it all in. Hayley—in a super short, super tight aqua minidress. So much makeup and black eyeliner she looked like a clown. Strappy high-heeled sandals.

And, behind her in the distance, the low hum of a car's motor, lights off in the driveway.

Waiting.

"You're—sneaking out?" The words rolled out of Natalie's mouth as if they had a mind of their own.

"I—"

Hayley looked stunned. Quickly, her pointy purple nails slid from the handle.

They stared at each other there in the kitchen, with only the soft glow from the stove's range hood and the dim porchlight allowing their eyes to lock.

"I—wasn't."

Natalie barked out a humorless laugh. "Explain."

"A . . . friend just came by to say hi." The words tumbled from Hayley's lips like they were rehearsed. "I couldn't sleep and was messing around with clothes and makeup. Homecoming outfits and all. I wasn't sneaking out."

Natalie crossed her arms. "That's no Homecoming dress and you know it."

"Nat." Hayley's eyes were pleading, and they darted toward the door. "I wasn't. Let me just tell her to go."

As if on cue, someone revved the engine motor.

Fury built inside Natalie like a tidal wave. Before she could think, she ripped open the door and marched out in her pajamas until she was right in front of the car. It was a red car, that much she could see, and whoever was inside must think she's a maniac.

"Go." Natalie pointed toward the road.

The driver complied, backing up and peeling out, gone before Natalie could catch her breath.

Hayley's face was a mask of anger when Natalie got back inside.

"You had no right. That is *my* business." Hayley's hands were clenched but her voice was low.

Natalie's voice hissed low to match. "Well, you know what? You're *my* sister, and somebody's got to look out for you. Mom and Daddy have enough going on with Ashley than to worry about one of their supposedly well raised daughters sneaking out like some—some—"

"Some what? I'm not a baby anymore!" Hayley was seething now. "You don't know anything!"

"I do know this is at least the second time I've seen you prancing around in an outfit like this. Third, if you count what I'm told you were wearing at the gas station the other day. What's going on with you, Hayley? Are you trying to get yourself murdered? I mean, you read the headlines."

Hayley shook her head, as if thoughts were whirring around inside her brain like a helicopter gone haywire.

"Just you wait till Mom learns about this," Natalie said.

She watched as her sister slipped off one high heel, then the next.

Then, with what seemed like every ounce of wrath churning inside her, Hayley cocked her head and narrowed her eyes, looking straight at her sister. Her eyes were so cold they didn't even look blue anymore.

"You breathe one word of this to Mom and we are done. You hear me?"

And with that, Hayley turned on her heel and dashed upstairs to her room, shutting the door and twisting the lock behind her.

CHAPTER 31

Natalie

All night Natalie tossed and turned, wondering what to do. Tell Mom? Mom and Daddy? *This isn't just teenage drama anymore.* Hayley was on a bad path—she'd be blind to miss that.

Just before dawn, her brain finally settled down enough for an hour or so of restless sleep. By the time her alarm went off and she made it downstairs, hoping to catch Mom before she headed off to the elementary school, she'd just missed her.

"Great." The word tumbled from her lips as she watched Mom's brake lights gleam in the early morning sun before turning right onto Spruce Street, heading toward Main.

She could call her. *But what good will it do now?* She'd catch her after school, sit her down for a talk. Better yet, she'd call and schedule a chat, see if Mom would meet her at Ashley's.

Ashley's. Natalie grimaced. She wished she could call her, but Ashley had to rest before her third round of chemo this week. This was the last thing Ashley needed to worry about on top of everything else.

She remembered her dream—Ashley in the morgue—and shuddered.

No, she'd see if Mom could come over to the shop. They could chat there. Then maybe they could go together back to the house, sit down with Hayley. See what was really going on. At least they could set some ground rules.

She realized her hands were shaking and decided to go back in, make herself a real breakfast instead of the breakfast bars she'd been grabbing lately. She made enough bacon and eggs for Daddy, too.

Then, bringing her coffee mug with her, she headed upstairs to shower and dress for the day.

A few minutes before ten, she popped into Joe Mama's, hoping Laney could close up at Sunstrokes this evening.

Only, instead of Laney behind the counter, she was surprised to see Finn.

A warm jolt of something—nerves?—sent a shimmer through her insides.

"Hey." He cocked his head at her, somehow friendlier than he'd been the last few weeks, though maybe it was her imagination. Or maybe he was just over it all by now. *Just as well.*

She felt her brow pinch as the words tumbled out. "Is Laney around this morning?"

He shook his head. "No, I sent her and Bev for supplies. She'll be back around four or five, sometime before the aftercare ends at school."

"Ah." Natalie bit her lip, thinking. *Maybe Mom can just come here and I'll fill her in, let her do whatever she thinks is best. It's not like she needs my help parenting, for goodness sake.*

"Sorry. Everything okay?"

She was turning toward the door, but something in his soft brown eyes had her suddenly telling him about Hayley and the fight and everything else bottled up inside until she realized he was just staring at her, a frown creasing his eyebrows.

"I've told you way more than you want to hear." She wanted to smack herself, settling instead for a sheepish grin.

"Uh, no—I. I'm glad you did. That sounds . . . rough."

She made a little pffft sound, shaking her head slightly. "Yeah. It is. But I know you're busy. I guess I was looking to see if Laney wanted to work tonight so I could go home, try to talk with Mom a bit, maybe even sit down with Hayley together. But I'm micromanaging, I'm sure. Mom can handle this without me."

She glanced around, grateful no one was in earshot. The last thing she needed to do was spill their family drama in the middle of the town coffee shop. Besides, it probably wasn't anywhere near as dire as she was making this all out to be. What had Mom said just a couple weeks ago about raising teens? Nat herself had been a handful at seventeen, too.

Only she didn't remember ever sneaking out of the house dressed like, well. That.

Finn was looking at her like he wanted to say more. Finally, his eyes went all soft again.

"How's Ashley?"

"Doing okay. She has a scan in another few weeks, and hopefully everything's gone. She's pretty tired, though."

"I bet."

They were quiet a long moment, him behind the counter, fiddling with the dishrag like it was a belt or a knot. Her, fidgeting with the handle on her tote bag like it was a combination lock with the key to all the answers in the universe.

Her throat went dry, and finally she cleared it, smiling up at him.

"Well, gotta go open the shop for the day. See you." At the door, she paused. "Thanks for asking."

"Anytime." His gaze was long, and his eyes didn't leave hers. "And Nat. Pop over again, okay?"

She nodded, willing her cheeks not to flush. "Okay."

Once inside Sunstrokes, her heart felt like it was hammering ninety miles an hour. *Get it together, Motts.*

She stowed her tote in the back and busied herself wiping down the tables, flipping the sign from closed to open, adding water to the two jumbo ferns beside the door. The ferns Ashley had given her just a few months ago, her good-luck gift for opening the shop in the first place.

How far we've come since then, Nat thought, her eyes scanning the sunny, airy room. Tables on the side and in the back, ready for students, and nearby, half a dozen easels all set up with blank canvasses. Wide-beam shelves held acrylic and watercolor paints, and in the back and all along the walls was artwork of every kind imaginable—her own and Laney's, a few from Ashley, and a whole array of sample pieces for the Open Paint classes, from owls and cheerful daffodils to beach scenes and flipflops.

And there, on the back right, a few with scripture messages. One in particular caught her eye now.

"Don't worry about anything; instead, pray about everything. Tell God what you need, and thank him for all he has done," she read, with the verse, Philippians 4:6 (NLT), scrawled below.

It was the one Laney'd done at that first Open Paint, and the words "Instead, Pray" were big and bold and cheerful red, lines swooping like graceful birds until they looped around with curly ends at the top and bottom of the canvas. The rest of the text was a buttery bronze, with sparkles for accents.

"That's one of my favorites," she remembered Laney telling her that night, her face flush with color. "Helps me keep my priorities in check. I mean, what can I do on my own, just me? But the God of the universe. Now, that's a different story!"

At the time, Nat had marveled at the peace that seemed to wash over Laney's face like a glowing beam of light.

Now, she closed her eyes a moment, taking a deep, steadying

breath.

"God, help give me the words to tell Mom what's going on. And help me love Hayley well in the middle of all this. Amen."

Outside, through the wall-to-ceiling glass windows lining the front, she could see a white minivan pull into the parking lot, and what looked like a mom slide out.

Quickly, before she could forget, Natalie slid her cell phone from her pocket and typed a text to her mom.

"Can you pop over to the shop after work? Need to talk about Hayley stuff."

Mom's reply—"sure"—came right away.

The day passed in a blur, and Nat stayed busy most of the afternoon with a preschool field trip.

Around four, Mom still hadn't shown up.

"Sorry, one of the bus drivers quit, and I'm staying late," Mom told her breathlessly over the phone. "Let's talk at home."

When they finally talked, standing at the kitchen counter chopping tomatoes and onions for homemade spaghetti sauce, Mom listened fully.

"I'm just . . . worried. Something's up, and I'm pretty sure she's getting in over her head." Natalie scrunched up her nose, glancing over at Mom to gauge her reaction. "I'm hoping we can do a sit-down. She's on the wrong track, I just know it."

Mom grimaced. "Well, she's staying at Zoe's for the next few days."

"Zoe's? I thought . . .?" Nat blinked.

Mom shrugged. "I guess they patched things up. Apparently, they're doing some lake thing Saturday morning, and Hayley's going to school with them tomorrow and then driving straight from pickup to that cabin their family has over on Lake Wateree. She'll be back Sunday."

"Well, I guess that's way better than how I thought this weekend was going to go."

Mom put a soft hand over Natalie's. "Thank you for telling me. My head's been all upside down between Ashley and back-to-school and, well, everything else. Did I tell you Aunt Doreen and Uncle Allen are coming for Thanksgiving, now, too? Got to whip this house into shape between now and then, and you know me."

Nat smiled and surprised herself by hugging her mom hard. "I do know you, Mom. And I love you. Thanks for listening."

"Anytime, my Natty Girl. I'm glad you're back home."

The childhood nickname made her grin.

"Me, too, Mom. Me, too."

The next afternoon, she and Laney were knee deep in preparations for that night's Open Paint. Lissa was in the back, helping set out cups of water at every place, and Laney was at the shelves pouring streams of vibrant red, crystal blue, and sunshiny yellow into mini palettes.

Natalie's phone buzzed, telling her she had a text, but she ignored it, instead speaking into the shop phone.

"Three more? Absolutely we can fit you and your daughters in. Thanks, Mrs. Patella," Natalie said into the receiver, writing three more names onto tonight's reservation list.

She was in the back, pulling out a few more canvasses for the tables, when the cell phone's texts turned into a ring.

"What's up?" she asked breathlessly, noticing Mom's name on the screen.

"Nat, I just ran into Shana at Smathers' Grocery." Mom's voice was high-pitched, and she sounded like she'd just run a 5K.

Shana. "Zoe's mom?"

"Yes! Hayley's not with them this weekend. They're not even

going to the lake!"

Natalie paused, the weight of Mom's words sinking in. "If Hayley's not with Zoe . . ."

Mom's voice bordered on tears. "Then where in God's name *is* she?"

CHAPTER 32

Laney

LANEY WATCHED HER BOSS CLUTCH the phone, her face suddenly pale. It didn't take a rocket scientist to figure out what was happening, and she could tell from just the few times she'd met Hayley the girl was dancing with trouble.

"Go home, Mom, and call every one of her friends," she heard Natalie say into the phone. There was a tremor in her voice, but her eyes were intense, and her grip on the phone tight. "I'll meet you there in twenty."

Natalie hung up, gaping across the room at Laney.

"My sister. Hayley . . ."

Laney was instantly at her side. "Go. Be with your mom. I've got this."

Natalie's eyes were round, but she nodded. "You—sure?"

Laney lifted her chin. "Absolutely."

She watched Natalie collect her purse and head for the door. A moment later, her SUV was barreling out of the parking lot, tires squealing.

"Come on, kid. Don't do this," Laney muttered to herself, then felt a little hand tugging at her shirt.

"Mama?" Alissa stared up at her, little eyebrows all quirked with worry.

"Miss Natalie had to go home, sweet girl. Family emergency."

"At the hospital? Like Miss J?" Lissa's face scrunched.

Laney smoothed the hair from Lissa's face, tucking the wispy locks behind her ears.

"No, no, nothing like that. Just something Miss Natalie has to help her own mama with. Do you want to be my helper tonight still?"

Lissa's smile reminded her of fireworks. "Yes!"

"Okay, then help me put these canvasses out. Just be careful," she warned, snagging the pile of canvasses from where Nat had set them down on the front counter and passing one to Lissa to carry.

"I'll be cayer-fool, Mama," Lissa said, overenunciating the word so much Laney couldn't help but smile.

Two hours later, the paint party was just starting to wind down. The place looked like a colorful disaster, but from the smiles and laughter, Laney could tell everyone had a good time. She was too worried to celebrate, though. Natalie hadn't texted her back.

Maybe it means they tracked the kid down and are too busy giving her a what-for to reply. Laney frowned, collecting the discarded palettes and slipping them into the sink one by one, watching as Lissa went from person to person, each one placing their paintbrushes into the big plastic cup half-filled with water.

"You can feel free to leave them here to dry and pick them up tomorrow or next week," Laney told them. "Just make sure you sign your name on the bottom."

"Like a real artist," said one of the ladies, a redhead with spiky short hair and chin length dangly earrings, elbowing her friend.

"You bet."

It felt like another hour passed as everyone oohed and ahhed over each other's work and Laney was finally able to close the door and lock it up tight after the last customer had left.

Lissa had paint on her forehead and a dot of hot pink on the tip of her freckled nose, but she looked ready for action.

"Can we go to McDonald's for the slide? And sundaes?"

Momentary panic slid over her as she realized—not only was she closing up alone, but they didn't have a ride home.

Laney chewed on her lip, thinking. Cha Cha was long gone, and the coffee shop had closed over an hour ago. It was still light out, so they could hoof it if they had to, but they'd have to pass the laundromat, and the guys hanging outside, and . . .

First things first, she reminded herself, borrowing a line from Miss J. *Don't go worrying about tomorrow when you're still dealing with today's mess.*

"Come on, help me finish cleaning up," she told Lissa, and the two of them got the canvasses on the drying racks, the tops on all the paint bottles, and the brushes and palettes all washed and rinsed and set out for tomorrow.

Lissa collected all the water cups, pouring them down the now-empty sink and popping them in the trash can, and Laney sprayed the tables with cleaner, wiping up so everything looked fresh and brand-new.

"There." Laney gave the room a satisfied once-over.

Worry—this time about Nat—pricked her mind. She picked up the shop phone and dialed her boss's number.

"Did you find her?" she asked when Natalie answered.

"No. And for the life of me, I can't figure out where she could be." Natalie's voice sounded extra-young. She's scared, Laney realized.

And she should be. The thought, unbidden, catapulted though Laney's body, but she pushed it back before it could ramp up her anxieties even higher. *You don't need to go reading into everyone else's situation like it's a repeat of your own, Laney Ricks.*

Only, she'd seen what happened to girls like Hayley—over and over again.

A flash of Carla, left outside the hospital all those years ago, seared through her mind like a hot boil. Dead, far too young. Dead, like so many of them. Unwanted trash, Ethan called them once. Discards. Runaways.

But for all they knew, they had sisters like Natalie, families who cared, who wondered, who worried . . .

"I want to help." The words barreled out. "Nat, please. Let me help."

"That's sweet, Laney, but . . . oh. Oh! Oh, my gosh, you're stuck at the shop. I completely blanked!"

"I can call a cab, or walk—"

"No, no. I'm on my way."

The line went dead, and Laney stared at it, huffing out a breath.

Nat was there in less than five minutes. "I'm so sorry, Laney—"

"Nat, I mean it. I want to help you."

"How?"

Laney glanced at her over Lissa's head as she buckled the little girl into the back seat.

"Have you looked through her bedroom? Thoroughly?"

"I mean, enough to figure out she packed for a weekend away."

Laney's lips tightened. "Do you . . . mind if we go back to your house? I might have some ideas."

Natalie blinked but nodded. "Sure. I guess we can use all the help we can get."

Natalie's house was even bigger than Laney had pictured. Two whole stories, all painted a crisp white with cheerful blue shutters, with an actual white picket fence outside and a garden brimming with flowers.

Inside, the foyer had one of those rugs where people left shoes by the door so you didn't mess up the fancy hardwood floors, and the staircase looked like something Scarlet O'Hara might have sidled down. Pictures of Natalie and her sisters were everywhere, all decked out in pretty dresses, their straight white teeth and waved hair screaming "perfect family."

"Laney, these are my parents. Mom, Daddy, this is Laney and her daughter, Lissa, from my shop."

"Nat, honey, now's not the time for—" Mom began, panicked eyes catching her husband's in the recliner next to her.

But Natalie held up a hand. "Can Lissa sit with you a few minutes?"

Before she could answer, Natalie was pulling Laney up the long staircase and into a purple-and-white girl's bedroom, the door slamming shut behind them.

CHAPTER 33

Laney

Inside, Natalie paced the room. "I just have no clue where she'd be. Ashley hasn't seen her, and Mom got nothing from either of her best friends. She's been hanging out with some girl, Jasmine, but I don't know anything about her other than she drives some fast red car. Not even her last name."

Laney frowned. Sometimes, it was the guys who brought in the new girls, got them all trusting and broken in. But other times, it was the girls themselves. Girls like her, befriending a lone wolf and bringing her into the fold. At first, they came for the drugs, or the community. By the end, they were so hooked they couldn't leave. Even if they wanted to.

Natalie picked up a ratty brown teddy bear someone had haphazardly dumped on the bed. She clutched it to her chest, her eyes a million miles away.

"Does she have a diary?"

Nat's eyes focused, and she nodded, dropping to her knees and fishing under the bed. She pulled out a box with a notebook.

But the last entry was the beginning of June—months ago.

"I told you. She's just . . . stopped. Everything she used to care about."

"Has she been using?" Laney asked it quietly.

Natalie sighed. "How would I know? I don't even know what signs to look for."

"What about boys? New guys suddenly hanging around? Or do you know where Jasmine lives, maybe?"

"I thought she'd been dating Ben Smathers off and on for ages, but Mom just found out they broke up pretty recently. I saw her out once with a much older guy. If there's a new boyfriend, I don't know him."

Laney looked around the room, taking it all in—purple ruffles and concert posters, fake vines behind the bed, stuffed animals and dolls all piled in one of those fancy baskets that must have cost a fortune. A big white vanity with Hollywood-style makeup lights around the mirror, the surface littered with makeup compacts, lip gloss tubes, and blush brushes.

Natalie slid open dresser drawers, then the nightstand, and gasped.

"Her phone!"

Laney glanced over to see a cell phone in Natalie's hand. "You're sure it's hers?"

Natalie punched some keys, then groaned.

"Yeah, but it's locked. None of her old passcodes work. Or, at least none of the ones she usually uses."

Laney drifted to the vanity, sliding open drawers. Looking for what, she didn't know, but looking nonetheless.

There was a jewelry stand to the left, near the closet, and Laney went to it, popping open the side door to find a strand of pearls and a dainty, colorful pink seashell necklace, one with half a gold heart that read "BE" and "FRI"—presumably, someone else had the other half spelling "best friend."

The bottom drawer contained a few notes, mostly love notes

from Ben, and a couple mementos from some sporty thing Hayley'd done.

Then . . . jackpot!

Laney lifted the top, and her heart went from a steady thrum to a jackhammer.

It can't be.

But what else could it mean?

Laney pulled a thin sapphire-blue triple-corded bracelet from the jewelry box, dangled it in the lamplight.

Her mouth went dry, picturing the one she'd worn on her ankle for years.

The same one Carla had worn. And Shaylene, in her skintight low-rise jeans. And Drexa, and Ximena, and Amber. And Candy, and Fantasia, and Jade.

"Oh, dear Jesus."

She sank to the floor, her legs collapsing beneath her as she stared up at Natalie.

Ghosts, there with her once more. Ghosts of the past, back to haunt her.

Laney stared at the bracelet. "I think I know what's going on with Hayley."

CHAPTER 34

Natalie

"A . . . DRUG RING? Trafficking?" Natalie's eyes were wide as she took in what Laney told her. *This—this can't be.* "Are you sure?"

Laney visibly swallowed, her eyes looking at least two shades darker than normal, and she clutched the bracelet like, if she held it tight enough, it'd provide answers.

Two bright spots of color flushed Laney's cheeks. "I think we need to call the police, bring them in."

Natalie nodded quickly. "I think you're right."

They headed downstairs, explaining the situation as quickly as they could to her parents.

Lissa was curled up on the sofa sound asleep, her honey-colored hair resting softly on a pillow, and Laney stepped to the girl, gazing down at her.

"Police? That's ridiculous," Daddy sputtered.

"Nat, honey, you can't go marching in telling Sheriff Zane something like that out of nowhere." Mom looked aghast.

"Mom, our family name's not at stake here. Hayley is."

"I just—"

Natalie locked eyes with her mom. "What did Arlene Smathers

say?"

Mom looked down. "I didn't call her."

"Mom!"

"I . . . didn't want to worry her unnecessarily. Ruin Hayley's chances with Ben."

Fury snaked through Natalie. "Hayley's chances with Ben are the last thing we need to worry about right now!"

"Your daughter's right, Mrs. Motts. Mr. Motts," Laney said softly, gazing at both of them.

They looked at her, and Natalie could tell what they were thinking, what was going through their minds about her purple-streaked hair and too-skinny frame, the hint of a tattoo peeking out from the edge of her tank top.

Natalie's lips pressed together.

"I'm going to the police with or without your permission, but I'd love your blessing."

A long moment passed. Then Mom sighed.

"I'll call Arlene. Let me know what the sheriff's office says."

Natalie clasped her mom in a quick hug.

"Can she stay here with you?" She gestured to Lissa on the couch.

"Of course."

On the drive to the police station, a hundred questions for Laney zinged through Natalie's mind like a pinball on overdrive. *How do you know all this? What happened to you out there? Is this why you're skittish around any man who gets within ten feet of you? How do you know about the blue bracelet?*

But she was afraid to speak, to ask. Right now, she was just going to trust—and pray for the best.

Laney waited at the door to the police station almost before Natalie'd unbuckled her seatbelt.

And when they stood in front of Sheriff Zane and his deputy,

Natalie marveled at the steel behind Laney's eyes.

"We have good reason to suspect Natalie's sister's being recruited by Ethan Sansone and his Overdrive Gang. And she's in danger."

Sheriff Zane blinked, and Natalie could tell they recognized the name.

"And you'd know this how?"

Natalie watched as Laney lifted her chin and took a steadying breath. "I'm in witness protection because I'm a former Overdrive. I'm the one responsible for putting him behind bars."

CHAPTER 35

Natalie

It's like a hive abuzz *with action—conscious, intentional action*, Natalie thought as she watched the flurry of activity all around her at the sheriff's office. She and Laney were now sitting across from Lieutenant Tracy Haynes, giving her a full list of Hayley's friends and their phone numbers.

"What about social media?" Lieutenant Haynes asked, typing everything in.

"I think she's on a few, but she's not really active," Natalie told her, finding Hayley's account on her phone and passing it across to the officer. "Maybe these?"

Lieutenant Haynes swiped through, then picked up the phone, giving whoever was on the other end Hayley's account names.

"We've got a team who specializes in criminal child exploitation checking into everything now, so we'll see what that brings up."

Laney cocked her head. "What about other accounts? Like, ones she really uses."

"We'll be looking for those, too." Lieutenant Haynes nodded.

Natalie blinked. "Like a private account?"

"Yeah. Here, let me." Laney took the phone from Natalie and

scrolled through. "Her best friends were who?"

"Zoe Wilson and Chelsey Arant."

Natalie gave Lieutenant Haynes the only photo she had in her wallet, Hayley's school picture from last year.

"We have more hard copies of photos at the house, and you have the ones I gave you off my cell phone, too."

"I think we're set for now," Haynes said. "We'll send an officer out in the next hour to collect her phone, laptop, anything else we can sift through. And Sheriff Zane will get with you on the FBI update as soon as he can."

Natalie nodded, the whirlwind of police layers dizzying to her. Earlier, after they'd questioned Laney privately, Sheriff Zane had disappeared to loop in their FBI partners, who apparently had a massive undercover operation going. Laney's mention of that gang, Overdrive, had pushed Hayley's case from a basic runaway to a top-level priority. Natalie still didn't know what it all meant, but she was thankful Laney did.

Next to her, Laney was on Natalie's phone now, scrolling through Hayley's Instagram contacts even as they walked out to Nat's car.

"Any weird childhood nicknames I should know about?"

Natalie frowned as their heels clicked against the tile of the entryway, through the double doors, and onto the sidewalk outside.

"Hay-Hay, Haygirl. For six months she had us call her Princess Hayliana, but it didn't stick. Um, her favorite stuffed animal is a ratty old teddy bear named Magoo, and she's got a bunch of dolls named after Muppets, I think . . ."

"Bingo!"

Laney showed her a screenname for a magoo_girl1114 with a sunset and a flower for the profile image.

"That's got to be her—November fourteenth is her birthday." Nat clicked the lock to her car, and they climbed in.

Ashley was there with Mom when they arrived, and both of

their eyes were red. Natalie had texted them both a full update earlier, and Mom put Lissa to bed on the pullout sofa in Daddy's home office.

"She's okay?" Laney asked about Lissa when they arrived.

Mom led her back to check on the girl while Ashley wrapped Natalie in a big hug.

"This is crazy!" Ashley said.

"I know. Thank God for Laney. I'll fill you in later, but she's been a huge help."

Ashley looked up just as Laney walked back into the living room. "I can't thank you enough, Laney."

Laney looked embarrassed, but she just shrugged. "It's the least I can do. I just—want to help."

"Want to gather her stuff with me?" Natalie asked Laney. "Then maybe I can drive you home."

They disappeared upstairs to collect whatever else the police might need—Hayley's laptop, her old diary.

Laney sat in the vanity chair and continued scrolling through Nat's phone, looking at whatever magoo_girl1114 had posted, mostly some artsy shots of the sky and a few of her and a blonde girl with lots of eyeliner and a penchant for low-cut shirts.

"I bet that's Jasmine," Laney showed her.

Hayley'd tagged someone named "flutterby17," presumably Jasmine.

"Probably." Natalie sighed, the stack of Hayley's items piled in front of her like a gift offering. "Then again, who knows? And who knows if her name is even Jasmine."

"That gives me an idea. Maybe I can check her direct messages on the social accounts, see if she's been making plans. Does she keep her laptop unlocked?"

They checked, but it was locked. Nat tried again with the 1114 combination, plus a few other variations.

"No such luck."

They carried everything down and put it in a crate for the officer along with Hayley's school laptop and backpack.

The officer grabbed a few more things from the bedroom when he arrived.

"I'll keep you posted daily, ma'am, sir," he told Natalie's parents.

"We found this, too. Apparently her 'real' social media account." Natalie scrawled the screenname on a slip of paper for him.

"We thought we could get into her DMs, but we can't access anything."

When he'd gone, they all sat a moment on the couch, defeated.

"I just didn't see this coming." Mom fumbled with the tissue on her lap.

"Mary Lynn, you couldn't have." Daddy cleared his throat, then stood. "I'm going to take a walk."

Natalie glanced at Laney, sensed her exhaustion. She'd always been thin, but tonight she looked extra-thin. Extra fragile.

Witness protection. A gang. *What in the world?*

And yet somehow, Hayley was caught up in all this. Somehow, God was using Laney to help her—to help Hayley. It couldn't be coincidence.

She could only hope that help wasn't too late.

Ashley rose, collecting her things, and Natalie looked at Laney. "Come on. Let's get Lissa into the car and get you home."

They stayed quiet on the drive, and Natalie cracked the window, letting in fresh air that hinted of the fall to come.

Laney sagged in the passenger seat, gazing out at the rows of houses they passed.

This has to be hard for her.

When they pulled up at Laney's apartment, Natalie put the car in park.

"Thank you, Laney." She spoke softly. "I—I really just can't thank you enough."

Laney turned, but her gaze fell short.

"I thought coming here, starting over . . . I thought I'd never have to tell anybody. Now I feel like, I don't know." A short laugh escaped Laney's lips as she studied her hands. "Like I want to be anywhere but here."

"No one has to know. I mean, I'm not going to say anything. And it's not like Sheriff Zane will. Isn't witness protection ironclad?"

"It's supposed to be, but that's not the point. I'm connected, and they know it." Laney rubbed at her eyes, visibly swallowing hard. "I'm probably on their radar now."

Laney glanced back at Alissa, still conked out after a long day of kindergarten, afterschool paint, and finally Natalie's house to top it all off.

"Kids are resilient, you know," Natalie said.

This time Laney met her eyes.

"They are. But I'm not sure how resilient I am."

Laney unbuckled her seatbelt and slipped a drowsy Lissa from the backseat, setting her down on the pavement.

As Natalie drove off, she glanced back through the rearview mirror, watching them walk beneath the flickering light of the apartment sign. The Z in the sign still made the name look more like Lion Apartments than Zion. The pair of them looked incredibly tiny beneath the overhang. And soon they disappeared, somewhere into the depths of the building.

Natalie shivered, finally pulling over on the side of the road and bowing her head.

"Please, God. Give Laney peace tonight. And please watch over Hayley. Protect her. Help us get her back."

But somewhere in the shadows another voice whispered, sowing doubt. *It's too late . . .*

CHAPTER 36

Laney

Oh-God-oh-God-oh-God-oh-God. That night, long after she should have been sound asleep, Laney perched by her bedroom window watching the street. Pressing a fist to her mouth, she willed the tears to stop, but they wouldn't. Tears never helped, and right now, they were doing nothing but distracting her from her ability to plan. To think. But right now, they wouldn't stop coming.

There were a million other things she could have said in that sheriff's office besides give up her one safe haven. But of course she hadn't done anything crafty or reasonably intelligent. She'd just spilled the beans about witness protection, shoving her barely cracked door open wide for all the world to see.

Natalie's face was what did it, really—the small O her mouth had made, the way she'd folded her hands in her lap, looked away. On the surface she'd been nothing but nice. Grateful. Extra kind.

But Laney knew the maelstrom that must be whooshing through her boss's brain. Imagining her, Laney, doing rotten things. Evil things.

Things she wished she could forget, wash away like the flood from the Bible that swept the earth clean all those years ago.

And to think she'd just started getting comfortable here, in Dahlia. With Lissa in school, and that Bible study, and even Bev and Finn at the coffee shop. But she'd been stupid. Stupid!

Laney dug her fingernails into the fleshy part of her palm until it hurt, staring out at the dark night beyond the window.

Stupid to think she and Lissa could make a life here in Dahlia for good. Join the church.

The night was warm, but with the fan on, Laney was cold, so chilled she got in bed and pulled the comforter all the way up to her chin. But the shaking wouldn't stop.

Across the bedroom, Lissa slept like she hadn't a care in the world. What would she tell her baby girl about why they were moving? Other than Sunrise House, Dahlia was the only home Lissa'd ever known.

Sunrise House. Besides the women's prison, it was the only place Laney had ever felt truly, fully safe. Even here in Dahlia, she was always looking over her shoulder, waiting for the other shoe to drop. Like when Ethan got out of prison—hadn't she expected this somehow, some way? Hadn't she expected everything to come crashing down, like it always had?

In a way, she was relieved. *Of course this was going to happen,* she told herself. It was only a matter of time before the truth came out.

If she was honest, even when Mama was alive, even with all her secret fantasies about her and Zeb and Mama and Baby Henry being one big happy family, even then she'd known it was all a pipe dream. A joke.

It's better this way. Better now than later, at any rate.

People like Laney didn't get big happy families. They got second best. Leftovers. Whatever remained.

It'd be different for Alissa, she'd make sure of that. Somehow, some way.

But for now, for Laney, it was time to cut ties. *I'll do what I can to find Nat's sister. But after that . . .*

A flash of the sapphire-blue bracelet zipped through her mind. At first when she'd found it in the girl's jewelry box, she thought she was having a weird nightmare or flashback, some vision. But it wasn't a vision—it was real.

How? Overdrive, Ethan, the Jersey ring, the other guys—they'd all gone down. She'd helped make that happen. So how in the world was some kid like Hayley, a gazillion miles from where everything started for Laney herself, involved in all this?

The next morning, Laney finally let herself pick up the phone and dial Miss J. Whoever answered at Sunrise gave her the number to Miss J's daughter, Rosa, who answered on the first ring.

"Of course I remember you," Rosa said, and Laney could feel the smile in her voice. "Here, I'll get Mama."

When Miss J got on, it was like she already knew, though how that was even possible, Laney didn't have a clue.

"Honey, you are welcome back at Sunrise whenever you want or need. Though this time I'm hoping it's to lead the way, not just escape."

Laney burst into tears and told her everything. And by the time they'd finished talking, she had a plan in place.

"I'll see you next Saturday, sugar. Bright and early."

"See you then."

Laney hung up the phone, the tightness in her chest already dissipating. The end was in sight.

Time for a new start.

CHAPTER 37

Natalie

THE NEXT MORNING, Natalie sat at the kitchen table with Mom, Daddy, Ashley, and Matt. The twins were in the living room, and every once in a while she could hear the crash from their Jenga blocks, but at least for now they had some quiet time.

Time to think, and to plan.

"When's the officer supposed to call?" Matt asked.

Natalie shook her head. "All he said was he'd keep us updated every day, and we should stay in touch with her friends, spread the word."

"Spread the word." Mom pressed her lips together. "Everyone in town's going to know about this by nightfall."

"That's a good thing, Mary Lynn." Daddy placed a hand over his wife's. "We'll find her, and that's really all that matters."

Natalie looked at her father in surprise. *He's come a long way.*

Ashley cleared her throat. "I was thinking maybe Matt and I can drive over to Aberville, check the mini mall and that place you told me about where you spotted Hayley that one night."

Nat looked down, flushing. "If only I'd spoken up back then about it."

This time it was Mom's turn to surprise her. "Nat, honey, I don't think it would have done a thing other than make this happen faster. Let's keep our sights going forward, not backwards."

She was right, Natalie realized, looking around at her family in gratitude.

They made a plan—Ash and Matt and the twins would head to Aberville, Mom would make the rounds talking to Hayley's friends, and Daddy would head to the station and check in.

As for Natalie, she'd head to the shop for a couple hours, see if maybe Laney would cover for her. Then she'd do some of her own searching.

Please, God. Don't let it be too late.

At the shop, she had a few minutes to herself before Laney showed up for her Saturday shift and the store opened. She checked her email—nothing yet. Last night, when she couldn't sleep, she'd been all over the internet, trying to figure out how police located trafficking victims.

That's when she discovered the regional counter-trafficking initiative, and emailed them.

Laney and Lissa walked in a few minutes before ten.

After she got Lissa settled in the back, Laney approached. "Look, whatever I need to do today to help, count me in. I'm happy to run stuff here so you can get out and do some searching."

Nat made a face. "That's just the problem. I don't even know where to search. I did, however, uncover this."

She pulled up the counter-trafficking group's website and swiveled the laptop so Laney could read.

"This is good!" Laney met her eyes.

Natalie dialed the number on the website, but no one answered.

She left a brief message on their voicemail asking for a callback.

She bit her lip, thinking hard. "Laney, remember you said you saw Hayley at the gas station that day with that girl, the one with the red car? I wonder if they have surveillance outside."

"That's a good thought!" Laney perked up. "I bet the police can access it."

Nat left a message for Lieutenant Haynes, and a second one for the sheriff. Parents and kids started to arrive for their eleven o'clock kid paint. A restless energy hummed inside her.

Laney noticed. "You'll feel better if you get out, drive around a little. I've got this." She thumbed to the room beyond. "Really."

"You sure?"

"Positive."

Natalie spotted Finn coming out of Joe Mama's as she clicked the button to unlock her SUV.

"Wait up," he called, jogging over.

His face looked worried when he got close. "I heard about Hayley gone missing. Your mom was in earlier, putting up flyers."

Natalie's brows lifted, but she was relieved. *They'll find her faster if the word's getting out so fast. Won't they?*

Finn peered at her, his face concerned. "Do they have any ideas where she might be, who she's with?"

Natalie hesitated, then blurted out the truth. "They think she might have gotten involved with some gang. Well, Laney thinks so, and it all seems to add up."

Finn frowned. "Laney?"

She told him the basics but stopped herself from saying too much. Laney's business was her own. "She's right, honestly. She spotted her with some rough crowd last week or so, and we all kind of put two-and-two together based on how she's been acting."

His eyes grew soft. "Nat, I—I'm so sorry. Look, I want to help. I've got two employees today who can cover everything. Let me tag along with you, even if it's just for moral support."

She was tempted, and she could see he knew.

"Come on. Please, Nat. You don't have to do it all yourself."

He's right, she realized. "Okay," she murmured, her chest thrumming with . . . what, she didn't know. Nerves, and worry, and relief, and butterflies. Everything, all at once.

She let him drive, and they took his truck—first to the gas station where Laney'd seen Hayley, then to the sheriff's office, then to the high school, around back where the track team practiced. The track was empty, and Natalie gazed at the dusty ring, remembering the meets she'd grudgingly attended in the spring, cheering her kid sister on.

Remembered Hayley, looking like a young horse, all long legs and tanned skin, her hair pulled back high and tight, muscles rippling.

"Why would she do this?" Natalie shook her head, barely aware she'd asked the question aloud.

"After my dad left, I went through an angry period." Finn sighed. "I can't imagine understanding what's going through Hayley's head, but sometimes we lash out at the people closest to us, think pushing them away's easier than letting them leave us in the dust."

Natalie considered it—Ashley sick, Natalie home, Mom and Daddy busy. Distracted.

She thinned her lips.

Her purse buzzed, and she jumped, realizing someone was calling her cell phone. *Please, be Hayley*, she begged silently.

Instead, it was the human trafficking coalition.

"I'm Ana Montoya," the woman told her, explaining how they worked and how they could help. "Tell me everything you know."

She did, from the bracelet and Laney to the red sports car.

"It used to be men doing most of the grooming, but these days, the women are just as bad."

"Grooming?"

"It's psychological mostly, like dangling a carrot in front of someone, whether that's expensive gifts or the promise of a new lifestyle—a boyfriend, a group of new friends, or a big dream come true. Did your sister get any fancy gifts recently?"

Natalie remembered the sparkly H necklace, mentioned that, plus the rift between Hayley and her friends over the summer. "Oh, and manicures."

Grooming, indeed.

"Divide and isolate. Like how wolves separate sheep from the pack, then close in for the kill."

Natalie shivered, thinking of Hayley as some lone sheep, preyed upon. Vulnerable. Alone.

"The good news is we've got lots of resources," Ana told her.

Natalie told her about the screenname they discovered last night, and the girl she'd tagged in those posts.

Ana promised to get back with her as soon as she could.

"For now, just keep your phone with you, your eyes peeled, and your prayers strong."

When she hung up, Finn was pulling up something on his phone. "Speaking of social media, we need to get the word out there, too. Flyers are good, but these days, we can get faster traction with a strongly worded post than you'd imagine. Can you text me a picture of Hayley?"

She did, and within minutes, he'd posted it on both his personal and business social media accounts.

"Like and comment. It helps the algorithm." He motioned to her own phone, and she did, sharing the posts as well.

Within fifteen minutes, they'd gotten dozens of comments.

"The more comments, the faster it spreads," Finn told her.

Laney looked like she was about to burst when they returned, Finn following on Natalie's heels.

"Did Officer Scott call you?" she asked. "He was just here."

"No." Natalie's eyes were wide.

Her phone buzzed in her hand. Mom.

"They think they tracked down the girl she's with. A trafficking coalition pinged the license plate off surveillance video from the gas station. Tracked her car outside some sketchy motel chain toward Dillon. Investigators have been fishing around for weeks there, think they're super close to nailing them."

"Dillon?" That was halfway to Myrtle Beach. "Oh, my goodness, Mom!"

They hung up, and Natalie shared the news with Laney and Finn.

Laney nodded. "I'm not surprised. Overdrive travels fast. And look."

She pointed to the laptop, which was streaming the local news station out of Charlotte. A reporter onscreen shared the latest about Hayley, her picture filling the monitor. She wore the topaz pendant—her birthstone—that she'd gotten last Christmas, and she looked super young and incredibly wholesome, not the kind of photo Natalie was used to seeing on television news. Another photo flashed across the screen, one taken at Easter with Hayley in the center, Ashley and Natalie on either side, all of them dressed up for church. The reporter went on to share information about how she was considered "endangered" and possibly with others considered dangerous, offering a sizable reward for information.

"They'll find her soon, at this rate," Laney murmured, her eyes locked on the screen.

Finn didn't say anything, just stared at his shoes like he was scared or nervous or just plain freaked out by the whole thing.

He surprised her by holding out one hand to her and one to

Laney.

"Only one thing we can do at this point," he said. "Let's pray."

Around one, Ashley and Matt got to the shop. Paisley and Peter raced for the back, where they joined Lissa in the kid craft area.

"Mom should be here shortly."

As if on cue, Mom walked in, Daddy with her. It was maybe the second time he'd seen her shop, and he got out of their champagne sedan, glancing around at the signage and the cheerful welcome sign.

"Place is looking good," Daddy told her when they entered.

Natalie gave him a quick hug.

"Mom, Daddy, you remember Laney from last night. And this is Finn. He's a . . . friend, and he owns the coffee shop over there." She pointed in the general direction, and they all nodded, shaking hands.

Laney looked a bit uncomfortable, but she hung in there. Natalie was proud of her.

"How's it going?" Matt asked them.

"Officer Scott promised he'll call the second they hear anything about the motel sting . . ." Mom said.

"So now we wait," Daddy added, putting an arm around Mom's shoulders. For the second time in the last two days, Natalie was struck by how tenderly he seemed to treat her.

Funny that it took a tragedy to notice this stuff.

Mom cleared her throat. "I had a good long talk with Zoe and Chelsey this morning. Apparently Hayley was pulling away even before the broken leg, but after, they said she just stopped engaging entirely. They didn't know it was this bad. Now they're beating themselves up for not telling us."

Natalie frowned. "It's not their fault. What about Ben?"

"That's been off for a while, too, also before the broken leg. They had some big fight, something to do with someone she was talking to on the internet. I—I just feel so stupid. All this time, she's doing this stuff right beneath our noses, in our own home!"

"Mrs. Motts, you didn't do anything wrong." Laney stepped to the counter, now looking directly into Mom's eyes. "These people—they're predators. For whatever reason, they found Hayley, and they zeroed in on her like a target. They know how to work people."

Mom sniffled, dabbing at her eyes with a tissue. "You sound like you know what you're talking about, sweetheart."

Laney took a breath. "I . . . do."

Slowly, everyone turned to look at her.

Natalie stepped closer to Laney. "I mean, she knows a lot about all this stuff and—"

Laney put a gentle hand on her arm. "Nat, it's okay. What I mean is, what's happening to Hayley happened to me, too, a long, long time ago. These people she's with?" Her voice got shaky, but not from sadness or fear, Natalie could see. It shook from rage.

Laney glanced toward the back to make sure the kids were still playing, then continued.

"They're monsters. Evil, evil people, and they have one goal: to take and use innocent young girls just because they can. I got out when I got pregnant with Lissa, but most girls aren't so lucky. But Hayley is—we're going to find her. They're going to catch these people. And mark my words. We're going to take them all down."

Tears spilled from Mom's eyes, and she wrapped Laney in a hug. Laney hugged her back.

Just then, Daddy's phone rang. He answered, clutching the phone tight.

"Oh, dear Lord." Daddy's face went almost gray, and he passed the phone to Matt.

"What's going on?" Matt said into the phone, listening intently. He hung up, then turned to face them.

"They raided the motel, arrested three—two men, one woman. People ran out, and they're actively combing the area. But in the search, they . . ." Matt stopped, the words appearing to catch in his throat.

"They what?" Ashley clutched his arm. "What?"

"They found a body in the woods. A young woman. They—they need one of us to come."

CHAPTER 38

Natalie

NATALIE FELT LIKE SHE WAS UNDERWATER as the words wafted like air bubbles slowly from her lips.

" . . . I'll go."

"No, no, honey, it should be me—" Daddy slumped into the chair even as he tried to protest.

Mom was crying, and Ashley'd gone white.

Matt stepped up. "I'll go with you."

But Finn put a hand on Matt's arm, motioning to Ashley. "You need to stay with her. I'll go with Nat."

"I want to come, too," Laney added. She turned to Ashley. "Can Lissa stay with you?"

"Of . . . course." Ashley just stared at Matt like he was speaking nonsense. "Matt, this can't be. It's got to be someone else."

"And maybe it is someone else," Finn said, his voice reassuring.

Natalie felt him take her arm, ask for her car keys.

Within five minutes, she, Laney, and Finn were driving southeast on Highway Nine toward Dillon County.

"It's a fifty-minute drive," Laney said from the center of the rear seat, leaning forward so she was almost between them. She plugged in the address on the GPS in Finn's phone, then passed it up to them.

Finn put it on the dashboard, the robotic voice ordering, "Turn left, then turn right in point-two miles."

He jabbed down the volume. "We're just going to drive and see," he told them. "It doesn't mean anything."

It's not her. Natalie didn't know how she knew this, but she did. She felt a gentle press, almost an invisible caress, on her head and closed her eyes, listening to the tires on the road and the smooth click-click of the turning signal as they quickly made their way out of town.

Laney didn't say anything, but every time Natalie turned her head, she saw Laney clutching the cross around her neck, praying silently.

It's not her. It's not her. It's-not-her-it's-not-her-it's-not-her-it's-not-her. The words echoed in her mind, keeping time as the car moved them closer and closer still.

At one point she felt Laney slip Natalie's phone from her console and answer it, tell whoever was on the other end they were about ten minutes out.

And then they were there, pulling up outside a motel, the faded blue sign out front advertising the Swamp Fox Inn. Half a dozen police cars filled the parking lot, a few with lights flashing. The place was seedy at best, a rundown concrete stretch of nondescript rooms.

Nat slipped out of the car and peered up to see police tape stretching across a second-floor hotel room, and in the distance, she spotted a news camera, the reporter describing the scene behind her for on-air viewers.

An officer met them and escorted them around back, where Natalie saw Lieutenant Haynes and what looked to be FBI agents. A coroner's van was parked nearby, and an ambulance, and someone in uniform was snapping photos of the scene, documenting evidence.

With every click of the camera, Nat wanted to jump out of her skin, but she allowed Finn and Laney to guide her where they needed to be.

"We don't think it's her," Lieutenant Haynes told her as they walked toward the bank of the creek, "but we need to be certain."

Not her. Not her. They stepped closer, knelt in the soft dirt. Before them was a plastic tarp. She didn't want to see. For the life of her, really-really-really didn't want to see.

But for Hayley's sake—for her parents' sake—she had to.

A flash of Stacey seared through her mind then, Stacey on the cold slab in the county morgue all the way in Nashville. Nat started to stand and then stumbled, catching herself. She took a breath, one knee in the dirt. *Just do this. Do what you have to do.*

The coroner had his hand on the tarp.

"Just let me know when you're ready," he told her.

She took a deep breath, then another. *How do you even get ready for something like this?*

Then came the crackle of the lieutenant's radio, a short bark of airwave.

"We've got her! We found the kid, over."

"Roger that."

"En route now."

Lieutenant Haynes paused, one hand out. "Hold back a moment."

"Nat, look!" Laney pointed up the bank.

Natalie looked up, but she couldn't see.

Finn took her hand and guided her up, to the top of the bank.

And then she could see—it was Hayley! Hayley, being led from the back of the police car. Hayley, a thin blanket around her shoulders, hair all stringy and every which way.

"Hay!" she cried out, but the words only crackled past her lips.

And now she was running, running as hard and fast as she could, running toward her sister.

Hayley was running too. Straight for her.

They collapsed, sobbing in each other's arms.

"You're okay! Oh, dear God, you're okay!" Nat was crying and touching Hayley's face like she wasn't real, and Hayley was crying and laughing and clinging tight.

Finn was there now, and Laney, and Lieutenant Haynes, all of them in one big circle there in the back lot of the seedy motel.

"Come on."

Lieutenant Haynes ushered them over to the makeshift base, where a medical team checked over Hayley and doctored wounds and gave them apple juice and tiny paper cups of freezing-cold water.

Natalie wouldn't leave her sister's side.

Laney held out Natalie's cell phone at one point, and they said hi to their parents on speaker phone.

"I'm sorry, Mommy—I'm so so sorry." Hayley dissolved in tears then.

Natalie just held her close. None of it mattered anymore.

Hayley was safe.

She glanced down the bank of the creek, toward the body of some other poor, poor girl. It wasn't Hayley, but she was somebody's baby.

Somebody's girl.

But not hers. Not her Hayley.

CHAPTER 39

Laney

Finn drove Laney back in Natalie's SUV as they followed Natalie and Hayley in the county ambulance. Hayley had to get checked out fully before release, plus give her statement and anything else police needed. Natalie's parents would meet them at the hospital.

She wasn't the only kid they'd recovered that day, Lieutenant Haynes told them quietly as they stood outside the ambulance, waiting for crews to get Hayley strapped in for the ride. Two other girls were rescued as well, one just thirteen years old.

Laney swallowed, a knot in her belly reminding her she hadn't eaten since breakfast. Not that she could manage anything.

"What about the other girl? The one . . ." Her glance toward the creek said all she needed to say.

"We don't know yet, but it appears she's been on the road awhile. Appears to be an overdose, but we'll know more soon." Lieutenant Haynes pressed her lips together, then told them they could go.

"Come on. Let's get you back to your girl," Finn said, then looked at the lieutenant. "Thank you."

"Of course. And Laney?" Lieutenant Haynes put a hand on Laney's shoulder. The touch felt kind, almost sisterly. "Thank you.

The information you volunteered—it made all the difference in how quickly we were able to recover these girls."

Laney didn't even have the words to reply. She just stared blankly after Lieutenant Haynes as Finn escorted her to the car.

"I'll drop you off at the shop, then head over to the medical center to be with Nat," Finn said as they pulled onto the road.

They didn't talk on the ride, though once Laney glanced over to see Finn giving her a thoughtful look.

I'm a scumbag, and now everyone knows it. Funny—she should care more that her big secret was out. But somehow, knowing Hayley was alive and okay and back with her family, somehow that made everything better. Besides, Miss J already told her she and Lissa had a place at Sunrise House as long as they wanted. Assistant director, that was her new title, at least until Miss J officially retired. She'd learn from the best, spend the rest of her days making sure girls like her really could get back on their feet.

And making sure Alissa never had to worry about any of it in the first place.

She couldn't think of anything else she'd rather do.

At Sunstrokes, she practically flew from the car and into the shop, where she wrapped Lissa in the tightest hug she could get away with.

Lissa giggled like it was a big game, hugging her back. "Mommy!"

"I missed you, baby girl. My smart girl." Laney knelt down, gazing into her daughter's eyes.

"And you're a smart mommy girl. The smartest mama ever." Lissa poked Laney in the chest.

Laney kissed the tip of Lissa's nose.

Out of the corner of her eye, she could see Ashley and Matt watching, their arms around the twins.

From the door, Finn gave a little cough.

"Uh, see you Monday?"

Laney stared at him.

He just waited, brows raised expectantly for her answer, like it was a perfectly normal question.

"Ah, sure, if I still have a job."

Finn gave her a look like she was crazy. "Of course you do."

And then he was gone, Laney staring after him, wondering what and why but too stunned to care anymore.

That night, long after Ashley'd dropped them off at home, long after Lissa's grape-scented bubble bath and their hot dog and mac-and-cheese supper and the Bible bedtime storybook and at least three more oddly similar princess-dog-rainbow-themed board books, Laney sat on the floor across the room, watching her baby sleep.

Lieutenant Haynes had called just before dinner with an update. It had been their biggest bust in eighteen months, and all the ringleaders had been captured and were now behind bars, including Jasmine, whose real name turned out to be Simone and who'd helped lure all three of the kids police rescued that day.

Ana Montoya had been right.

Ethan was nowhere close, and local police confirmed he was across the state in some halfway house and had nothing to do with any of this. He had to wear an ankle monitor for the next ten years, Haynes told her.

"Call me Tracy," she'd told Laney as they wrapped up the call. "You know, your identity's still safe."

"I guess."

"That's my point. You don't have to guess."

"But my secret's out." Laney had stirred the macaroni at the stove, looking across the small apartment at Lissa, who was playing with a Barbie doll on the couch, lost in the game.

"Maybe that's a good thing."

Now, her words echoed in Laney's mind as she sat across the bedroom, watching Lissa sleep.

From somewhere below, a woman let out a fierce string of curse words, ordering some no-good-jerk off her property for good.

"And don't come back. Ever!" she hollered.

A door slammed loud, and Laney could hear heavy boots stomp down stairs. She peered out the window, watching a big man slink into his truck and take off, his tires peeling out in the warm late-summer night.

You go, girl, Laney congratulated her nameless neighbor.

Standing up to bad guys—and girls, girls like Simone—started just like this. With one person deciding she'd had enough and was holding her own. With one person leaving The Life, starting over for the sake of an unborn child.

And maybe, just maybe, with one former victim deciding it was time to come clean and claim her past for the sake of another girl in danger.

Maybe that's a good thing. The lieutenant's words blazed across Laney's mind as she wrapped herself in the fleece blanket from her bed and gazed at the stars beyond her window.

Maybe so.

CHAPTER 40

Epilogue

It was a chilly December Saturday as Natalie stood on what used to be Old Man DeLuc's property. Finn was at her side, and he'd slipped his gloved hand into hers, something new between them. She glanced up at him, a thrill zipping through her.

Before them, Helen Chastain, Pastor Dave, and Rev Bryant had just finished giving an update on the building, which was far ahead of schedule. The walls were up, and Tikvah House was now officially dried in. Crews would spend the rest of the winter finishing up the interior, with painting and furnishing. Their big launch was scheduled for spring, hopefully just after Easter.

"Is she here yet?" Natalie whispered.

Finn shook his head. "I don't see her."

Laney was supposed to call when she got into town that morning for the Tikvah House ceremony, but it was almost noon, and so far, there'd been no sign of her.

They were breaking to head to the church for lunch when the blue sedan pulled into the lot and Laney jumped out, followed quickly by Alissa.

"Auntie Nat!" Lissa barreled into Natalie's arms, and Natalie picked her up, swinging her around.

"There's my girl!"

"Flat tire. Sorry we missed the big event," Laney said sheepishly.

"As long as you're here. Besides, you only missed half of it." Nat grinned and slung an arm around her friend. "How's Columbia treating you?"

"Sunrise House is way better than the Zion Apartments, not to brag or anything." Laney stuck out her tongue as they all walked toward their cars. "And I'm learning a lot. Miss J is a great teacher."

"Still think you'll be ready to move back to Dahlia this spring?" Natalie asked.

Finn added, "You know they can't open this place without you."

"There's our new director!" Helen Chastain spotted them, waving, with Marla Bryant and Devon close behind.

Laney had agreed to take the position as Tikvah House director on one condition—she could go back to Columbia for the fall and winter and train under Miss J, both until Miss J could get back on her feet and until Laney felt she knew enough to run Tikvah properly.

Even though Laney didn't really want Lissa shifting back and forth between schools, they all agreed kindergarten was a better time to do it than any other grade. And besides, she and Lissa weren't leaving Dahlia for good. Only a few months and they'd be back again.

"It's like a vacation. An adventure," she'd told Lissa, just like her own Mama had done with her all those years ago.

Only out of Laney's mouth, the words were true, not just some line to make running away seem fun and exciting. Living in Sunrise House, learning at Miss J's knee, it really did feel like an adventure. Even Lissa got to help out, making the other kids who came to stay feel comfortable. Secure.

Just like they were.

Natalie's mom met them at the church door, ushering them in. Hayley was there, too, and Ashley. She'd finally just stopped wearing her wig, her cropped blonde hair poking cheerfully out behind a bright pink headwrap.

"Lissa!" Paisley spotted them across the room and raced over, Peter on her heels.

"I hear you got to ring the bell," Laney told Ashley as they hugged.

"Yep! I'm officially in remission."

They all jumped in, helping Helen and Marla set out the casseroles and pies and other dishes, then everyone dug in.

When they'd mostly finished eating, Rev Bryant and Pastor Dave made their way to the podium.

"She doesn't know this is coming, otherwise maybe she would have stayed away," Rev began with a laugh after everyone quieted down.

"Oh, dear, please tell me they don't mean me," Laney murmured to Natalie, who just smiled mischievously.

Pastor Dave motioned to Helen, who guided a red-cheeked Laney toward the front of the room.

"We know you're busy training down in Columbia to be our new director," Pastor Dave told Laney when she joined them at the podium. "But thanks to the phenomenal fundraising skills of our Development Chair, Natalie Motts, we've raised enough funds to establish a children's reading and craft room. And we'd like to name it Laney's Lair, in your honor."

Pastor Dave motioned to an easel covered in cloth, which Rev pulled away to reveal an artistic rendering of a children's room for Tikvah House.

"Laney's Lair" it read at the top, the words all animals shaped creatively into letters.

"Natalie has agreed to do the mural, and we'll officially open

Laney's Lair when the rest of Tikvah House opens this spring. It'll be a haven for moms—and their kids."

The room erupted in applause, and even Laney found herself grinning.

"It's weird to have a room named after you, but I think I can get used to it," Laney told Finn when they were all chatting after.

There was a big cake, too, and Cheyenne Tillman brought her guitar and strummed some tunes while a few girls from the high school sang. Hayley stood on the outskirts, clapping and taking pictures. She looked subdued—the last few months had changed her sister. Gone was the bright-eyed, carefree teen, though the young woman who now stood in her place displayed a strength Natalie appreciated. Admired, even.

"Thanks for being here, sis," Nat whispered.

Hayley just smiled, her blue eyes steady.

Laney saw Finn watching Natalie with her sister across the room, and she elbowed him.

"You two together make me so happy."

Finn laughed out loud. "You know what, Laney? Me, too."

Natalie caught his eye and strolled over. And together, the three of them gazed around the room, taking it all in. All they'd done.

Together.

Planting seeds for a new tomorrow.

The End

About the Author

Jessica Brodie is an award-winning author and journalist with thousands of articles to her name and a huge heart for people and their inspiring redemption stories. She holds a master's in English and a bachelor's in communications. A native of Miami, Florida, she now makes her home in South Carolina with her husband Matt, four children, three misfit cats, and one giant German Shepherd. Find her at JessicaBrodie.com.

Book Club Discussion Questions

1. Natalie returns to Dahlia carrying two losses at once—grief over Tucker and Stacey's deaths, and the betrayal of discovering their secret. Which wound do you think was harder for her to heal, and why?

2. Laney is described as someone who wants no one to know anything about her past. Did you find her protectiveness of her story understandable, or did it ever feel frustrating? How did your feelings about her shift as the book went on?

3. Finn is quietly present throughout much of the story. What drew you to him as a character, and what do you think Natalie needed from him that was different from what she'd had before?

4. Art and creativity serve as a source of healing throughout the book. Is there something in your own life—a hobby, a routine, a place—that functions the way Sunstrokes does for Natalie?

5. Both Natalie and Laney are rebuilding from scratch, but in very different ways and from very different circumstances. What do you think they gave each other that no one else could?

6. Forgiveness is a quiet but powerful thread in the story—Natalie forgiving Tucker, Laney learning to forgive herself. Did either of those journeys resonate with you personally?

7. The book deals honestly with human trafficking without being gratuitous about it. Did reading Laney's story change or deepen how you think about that issue?

8. Natalie's parents respond to her grief and her business plans with doubt and worry. Do you think their concern was fair, or did it feel dismissive? How does the family dynamic shift by the end?

9. When Laney comes forward to help find Hayley, she risks everything she's built. Do you think she had a real choice in that moment, or did it feel inevitable given who she'd become?

10. The title *Hidden Seeds* and the closing image of things blooming under rocky soil ties both women's stories together. Whose "hidden seed" stayed with you more—Natalie's or Laney's?

11. If Sunstrokes were a real place in your town, would you go? What kind of class or event would you sign up for?

12. Which character—Natalie, Laney, Finn, or someone else—would you most want to spend an afternoon with, and what would you talk about?

Acknowledgments

So many of us have shameful, scary stories from our pasts—stories we're frightened to reveal, stories we think might change other people's opinions of us, stories that haunt our dreams and keep us up way past our bedtimes, worrying and fretting over what-ifs and if-onlys. Perhaps those stories are mundane, impacting only us. Maybe it's that lost love who got away, or the job we didn't take a chance on.

But others go to great lengths to conceal terrible circumstances from the world, and even their close friends, whether that's abuse, incarceration, mental health issues, or struggles with substances. That's where *Hidden Seeds* originated—in the idea that walking around with us every day at church, in our workplaces, and in the grocery store are people concealing great hardship and pain. Many beat themselves up internally, berating themselves for what they consider to be bad choices or plans gone awry. Others simply hide behind their secrets, terrified that if they reveal an iota of their circumstances they'll be treated like a pariah. In the process, they never taste the liberation of new life in Christ, nor do they allow God to use them to their full potential. They're too busy with the past.

Yet through my work as a journalist, as well as through nonprofit ministries my husband and I have been involved with—particularly Killingsworth Home and Lighthouse for Life in Columbia, South Carolina—I've seen so much hope. I've seen women, and men, heal after tremendous hardship. I've heard testimonies and watched people soar with the freedom that comes from living in the light after so much darkness.

Grace, not only that which we extend to others but that which we extend to ourselves, is critical. You never know what caused someone to make the choices they did or end up in the life they're living. New life is possible. Second chances—and third! and fourteenth!—are possible.

It's a beautiful thing to watch someone embrace transformation, and to see other people walk alongside them in Christian love to help make that happen.

This book started as two separate stories that ended up merging into one novel. And like everything else, it wasn't written in a silo. A huge thank you goes to countless loved ones and colleagues who helped me along the way, whether through prayer or encouragement.

First, my biggest thanks go to God—for his love, grace, mercy, compassion, and forgiveness.

Thank you to my best friend and the love of my life, my husband Matt Brodie, for giving me the foundation and the steady love that enables me to craft stories securely and with wholehearted freedom. Thanks to my kids, Cameron, Avery, Allison, and Will; to my mom, Kathleen; to my sister, Sara; and to my sister-friend, Katy Haddad (whose prayers are clearly superpowered!).

I also want to thank my parents-in-law, who are two of the best human beings I have ever known. You welcomed me into your family with so much love and acceptance and grace—and took in my kids as your own, too. You both are a blessing to me and teach me so much about steady and steadfast love. I love you! I also want to thank my stepdad, Frank, whose constant love over the years has been a rock in its own way. I appreciate you and love you more than I think you'll ever know.

Thanks also to my writing groups and writer friends, who help make what can sometimes be a solitary craft into a real community. Big thanks go to my now-dissolved conference-call group (Diane Thomas, Gene Wright, Donna Warner, and Marilyn Staats) and to my current group, Lexington Word Weavers.

To all who care and who help me grow as a writer and as a human—thank you. I love you and appreciate you more than you know.

Jessica

THE DAHLIA SERIES

The Memory Garden: Book One

The Memory Garden, the Amazon-bestselling first book in the Dahlia Series, is a gripping Southern novel following a broken journalist who finds unexpected purpose in a small town when a troubled boy's dangerous secret puts them both at risk.

Tangled Roots: Book Two

In *Tangled Roots*, Tiff Steadman thought she'd escaped her shameful past—until her recently paroled brother James arrives in Dahlia, threatening the respectable life she's carefully built. As wedding plans and buried secrets collide, these two siblings must confront the truth they've both been hiding and decide if redemption is worth the cost.

Hidden Seeds: Book Three

Returning to Dahlia after tragedy exposes her fiancé's betrayal, Natalie Motts rebuilds her life through art and unexpected friendship with Laney, a trafficking survivor hiding a dangerous past. When Natalie's teenage sister vanishes, Laney must choose between protecting her hard-won safety and stepping back into darkness to bring the girl home.

Book Four: Coming 2027

Marla's story . . . to be continued.

Paperback, e-book, and audiobook available.

Sign up for Jessica's Dahlia Email List and stay notified about her latest releases. Visit JessicaBrodie.com/Dahlia

www.ingramcontent.com/pod-product-compliance
Lightning Source LLC
LaVergne TN
LVHW010646110826
845149LV00014B/2969

* 9 7 9 8 9 9 2 9 0 0 8 4 2 *

Praise for Hidden Seeds

"*Hidden Seeds*—the title alone struck my curiosity, and the deeper I dove into the work, the more my curiosity grew. Jessica Brodie spins a tale that keeps you wondering what will happen next. Intrigue, mystery, and lost love haunt you as you walk Natalie Motts' pathway to healing. Brodie has developed a character in Natalie Motts that digs into your heart and forces you to cheer her on to a happy life. This must-read will open your eyes to the depths that we must sometimes go to in order to find who we are and what our happiness is. A winner that should be on every reader's nightstand."

Cindy K. Sproles, bestselling author of Appalachian historical fiction

"Jessica Brodie weaves a riveting tale of tragedy and triumph into her latest novel, *Hidden Seeds*. By the end of the book, her skillful story telling had stitched her characters into my heart. Even when I wasn't reading, I found myself thinking about my new friends, worrying about them, and cheering them on. I appreciate that Brodie isn't afraid to address hard topics in a fictional setting to help us all become more aware of the culture in which we live."

Lori Hatcher, bestselling devotional author

"Jessica Brodie has a beautiful, captivating voice and a skill at crafting stories with the perfect blend of depth, nostalgia, Southern charm, and hope. I adored Natalie from *Hidden Seeds* and found myself rooting for her from page one."

Jennifer Slattery, multi-published author and speaker

"Jessica Brodie has a unique way of handling tough, real-life emotions and situations that is equally real and raw, and yet full of hope and redemption. In *Hidden Seeds*, she tackles grief, betrayal, and what it looks like to really start over, in a way that makes you relate to the characters on a deep level."

Krystina Renae Rankin, author, *Worthy of Redemption*